THE ᴇMERALD AFFAIR

Jane Williams

ISBN: 9798407866879
Lord Toad Publishing

DEDICATION

To Steve - mon crapaud bien aimé!

To David, Denise, Charlotte and James - you are
so loved.

.

ACKNOWLEDGMENTS

To Steve… for everything.

To Jane and Olivier… for friendship, assistance and support.

Finally to Christine… who was there at the duke's birth!!

TABLE OF CONTENTS

MAP

■ Denbrugh Place
◆ Solworth Manor
● Stanford Park
▲ Folly Hill

Oxford

RIVER

Oxfordshire

Buckinghamshire

THAMES

Wallingford

Berkshire

Henley
on
Thames

Pangbourne

Bath

Reading

Windsor

Hampton
Court

London

Surrey

Descent of the House of Vénoire

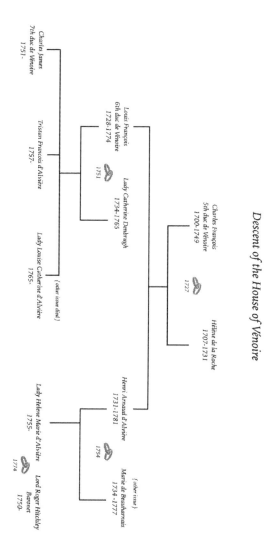

Charles James
7th duc de Vénoire
1751-

Louis François
6th duc de Vénoire
1728-1774

Tristan François d'Alvière
1757-

1751

Lady Catherine Denbragh
1734-1765

{ other issue died }

Lady Louise Catherine d'Alvière
1765-

Charles François
5th duc de Vénoire
1700-1749

1727

Hélène de la Roche
1707-1731

Henri Arnaud d'Alvière
1731-1781

1754

{ other issue }

Marie de Beauharnais
1734-1777

Lady Hélène Marie d'Alvière
1755-

1774

Lord Roger Hitchley
Baronet
1750-

11

OVERTURE

Denbrugh Place Lodge; Spring 1782.

Thoughts of the duke's old nurse.

The unexpectedly bright spring sunlight was being used to advantage as the gnarled, old hands set the tiniest of stitches in the wristbands of the fine lawn shirt. Shaking out her work, Mrs Mary Threadgold stood easing out the strains in her back. Folding the finished shirt, she set it carefully on the dresser. It would need to be taken up to Denbrugh Place soon if all the bustle meant what she thought it did.

The Lodge House was silent at present, discounting the ticking of the grandfather clock. She was so accustomed to this that it failed to register anymore. As she stood gazing from the window, her mind was far away. It was not the present spring flowers she saw but those tended by her mother-in-law nigh on fifty years ago. She had been eighteen then, a newly arrived bride, proud of the fact that her husband Tom was the Lodgekeeper's son. She had been born the daughter of a tenant farmer whose family had farmed land on the estate of Denbrugh for several centuries. The estate which had the backdrop of the pleasant Chilterns Hills, and the noble family who owned it, had been her universe. If things had followed their normal course, Tom would have become Lodgekeeper on his father's demise. This was not to be. They had been married for just eighteen months, when Tom was thrown from the gig returning from market. Earl James, the then master of Denbrugh Place had even sent his own physician - to no avail. Tom never regained his senses, leaving his young widow, their month-old son and his devastated parents to mourn his loss.

However, Denbrugh looks after its own. The earl and countess had begun readying their nursery for the arrival of an expected heir. Fate is no respecter of mortal plans. The noble couple were blessed with a copper haired girl after a gruelling birth. There was an immediate need for a wet nurse and at the Lodge, Mary Threadgold was nursing her month old son with milk to spare a plenty. So it was that she and Ben moved into the nursery on the top floor of Denbrugh Place, little realising how her status within this world was about to change. At first it was hard to accustom herself to living in the Palladian splendour of the big house, albeit on the Nursery floor. She was starting to adjust to a different life, when another momentous change occurred. The Countess Lucy, failed to recover from her birthing ordeal, dying within the month. Indeed, the years of 1734 and 1735 were as black for Denbrugh Place as they were for the Threadgold family. Just as Ben had been left abruptly fatherless, so was Lady Catherine left motherless. Death the great leveller.

The maternal role was to be filled on the nursery level by Mrs Threadgold. So close did she and her charge become that Mary maintained her position even when the school room and a governess beckoned. After Lady Catherine's coming out at eighteen resulted in a love match with a French duke, the English nurse travelled with the new family. Her duchess's children were fondly given into her charge, as was overall responsibility for the other nursery servants. Despite this well-ordered world of love and wealth, from the duchess's eight pregnancies only three children survived. Her first born, Charles, her fourth Tristan and her youngest, a daughter named Louise who was to be the cause of her death. Louis-François, 6th Duc de Vénoire and her grieving widower, was to remain inconsolable and taciturn for the remainder of his life. It was Mrs Threadgold's belief that his three children had suffered because of it. Charles, the present holder of the titles Duke of Vénoire, Earl of Denbrugh seemed to his old nurse to be suffering still.

The old lady sighed as she heard the back door open and close. Rousing herself from her memories, she went into the scullery. Here she found her daughter-in-law Fanny, setting a new crock of butter in the pantry. At forty-eight, the same age as her husband Ben, her figure had thickened but the smile which had first caught his attention was ever present.

'Something smells good for later, Ma! You've been busy, seems. None of them back yet?' She began cutting a loaf as Mary drew off a jug of homebrew. 'I saw our Jim as I come across the Park, he said as he'd be in for a bite soon. He was going to lead the blacks up to the stable yard first.'

Jim was the seventeen-year old middle son of the Threadgolds, an under-groom in Denbrugh stables where his elder brother Dickon at four and twenty had recently been appointed head. A matter of pride within the family as the present Duke of Vénoire, Earl of Denbrugh, did not trust his blood stock lightly to any but skilled hands. Most of the duke's circle would have been surprised to learn of the loyalty he inspired in his retainers. His cynicism and boredom with the social round did not extend to his estates. They would not have been surprised, however, by the caprice which was currently setting everyone by the ears! Having declared he was remaining in the country for the start of the Season, declining all invitations for events in Town and being closeted with his agent most mornings, of a sudden he had issued new orders.

He would go to his Grosvenor Square

town house after all and as soon as may be. In order to make this happen smoothly as was expected, help had been called for in all quarters. Instead of tending the main entrance gate, Ben Threadgold had been helping footmen shift the many packed valises, trunks and boxes from house to stable yard, whilst his youngest son, fourteen-year-old Daniel had been bidden to leave his garden work and help to ready the carriages.

Just then, the four Threadgold males entered the scullery by the back door, accompanied by laughter and the clattering of discarded boots.

'No need to open the gate for anyone was there, Ma?' Ben asked, entering the scullery.

His mother shook her head as she gave each of the four a tankard poured from the jug.

'As quiet as can be.' She replied.

'Wish it were the same up the drive! Mr Wilkes keeps changing his mind about which luggage goes where.' sighed Dan. 'That's 'cos Mr Ferris keeps on bringing more!'

Wilkes had been head coachman since before the old Earl's death in 1774, whilst Ferris was the duke's longstanding valet. Mary paused in passing out the plates of ham and bread to her son and grandsons.

'So, he's still set on going then, not changed his plans?'

Ben shrugged, running a broad hand through his short, grey curls, 'Well, I don't say as I'm privy to his grace's plans, exactly but with all that's going on, I reckon he has not.'

Dickon, with due ceremony, consulted the pocket watch he had received from his master on his appointment as Head Groom and said proudly, 'If'n it helps to know, Mr Wilkes wants the blacks in harness by two. Tomorrow, I'm to take the riding horses up and I'm bid to bide at Grosvenor Square Mews until I'm told different.'

There was a flurry of exclamations from the females of his family at this remark, by which reaction he looked surprised, yet stoical. He divulged that Mrs Chambers, the housekeeper at Denbrugh, was packing all the travelling servants' liveries and as an afterthought he mumbled that Bess had already offered to pack what he needed from his room above the coach-house. Ben exchanged a speaking glance with Fanny but that did not prevent his mother from exclaiming,

'So, that's the way of things, is it?'

Jim and Dan hid telling smiles in their tankards as Dickon hurriedly entered the passage to put on his boots and hide the fact that his face was red. He and the coachman's daughter, Bess Wilkes, had been seen a lot in each other's company of late. She was a sewing maid, whose needlework met with his grandmother's approval.

Mary had followed Dickon out. 'Orders is orders, don't you go being late with those beasts.' She hesitated and almost against her will enquired, 'Did his grace give you your orders himself?'

'Nay, Gran. Mr Ferris.'

She sighed deeply, gave her head a shake and bade him hurry.

Mary's son dropped his hand on her shoulder as he came behind her. 'What's amiss, Ma?'

There were a few moments of silence before she sighed once more. 'Naught's amiss with me! It's just…First he's in France, then it's hunting, next he's here, now it's another Season starting! So restless. What's to become of him, that's what I'd like to know? I wish he were happy. I wish someone else could see that there's more to him than his titles and his fortune. I do so long to see him set up his nursery before I'm past helping!' Fetching another deep sigh, she smiled tremulously at her son. 'You and Fanny'd got Dickon and Jim by the time you were one and thirty!'

Her son gave her a quick squeeze as he smiled at her, 'Ah, well, you always say as how Quality's different. You a werritin' won't make a ha'p'orth of difference to how he lives his life.' Ben shouted his goodbyes to his wife, calling to Jim and Daniel to hurry if they were to walk together across the park.

Mrs Threadgold watched the three stockily built men walk rapidly away from the curve in the gravel drive, heading for the path through the wood on the edge of the park. She noted that Daniel would probably be the tallest of her grandsons by the time he'd finished growing. Strange the way looks, in the main, followed down the generations. From behind, Ben's hair grew to a point in the nape of his neck, just as her Tom's had. It had been passed on to the two eldest, but Dan favoured Fanny's side.

The duke had inherited his looks and height from his father, showing not the faintest resemblance to his mother, save for his slender fingers. Even in the cradle he had been long and fine boned, a totally different bundle to nurse then her own baby. A shock of blue-black hair, which now took a lot of powdering by Mr Ferris. A blue eyed gaze which he so frequently hid beneath lowering brows. Such long lashes which were the envy of many a female. His figure was muscular and elegant, setting off anything he chose to wear. To say that he was a catch was no exaggeration. The fact that this was said by so many hopeful mammas was part of his problems. He had inherited a vast double fortune and two titles by the time he was three and twenty. Since then, he had had in his charge his younger brother and sister, their fortunes to manage, as well as his own and no one to gainsay his behaviour. His father had required him to live up to his own tenets of what it was to be a nobleman, old Earl James had had little time to soften these before he too had joined his ancestors in the Denbrugh burial plot. All this was eight years ago, now.

Mary's musings were broken into by Fanny placing a lined basket on the chair, 'Shall I take the finished shirts up to the house?' She nodded a glance at the grandfather clock. 'It wants half an hour before two o'clock. I'll be quicker than you could be, Ma.'

Usually, Mrs Threadgold resented any reference to her advancing years, but it was more important to her that her lovingly crafted shirts were safely stowed before the duke's departure. So having popped a lavender bag between them she shooed her daughter- in-law out of the lodge house.

This proved to have been a very sensible decision, as at a few minutes past the hour of two o'clock the old nurse heard the sound of carriage wheels on the gravel drive. She had been seated on the bench by the garden wall, half hoping to catch a glimpse of her nurseling, half wondering could she open the heavy wooden gate unaided. She need not have worried; Daniel sprang down from the box, as Wilkes slowed the four beautiful black horses. As the lad tended the gate, his grace Charles James seventh Duc de Vénoire, third Earl of Denbrugh, leaned forward to the lowered window above the crest panelled door.

He wore a simple royal blue frock coat, over a figured waistcoat, a plain tricorne and his caped greatcoat lay beside him. Raising his long fingered right hand to acknowledge her curtsy, the sun glinted on his grandfather's emerald ring, as his lace cuffs fell back. There was almost a suggestion of a gallant's bow in his action. She noted this with a half laugh.

'A bientôt, Nounou.' He bestowed on his nurse one of his rare, dazzling smiles.

Wilkes sprang the horses and they were gone in a flurry of dust as they swung out onto the Henley road.

Daniel had already started to run back towards the big house. His grandmother turned from the gate, hugging her fine, green wool shawl to herself, against the sudden breeze which tugged at the strings of her bonnet.

'Would that you could just find the right lady, my lordling.' She whispered to herself. 'What's to become of your life!'

INTERMEZZO

Grosvenor Square; three weeks later.

Thoughts of the duke and of his valet.

It had proved useless. Of course, it had proved useless! This was the repeated thought which was like the clash of blades in his head. As he stood before his library fireplace, he regarded the increasing number of gilt-edged invitations ranged on the mantlepiece, with a moue of distaste. Charles, duke of Vénoire turned abruptly to the claret which a footman had earlier placed noiselessly on the side table. His face was a blank as he sipped the damson-coloured wine. What was he to do? For how much longer could he postpone what he knew to be his duty? Not for the first time of late, he heard his father's icy voice in his ear.

'It behoves you to produce an heir! Find love where you will, but marry you must!'

Since this father of his had introduced him to his first fille d'amour as a coming of age present in Paris, Charles had not lacked for lightskirts. They would all have agreed that he was a generous and kind patron, terminating each individual relationship before forming another. His latest mistress, a shockingly expensive Parisienne named Célestine had recently arrived aboard his yacht to take up residence in a house rented for her in Soho Square. After visiting her last night, he had awoken late with the phrase, 'It had proved useless!' repeating in his brain. Pleasant it had certainly been but not enough to distract him from the expectations and demands of the Season. He had tried fencing, riding and cards but no matter where he found himself something served to remind him of what should be his course of action before the Season was out.

Only in recent days, his fencing partner had made mention of his sister's coming out ball. Sure enough, the recently delivered invitation glinted reproachfully amongst its fellows. Vary the hour he rode as much as he would, some girl of suitable rank and ton, properly escorted, appeared in the park to exchange bows. Even a hand of cards at Whites with his intimates had been spoiled by overhearing a bet being placed in the book, that he would be leg shackled by Season's end!

Vénoire had always realised that his rank was as a magnet yet had at first lived in hope that he would draw a bride who loved him in spite of this. Hope faded with each passing year, replaced by cynicism and ennui. Boredom was what beset him now, evincing itself as the constant restlessness which followed him everywhere. He was pacing the room when the door opened soundlessly and his butler, Downes, entered bearing a silver salver before him on which rested an engraved card. Halting his pacing, Vénoire raised a black eyebrow inquisitorially.

'Lord George Carshaw is below, your grace.'

'A visiting card, in the afternoon?' With a Gallic shrug, his master stated, 'I do not think I am acquainted with anyone who would show such a want of manners!' He dropped the card back on the salver.

Downes at his most urbane, bowed. The fact that he remained, provoked the duke to remark,

'Ah, there is something more?'

'His lordship begged me to inform your grace, that his elder son claims friendship with Lord Tristan.'

Vénoire laughed mirthlessly, 'That I doubt!'

The butler inclined his head once more, 'Lord Carshaw desires to leave an invitation to his daughter's coming out ball.' His utterance was wooden, but it demonstrated his feelings on such effrontery. Of late, his master's temper had been unpredictable, but he was not prepared for his outburst of genuine laughter.

'Such a desire! A veritable mushroom! An encroaching, shameless mushroom! Let him leave it then!' Another burst of laughter followed the butler's stately tread out of the room. The laughter died in the blue eyes as the duke stood drumming his fingers upon the mantelpiece. He felt the strongest desire to sweep the incessant invitations from the shelf and from his life. Several fell to the floor. Despite his inclinations, he bent to retrieve them.

Uppermost was one he recognised. It was inscribed in his cousin's flowing hand, the unseemly flourishes brought back some light to his eyes. Hélène d'Alvière had surprised everyone, not least her now devoted husband, by accepting his tentative proposal of marriage, defying all understandable opposition from her father. Her uncle, duke Louis-François, when appealed to, had shocked his younger brother Arnaud by sanctioning the match. In his position as the head of the family, he had insisted that this younger brother escort his daughter to the altar in the chapel at Palombières, their Loire château.

The Catholic baronet she had wed eight years ago was one Lord Roger Hitchley. It so happened that he was Charles' long-standing friend. Time spent in their company often lifted his spirits. Their small estate of Stanford Park in Berkshire often proved a haven, where no demands were made. This present invitation to a small country party had lain unanswered, tossed aside with the rest. With sudden decision, Vénoire pulled the bell-rope. Almost instantly, a footman appeared and went to remove the wine tray, he straightened betraying no surprise when the duke requested,

'Have Ferris come to my bedchamber.' With swift strides, his grace reached the door before the footman could open it for him, adding clearly, 'Ensure Wilkes has the carriage readied. Oh, also, cancel dinner!'

This last order had caused the young footman to blench. As he later confided over supper to the fellow he shared duties with, he had conveyed *that* message to Mr Downes himself. Not for anything would he have passed such a message to Monsieur Samson, his grace's French Chef! His temper was as bad as his dishes were said to be good. Not that the servants were favoured with tasting them. The assistant cook provided ample sustenance, much more to their tastes.

It was after the servant's meal the same evening, that Mr Downes inquired if Mr Ferris would care to join him in his pantry for a glass of brandy. The butler had held his position in the Grosvenor Square household since appointed by Earl James, when his present master was still in short coats. As such, he was staunchly loyal to the duke. He readied two glasses and unlocked his private dresser.

Tom Ferris had been appointed Vénoire's valet also thanks to the deceased earl. He had come to the post aged three and twenty, only five years older than his master. It had begun with a baptism of fire, as within weeks of settling in at Denbrugh Place, his master had been ordered to France by his father, who was a courtier to the Dauphin. That Ferris had met with this autocratic nobleman's standards of turnout for his son was no mean feat. Versailles was far more rigorously formal than St. James, yet he had passed the test. The brief nod which Louis-François had given, on seeing his son descend the staircase before his presentation had been followed the next day by a Louis d'or, under his seal. No message accompanied it, but Ferris had realised its significance.

Master and Man had been together day and night ever since. Friendship there could never be, but their bond was a strong one. Which was all to the good at the present time. Accepting the glass of brandy from the butler and seating himself in the fireside chair, Tom Ferris took a sip.

'I fear I have not seen Monsieur Samson

in such a passion for a very long time.' Thus did Mr Downes open the topic of conversation which was uppermost in the Servants Hall.

'Indeed. I am sorry that you should have borne the brunt of it.' Ferris shook his head. 'I really do not know....' Pressing his lips together, in order not to continue, 'an excellent brandy, if I might say so.' He sipped again.

'Ah, yes! His grace is normally most considerate, as we both know.' Downes turned the bottle in his hands. 'A gift on his last return from France.' Shaking his head, he continued, 'Sadly, I am beginning to recognise more of his late father in him, than of his late grandfather.'

Ferris stiffened, perceptibly, 'As to that, Mr Downes, I would have to disagree.'

Downes tried again, 'We, the Upper servants are all devoted to his grace but surely you would agree that today's happenings are a little disturbing, Mr Ferris? Setting out so late, with no footmen, nor yourself in attendance. It is not fitting to his rank! In such weather, as well!' He added as a rumble of thunder was clearly heard, even in the basement. 'Wilkes was worried for the horses, so I was informed.'

Ferris shook his head, giving his fellow servant the sort of look such a remark deserved.

He knew that George Wilkes, having been coachman to the family since Lady Catherine's marriage to her French duke, would never worry for his master's horseflesh. 'His grace would never risk the blacks, no matter his mood!' Again, he compressed his lips.

Downes gestured to Ferris's glass with the bottle.

'No, I thank you, Mr Downes. I must finish my own packing as I need to be away before dawn, if I am to reach Stanford Park by breakfast time. It seems to me that you may reassure everyone who is troubled by his grace's somewhat precipitous departure, that he is expected by Lord and Lady Hitchley. An oversight with the date, nothing more.'

They exchanged bows and smiled their good nights.

Tom Ferris thoughtfully climbed the back stairs to his comfortably appointed room, situated behind his grace's dressing room. Firstly, he looked in here, to ensure that the portmanteaux had been taken to the coach in which he and his grace's traps would be travelling come the dawn. Moving into the duke's suite he methodically straightened anything which was out of place. Several drawers still stood open, showing the strangely impetuous passage of the duke. He tutted to himself at yet another sign of his master's unusual lack of consideration. Ensuring that all was tidy, he sighed. Taking a small key from his buff waistcoat pocket, he returned to the dressing room. He unlocked the travelling jewel case, casting a well-trained eye over its contents.

Everything that might be required was in its place. His master had worn his amethyst and diamond pin to hold his jabot in place and his grandfather's emerald ring, which he rarely went without. Suppressing a yawn with long practice, he carefully removed his green broadcloth coat, brushing it before safely hanging it up for the night. His cloak bag was ready packed, but it had provided a useful excuse to leave the Butler's Pantry. Not for the first time during these several months he was nonplussed by his master's erratic behaviour. Certainly, he always required his life to run smoothly but usually showed consideration for his servants as they fulfilled this. Like Mrs Threadgold, he too was concerned about what was to become of the duke. Such restlessness of spirits betokened more than boredom; it showed a deep unhappiness. Not for the world would he voice his worries, not even to someone as partisan as Mr Downes undoubtedly was. He would fiercely protect his master, if he was able, especially from himself!

ONE
April 1782

Encounter with highwaymen.

A fitful moon pierced the rain clouds, illuminating part of the deserted, rutted road below. The nocturnal silence was broken by the sounds of a carriage, lurching its well sprung way along this, the London to Bath Turnpike. The high stepping black carriage horses had shown great aversion to the storm which had begun as they quitted Town. It had needed all of Wilkes's skill and coaxing to calm them. Having tired in their muddy battle they were content now to use their energy to reach stabling for the night. The coachman too was looking forward to the warmth of a fire and some supper. He was glad of the caped driving coat, tricorne and wig upon his head for providing some warmth. Allowing for the delay caused by the storm, he estimated that they were within a league of Stanford Park. Three miles was nothing for such carriage horses as it was his privilege to drive.

As they swung round a bend in the road, a gust of wind caused the coach-lamps to flare, silhouetting a rider against the lighter sky. He was standing in the middle of the high road, not much ahead of the powerful four being driven. This apparition startled Wilkes so much that he pulled unexpectedly hard on the reins. The horses plunged to a snorting halt, as he applied the brake, blowing clouds of steam from their nostrils. Wilkes silently cursed the decision not to have a footman along, as he slowly reached for the blunderbuss propped next to him. The well muffled horseman edged his wary mount closer.

'Do not attempt it!' He motioned with his pistol towards the ground.

In the short time it took for Wilkes to assess his adversary, an unobserved second figure emerged from the trees beside the road. This man clubbed the coachman senseless where he sat. Then moved to hold the heads of the mettlesome beasts.

The first man now wrenched open the crested carriage door with one tan gauntleted hand, pointing the wickedly glinting pistol muzzle at the recumbent occupant. The rider's fine boned chestnut horse fidgeted nervously.

On hearing the snorting of his horses and feeling the lurching of his coach, the sleepy duke had needed to grab the hanging straps in order to brace himself. When the carriage remained upright, he had assumed a relaxed position against the blue upholstery, sliding a languid hand beneath the rug lying next to his person. The pistol it now concealed was held across his thigh, unfortunately un-cocked. At present, the immaculately dressed duke regarded the muffled face, hovering on a level with his own.

He observed that the muffler was of good quality, the tricorne whilst not gilt edged like his was freshly brushed and the man's mount was a thoroughbred; all the while he kept his eyelids half lowered. The steely tone in his voice betrayed his alertness,

'Sir, you are delaying me for no good purpose. I fear you would have been better advised to await richer pickings than myself.'

He noted the restive shuddering of his attacker's horse, as its master nudged it back into the shadows with his knees. This nervousness was emanating from the rider, of that the duke felt sure. He continued to regard the rogue's face, fixing in his memory the grey eyes, which were all that was visible between the swathed muffler and the dripping tricorne.

'I want your ring! The emerald from your right hand.'

The occupant of the carriage made no move, save to leisurely raise his quizzing glass, observing the wavering pistol through it.

'My right hand?' A slight quirk of one finely arched black brow, 'Indeed, you are well informed. A very particular highwayman, are you not?'

Observing the slightly unsteady muzzle of the pistol as it clicked ominously, Vénoire decided it would be wise to comply. With languorous care, he removed the ring from his tapering finger. Dropping it into the upturned palm of the scuffed gauntlet, he unhurriedly retrieved his pistol from beneath the carriage rug. In the split second that it took for the brigand to turn his horse and surge into the darker woods, Charles had cocked his weapon and fired. The report had served to plunge the horses against the traces. Fortunately, the brake held, rocking the carriage so violently that Vénoire was sent sprawling with less than his customary dignity. Gathering himself together, he sprang down from the door, cursing as he landed in a mud filled rut.

He cast an assessing glance towards the shadowy woods but could discern no movement. A sudden late burst of rain spattered his amethyst velvet coat as he mounted the box. Here he swiftly took in the fact that Wilkes was unconscious. He carefully moved the undischarged blunderbuss. Distastefully, he felt Wilkes stubbly head where his wig should have been, finding an egg sized bump. He probed with strong fingers, which provoked a deep groan. A slight stickiness suggested blood. Thoughtfully, he wiped his fingers on Wilkes's livery. As he pulled his evening cloak over his shoulders, he mused,

'An unlooked-for encounter with an extremely particular thief! I wonder how many of my acquaintance could say for sure, on which hand I wear my emerald?' His voice elicited an incomprehensible mumble from his coachman.

The whickering restiveness of his horses broke in upon such thoughts. He regarded their rain-soaked rumps which quivered slightly. It would never do for them to take a chill.

'Soit!' He gathered up the reins, adjusting his coachman's inert form to a safe position against his own person. His horses recognised his sure touch on the leathers and eagerly responded as he disengaged the brake. 'En avant, mes enfants!'

In due course, the duke brought his carriage to a halt before the flambeaux lit porch of Stanford Park. There were no other equipages in sight, externally all was quiet, but violins could be heard in the distance. Despite the lateness of the hour, there was no need for the duke to sound the knocker of his cousin's stout door. A well-trained footman swung the heavy wood wide in impeccable fashion, to allow the new arrival entry.

Being divested of his cloak and tricorne, the duke said, 'You will find my coachman in need of assistance, on the box. See that he is well taken care of. My horses too, they must not stand for long.'

His grace of Vénoire began crossing the black and white flagged hall. His tall figure stood out against the panelling. At this moment, there was nothing in his demeanour to suggest that he had any other thoughts in mind than of a night's pleasure. The impassively faced footman did think he had discerned a whiff of powder-shot as he had received the new arrival's cloak but he knew better than to question any actions of his betters.

'No need to announce me.'

In stately and unhurried manner, the duke ascended the carved oak staircase. He was a sublime aspirant to fashion; his own hair, grey powdered and confined in a perfect queue, Mechlin lace at his throat and wrists, an amethyst velvet coat with ivory coloured waistcoat and breeches moulded to his form. If one happened to glance at his low-heeled evening shoes, one might be forgiven for thinking his stockings were mud flecked. However few people, once caught in his gaze would think to do so.

On reaching the half landing, Charles' features bore their habitual air of fashionable boredom. Those who passed him, bowing, thought nothing of his late arrival. Vénoire was Vénoire, after all. Of the thirty or forty people present, most knew of his quirks. He leant against the door frame of his cousin's salon allowing his senses to be assailed on numerous fronts. He heard a cacophony of well-bred voices, orchestrated by the scraping of violins. He smelt beeswax candles overlaid by a multitude of different perfumes. Fastidiously he lifted his own scented handkerchief to his chiselled nostrils, concealing a yawn at the same moment. Bleakly he realised he had been foolish to come. His actions had caused an unwarranted disturbance for his household and to what ends? He was contemplating the solitude which he knew Lord Hitchley's library could offer but good manners dictated he should at least greet his hostess first.

Of a sudden, his attention was caught by the trilling laughter of Lady Hélène, close at hand. She presented a vision in gold brocade and lace, her exquisitely small hands were resting on the arm of a callow youth, bemoaning his luck at Faro. Her laughter struck Vénoire as strained. The young man's cod-like eyes were riveted on his hostess's décolletage, which was dashing in the extreme. The more staid matrons of the district found an ever ready fund of gossip in her fast ways. Hélène administered a sharp rap with her fan to the besotted youngster, who far from being repulsed, continued to whisper in her ear. Charles moved across the room, raising his quizzing glass to survey the young pup. On lifting his gaze, this gentleman encountered one of the duke's most glacial stares. The combination of hauteur and contempt emanating from the older man served to send the sprig scuttling into a confused retreat.

'I had no notion that children were to your taste, cousine.''

Hélène shrugged, laughing but her laughter did not touch her blue eyes, 'Oh, he will have forgotten his nonsense by tomorrow. I must amuse myself, somehow.' Taking his offered arm she continued more seriously, 'Even for you this is a late arrival! We had quite given you up, especially as I must have mislaid your acceptance to the invitation.' Sensing her cousin stiffen she smoothly suggested, 'You are too late to take me into supper but you may procure me a glass of Canary.'

He allowed his veiled gaze to sweep the room, then requested, in a lowered tone, 'May I talk with Roger?'

She gave him a puzzled look but was suddenly attuned to his strange mood.

'He was playing Piquet, the last time I saw him.' Gesturing towards the anteroom, which was set out for cards.

'Ah.' Vénoire was about to continue, when Hélène turned abruptly in order to block him from a hawk-faced dowager who had been crossing the salon towards them.

'Go down to the Library, Charles. We cannot talk in this crush. I'll send Roger to you, as soon as may be.'

Grateful for her usual astuteness, he leisurely complied. His bows to left and right as he quitted the salon were perfectly judged. No one thought such stiff-necked behaviour unusual in Vénoire.

On entering his host's library, he was glad to see a fire still burned, as he suddenly became aware of the dampness of his coat. The decanter of brandy which stood on the side table was a welcome sight. He poured himself a glass, shaking out his lace cuffs which were also damp he now realised. Not suitable apparel for driving a carriage, he thought. He was frowning into his half-consumed glass, casting his mind back over the unexpected events of the evening when his host entered.

'Devil take it, Vénoire, what's amiss? Lena's most mysterious. Some nonsense about an urgent messenger needing to see me!' He looked around as if to reassure himself that this was a falsehood.

Lord Roger Hitchley was a tall, heavily built gentleman, a little florid of countenance with a pair of warm brown eyes which saw more than his demeanour would betray. With the physique of a horseman rather than a dancer, he was still unexpectedly debonair in evening attire. At two and thirty, he was a year older than the duke whom he had first met at school. That their friendship had outlasted school days spoke volumes about his personality, something that had been appreciated by duke Louis-François when he had welcomed his addresses to his niece, eight years ago. The steady, stolidness of this country gentleman was the perfect balance for Hélène's volatile nature. At present he had raised a branch of candles in order to see his friend more clearly. The muddied stockings did not escape his notice. 'Was there an accident? The blacks alright?' A note of genuine concern could be detected in his question.

Vénoire raised an eyebrow, 'I note your correct priorities, mon cher!' He proffered his filigree snuff box.

'It's obvious you've taken no harm!' Hitchley took a pinch of snuff with amazing delicacy for a man of his proportions. He flicked at the dust, where it marred his maroon silk sleeve and waited for enlightenment.

Dusting his fingers on his handkerchief, the duke began to recount what had befallen that evening. He finished by regarding the bare fingers of his right hand, 'Such a particular thief.'

'True enough, but you are not the first I've heard of being robbed in such a fashion. D' ye remember Halliday?'

Vénoire looked blankly. Roger shook his head, 'No matter, a neighbour. Took his wig and boots, nothing more!'

'Indeed. This intrigues. Are the Justices involved?'

His friend grunted, 'What d' ye think? Such an embarrassment, he hoped to forget it. Some young buck's prank, I thought. Are you of the same opinion?' He poured them both some more brandy.

'So, it would appear. I did not mention these events to Hélène. I feel no need to brut my discomfiture abroad.' The duke's voice took on a sardonic tone, 'Vénoire, bested by a High Toby! I think not... my reputation would be sadly bruised.'

Roger snorted, inelegantly, 'Much you care what people say of you!'

In a much more menacing tone, Charles murmured, 'Oh, indeed I have great care for what is said about me! I think no one should take me for a fool.'

Roger regarded him steadily, 'No one does, m' dear fellow.' He gestured towards the curtained windows, encompassing his land outside. 'Merely a local incident. We move in different circles in the main.'

This was said without rancour but on certain levels was true. The Hitchleys of Stanford Park were not accepted everywhere. Whig memories were long. Despite holding land given as a reward at the Restoration, a still Catholic family who had supported the Stuart uprising were not trusted everywhere. This affected Lord Roger not a whit, once his wife had made clear to him that she truly preferred a country lifestyle.

There was a discrete knocking on the library door, followed by the dark coated butler's entrance.

'Well, Westock?' Roger was abrupt at being disturbed.

'Pardon, my Lord but her Ladyship grows impatient at your absence. I thought it only right to appraise you of the fact.' Westock remained po-faced as usual, beneath his meticulously curled wig.

'Lord! That's all that's needed.' He glanced at the mantle-clock. 'Charles, I'll have to leave you. The guests will be departing soon, ought to be with Lena to say our goodbyes. You require anything, Westock will organise it.' He smiled affably at his friend, nodding to his butler, as he trod across to the door.

This elderly retainer bowed his master out, then turning he bowed again to the duke. 'Shall I bring coffee and some lobster patties from the Supper buffet, your grace?'

Vénoire nodded, 'An excellent thought, Westock.'

As he waited for his supper, his grace of Vénoire was deep in thought. He was certain that the rogue horseman was no ordinary Bridle-cull. The animal he had ridden had been of bloodstock, albeit too showy a chestnut for his taste. His clothes too, had been of a certain quality and silver engraving on the pistol stock had gleamed in the moonlight. There was nothing hooded now about Vénoire's clear, blue gaze as he recalled a pair of grey eyes staring at him above a woollen muffler. His own eyes narrowed at the picture in his mind of his emerald ring glinting in the scuffed and ridged palm of a tan leather gauntlet. Of a certainty, there was something more to this robbery. Attempting to resolve such a mystery might provide him with an escape from other thoughts this Season.

Westock returned to serve him a suddenly very welcome supper. Having trimmed a guttering candle and placed another log on the fire the butler made to leave but was interrupted by the duke's French accented voice, 'Wilkes, how does he?'

The impassive servant permitted himself a small smile, 'Also partaking of a light supper, your grace but sore headed.' Few aristocrats of such standing would concern themselves with a servant's wellbeing. 'I attended to him myself. When you wish to retire, your usual room is prepared, your grace. I have seen to it that there is a candle ready beside the door to the backstairs. The company should have left by the time you have enjoyed your supper.' He placed a fresh glass of brandy beside the duke's plate. Inclining his head with a nod of thanks,
'Just so, Westock, just so.

TWO

Encounter by the ruins.

Vénoire was awakened by the sound of his valet drawing back his bedchamber curtains, as he had been every morning of his life since reaching the age of eighteen. Tom Ferris had been chosen with care by his English grandfather, Earl James, who had also overseen his education in England. His father had raised no objections, initially being so devastated by the loss of his beloved wife when Charles was just fourteen. Their eldest son's world had shifted, too. Boarding school in a different country with the holidays spent at Denbrugh Place, had helped somewhat. Intermittently he had been summoned to Paris or Palombières according to duke Louis-François' moods. Thirteen years on and Ferris had been heard to say, he would not leave the duke's service for a thousand guineas. Those who had tried to lure him into their service received a polite but icy refusal, reminiscent of the duke's own tones. Although exacting high standards from his servants, Vénoire inspired devotion as well as loyalty. As he put down his empty coffee cup on the tray beside his bed the, duke inquired,

'Has Westock mentioned Wilkes? How does he?'

'Indeed, your grace Mr Westock mentioned Wilkes's mishap privately to me, at breakfast. He had advised him to remain resting but Wilkes could not settle until he had visited the horses.'

Vénoire nodded, 'Admirable Wilkes! And you, Tom, not too fatigued?'

Ferris had travelled the forty miles from Grosvenor Square with his grace's raiment, sleeping for the last four hours of the night in the

Berline. Now, neatly but soberly dressed in his smooth, green broadcloth coat, over buff breeches, he set about readying his master for his regular morning ride.

Moving the coffee tray to a side table, he replied, 'Perfectly rested, I thank your grace.'

Knowing that his master would reveal the source of Wilke's ills in his own time, he began the task of shaving the duke and ordering his hair, the latter still held traces of grey hair powder. Having removed this with deft brushing, he bound the thick, black locks with a leather thong. Later, only once his master was attired would he bind it into a neat queue.

The face reflected in the glass, as Ferris worked, bore no trace of the English heiress whom his father had loved and married. Hair, eyes, bone structure were all those of the autocratic sixth duke of Vénoire. Had the clothes which Ferris was assisting him into been those of a gentleman in attendance on King Louis XV, no one would have been able to differentiate between them. And yet… there was a softer set to his lips and around his eyes.

Easing the deep blue riding coat across his grace's muscular shoulders, Ferris stood back to admire the effect. The tall figure before him looked extremely well turned out when attired for riding, as he now was. From his dark, unpowered hair to his gleaming top-boots he met with his valet's approval.

Small wonder that he was the matrimonial object of numerous young ladies. Add his immense fortune to his good looks and it was no surprise that he was also the favoured choice of the mammas of these hopefuls. Despite a well-known penchant for gambling, prime horseflesh and extremely expensive lightskirts, their fathers still considered him a very warm man indeed. The double fortune cast into his pockets at the age of three and twenty, due to the demise of firstly his father, followed by his grandfather within four months, remained impressive.

This coveted prize regarded his valet with an amused twinkle in his deep blue eyes.

'Well Tom, will I do?'

His man gave a rueful smile as he smoothed the low crowned beaver hat which he was holding, 'I wish earl James could see you now, sir. He always said you'd cast the other young gentlemen in the shade.'

Vénoire laughed outright as he picked up his crop and gloves, 'Young Thomas, young? Spare me the compliments! I made sure I could rely on you not to flatter me!'

Certainly, with his striking features relaxed, a hint of laughter in his eyes and his habitual look of acute boredom vanquished, he did look younger and less severe. Ferris had also seen him numerous times of late after nights of dissipation when he looked far older. The polite world's reaction to his fortune and the possibility he presented as a matrimonial prize followed him on both sides of the Channel. This had encouraged a growth of cynicism within him which was in part rooted in his school days.

He had learnt there to distinguish genuine friendship from sycophancy. Any affection that his father had felt for his children had been extinguished with the death of his adored wife. Duty was all. The duchess's death had altered and prematurely aged his grandfather, too. It was all too easy to acknowledge that Charles, duke of Vénoire had good reason to view his world and life with cold eyed cynicism.

Proceeding down the staircase, he looked into the dining room. There was evidence of a light breakfast set out on a side table but no one seemed astir yet. Hitchley had indicated that he had a meeting with his agent, so would not ride with his friend this morning.

Making his way to the stables, Charles was pleased to find that the day was mild, with a blue sky washed by the previous night's rain. A groom had already saddled the bay gelding the duke rode when at Stanford Park. Before mounting, he strolled to the loose boxes used for visitor's horses. The four black horses whickered in recognition at his approach. They were boxed in their pairs and two ebony heads poked over each stall.

'Get over!' This order was followed by the sound of a slap on the rump. Inside the end stall, a wigless George Wilkes was checking the hind leg of one of the animals.

'An injury, Wilkes?' His coachman turned to bow on hearing the duke's voice, pulling down his shirt sleeves before exiting the stall.

'Appears not, your grace, all four are sound. Forgive my appearance your grace, Mr Ferris has taken my wig in order to clean it as well as maybe.' He started to shrug himself into his green coat, discarding the sacking he had been using to protect his buff breeches. Vénoire stayed him, turning him to view the side of his skull.

'And you, my good Wilkes, how sound are you?'

Gruffly he answered, 'I'll do, sir. I'm that sorry that I wasn't of help…'

Vénoire waved away what he was about to say. 'No import. A trifling accident. Caught by a low bough, were you not?'

The coachman regarded his master, repeating solemnly,

'A low tree bough, oh aye your grace!'

'Get you to breakfast. I shall not require your services today.' So saying, he returned to his tethered mount and springing into the saddle he set off at a smart trot.

It did not take him long to ease his horse into a canter. The Hitchleys' estate was not vast but its wooded park led unobtrusively onto the edge of the Berkshire Downs. Hedges sufficed as boundary markers. Setting his mount at such an obstacle, Charles cleared it, effortlessly, then gave the animal it's head across the open ground stretching before him. Ere long, a stream was reached and here he slowed to a walking pace along its banks. He had no particular destination in mind, so allowed the horse to follow its own inclinations, letting his thoughts turn to last night's encounter. The puzzle of the highway-man was intriguing, something must provide a key. He brought to mind the certain facts that he knew; the grey eyed thief had appeared well dressed, well mounted and well armed. He also was well informed about his victim's jewel! The bay dropped its head to pull at a tussock of grass whilst Vénoire sat frowning into the distance.

'It's medieval.' Stated a well-modulated voice from behind him.

'I beg your pardon?' He turned, with a chilling glance, to find a young woman regarding him with a slight smile. She appeared to be totally at her ease.

She pointed with the hand which held her shoes to a pile of stones and tumbled pillars ahead on the opposite bank.

'I thought that you were wondering about the ruin.'

Vénoire's gaze remained fixed on her, as his eyes travelled from the shoes with which she pointed to the neat, stockinged ankles, half submerged in the shallow stream. He raised an eyebrow; never had he been so accosted before.

'Were you not interested in the ruin, sir? Indeed, I sincerely beg your pardon if you were not.'

She began to walk away, not giving him a second glance, her demeanour unruffled by a stranger seeing her in such disarray. Taking in her simple muslin gown and glossy, undressed hair the duke surmised that she must be a servant companion. What she should be doing in middle of nowhere, he could not conjecture. Of a certainty, she had not been walking in the water for long, the hem of her slightly lifted gown did not appear very wet. Collecting his scattered thoughts he said, imperiously,

'Stay a moment!'

She turned her steady regard on him once more, her head a little to one side as she waited for him to continue.

For the fraction of a second, he was unable to recall what he wished to say.

'The ruin is medieval?' That was not what he had intended at all. Politeness bade him introduce himself but he merely continued to watch her as, of a sudden, she tossed her shoes onto the bank.

'Indeed. It was part of the Abbey once, before that became a house. I am firmly of the opinion that it was the distillery, though there are those who believe it was the infirmary, which may explain the reason it was left to tumble down.'

A governess then, thought Vénoire. If so, it was to be hoped she set a better example for her charges. Sensing the need for a response,

'The house?' He said. 'Ah, I collect there is a house nearby?'

'Why yes,' she was now standing on the bank. Her hem, modestly brushing the short grass.

'Would you like to look around the ruins? There can be no objection, in the least.' She turned, making her way towards them, without a backward glance, yet clearly expecting him to follow. He did so, dismounting once the stream was crossed, leaving his horse to graze at the water's edge. Feeling rather bemused, he could find no reasonable explanation as to why he was following a perfectly rag-mannered female to inspect a pile of stones in which he had not the least interest! On reaching where she was now seated, he saw that she had slipped on her shoes of grey kid and was regarding him with the slight smile he had remarked earlier.

'They were used to make mead, ale and herbal infusions here.' This was said definitively, with a disconcerting conviction. Perhaps he was conversing with a water nymph! Yet her mode of dress and forthright manner made him laugh at such a preposterous thought. She took the laugh to be one of disbelief. 'I assure you it is most certainly true. Look, here' Bending down to a clump of bushes at her feet, she broke off a handful of leaves, crushing them between her fingers. 'There you have it, wild thyme, do you see?'

It was true to say that his grace the duke of Vénoire had never seen nor smelt thyme - wild or otherwise - before, in all of his thirty one years; yet he found himself saying, gravely,

'Yes, I see.'

He also found himself noticing how the sunlight struck sparks from the curls of her chestnut hair beneath her simple straw hat, as she brushed the crushed leaves from her skirts.

'I have discovered pot shards, as well as the herbs, so you must agree it all points to a distillery.'

He found himself looking at her hands; slender and pale, with no sign of roughness. From her silent, candid gaze, it was clear that she expected some response.

'Of a certainty, a distillery.' He found himself smiling.

She smiled in her turn. 'Odd to think of monks living here in ages past. A peaceful life though, would you not think?'

Disconcerted at being expected to converse in such a manner, he decided to make introductions instead. Bowing, he said, 'Allow me to introduce myself, Charles, Duc de Vénoire.'

'Your grace,' she started her curtsy but cut it short on hearing the church clock strike the hour, 'Good God, I must leave you, I have lost track of the time!' She set off at a run across the grass before disappearing through a gate in a wall where it bounded the stream. Clearly the estate from which she had materialised was close by.

The duke found himself laughing, heartily. People reacted in numerous ways on hearing his name and rank but never had he received just such a dampening set down! She had hardly executed a suitable curtsy and either his title meant nothing to her, or the unknown young lady paid it no heed. Such a reaction provided a refreshing change and served to reinforce his opinion that the damsel was a governess, albeit a trifle young for such a post.

For a few moments he continued regarding the ruins, bending to pick a sprig of the wild thyme, cupping it to his nostrils to catch the scent. He must ask Hitchley whose land this was, there could not be many houses in the area which had once been an abbey. He was still smiling as he retrieved his straying mount and swung into the saddle.

A double mystery, it seemed but this one would surely be easily solved. Horse and rider now began retracing their steps along the edge of the stream. It had been his intention to use his ride to ponder the events of the previous evening, instead he found himself consumed by an uncharacteristic interest in the land around him. Far from his usual breakneck riding pace, he positively ambled back towards Stanford Park until the frustrated tossing of the bay's head and the jangling of the bit broke into his thoughts. He covered the remaining ground at a gallop. The groom was surprised on receiving the animal at its unlathered state.

Vénoire had found an appetite. He entered the house through the gun room, surprising a hurried curtsy from a maid at the still room door as he crossed the passage between the back stairs and the main staircase. Stanford Park was a small Carolean mansion whose passages he knew far better than the same regions in Denbrugh Place.

The family dining salon was situated on the ground floor at the front of the house. The hall footman made to open the door, but Charles indicated there was no need. The dining room was still laid for breakfast and here he found Roger partaking of cold roast beef and ale.

'Ah, so you're back. No need to change.' He gestured with his tankard to the side table, 'Help yourself, Charles, just call for anything you don't see.' He added, 'Lena was drinking chocolate in her chamber when I looked in on her earlier. She bade me tell you that she would see you at nuncheon.' His florid face clouded slightly, gruffly he continued, 'Thing is, Charles, we thought she was in an interesting condition again… until a se'night ago.' He covered his gentle brown eyes with his large hand briefly. Clearing his throat, he gazed unseeingly at his plate. Shaking his head, he swallowed hugely from his tankard. 'She takes it harder each time we are disappointed.'

Vénoire gripped his friend's shoulder, his face an impassive mask, 'There will be other children, doubt it not.' The gentleness of his tone belied his rigid attitude. Raw emotion was something he found difficult to cope with; his French sire had seen to that, beating him for any slight show of weakness. He cared greatly for the Hitchleys' sorrows. In their eight years of marriage, they had lost one son after a few hours and Hélène had suffered numerous miscarriages, which few knew about. As far as Society was concerned, she was a flirt and a social butterfly. There were even those who thought her feverish lifestyle betokened regret for marrying out of her rightful sphere.

Roger covered his friend's hand with his own broad one. 'Try the beef, it's excellent.'

Vénoire moved to the side table, 'I find ham more to my taste, this morning. Is it your own?'

Deftly the conversation moved on to more mundane matters.

Having changed from his riding clothes, the duke was later to be found seated in the library at the front of the house. He seemed to be contemplating the now smooth gravel drive, an open book beside him which was receiving scant attention. His face was shuttered and brooding when his host entered the room.

'What, reading, Charles, on such a day! D'ye feel like fishing? Or perhaps another ride? Halliday's Irish mare just dropped twin foals, good stock, thought you might want to ride over and inspect them. Got some hound pups I'm interested in too. Of course, I'd have to get 'em established before the hunting season starts.' His words tailed off as he saw that Vénoire was only partially listening. His open face was suddenly alert to the mood of his friend.

The duke closed his book with a snap, 'What can you tell me of Abbeys, Roger?'

'Abbeys?' A blink and a shrug, 'Not much, as you should know! Though I seem to remember being told our priest's hole linked to the ruins, time was. Didn't know you had any interest there, either.' Hitchley was at a loss to know where this conversation was leading.

'Aha,' a soft breath and a smile lit the

duke's eyes, 'Which particular ruins are those, mon cher?'

Moving to the map stand, Roger uncovered the plan of the estate, left out from his meeting earlier with his agent.

'Why, Solworth, of course.' His thick forefinger stabbed at the spot where the well-drawn stream curved around. 'Dempsters have owned it since the monks left. Doesn't seem right.' He shook his head, sighing.

Vénoire was regarding the plan intently but still caught the half aside.

'You have something against these Dempsters? I seem to recall you admiring hounds from that pack as well.'

'Egad, you recall me saying that do you?' He settled his form in the high-backed chair which Charles had recently vacated, giving him a long, steady look. His friend's face remained expressionless. 'You might not recall that old Dempster was Master of the Hunt here for as long as I can remember. He and m'father were at outs for years about who bred the better hounds. O'course, I never kept the pack up to such a standard, too busy chasing Lena across France, when the estate fell to me. Still, know I got that right!' He grinned, boyishly, 'And, I'm still more than solvent whilst old Sir Hugh left nothing but his pack of hounds and his debts to be settled. The Manor was the abbey proper, but the grounds are littered with ruins. Seems probable that the house might join 'em afore long.'

'Am I to understand that he left no one to rectify his-ah-blunders?'

'Well, there's Neville still up at Oxford, can't afford the fees now, I shouldn't wonder. The dowager Lady Dempster cannot control him, never could. She's a lot younger than Sir Hugh was. Also, there's the daughter. Last Season, I heard that Neville had fallen in with a rum crowd. God knows what he used for money, nor who sponsored him. Still, won't be there this year, have to kick his heels at home and stave off the creditors somehow. I've heard the pack of hounds are up for sale as well as the hunters. If it's a choice between those hounds and Halliday's, I know which my choice would be.'

The duke strolled slowly towards the door, turning as Roger finished speaking, 'I have a strong desire to own a Solworth hound! Yes, of a certainty.' He held up his hand to still the words about to be uttered by his friend. 'It shall become de rigueur for a hound to follow one's person this Season. I feel there must be room for a hound or two at Grosvenor Square. What, can you not picture it?' Laughing with real amusement at the expression on Hitchley's face.

'No…but… Vénoire…d' ye know, I don't think the pack can be split!' He followed the duke out and into the Hall, as he began mounting the staircase he heard him say,

'Then I must take the pack!'

Once changed for riding, the two gentlemen set off across the park, towards the lane. Hitchley cast a sideways glance at his companion. Abbeys and hounds! What new start was this? Not for a moment had he swallowed the idea that it was in order to set a fashion. That was not the duke's style.

'Idiotic!' He muttered.

'What is disturbing your thoughts, my dear?' Vénoire's studied drawl was present again, the blue eyes, hooded.

'No matter.'

A pause, 'Damn it, Charles. What are you about? And don't talk of setting a fashion, you know better than to cozen me!'

Riding level with each other, Vénoire gave a sideways glance, 'I am interested in ruins, Roger. It is a new... let us call it... a new passion with me.'

Seeming to change the subject he suddenly asked, 'Are there young Dempsters?'

Hitchley's horse pecked as he pulled too sharply on the reins, 'What the devil? I swear I cannot follow you sometimes, Charles! No, as I said there's Neville and of course, Juliet.'

It was Vénoire's turn to pull his horse up short, 'Why do you say 'of course'? I do not believe I am acquainted with....!'

Roger interrupted, 'No reason you'd remember but she was at one of Lena's picnics last year. Probably other occasions too. Not your social circle.'

Now it was Roger's turn to pick up on his friend's aside of 'A companion then, or chaperone!' by interjecting,

'Told you, dear boy, it's a mess. There's just the dowager, Neville, Juliet and their old nurse now. She got shot of everyone else. Not best pleased about that, Neville wasn't but impossible for him to do anything about it. Fait accompli by the time he came home for the interment, d' ye see.'

This provoked a short laugh from his companion, 'I see nothing and yet, perhaps I am beginning to see everything. Do you tell me it was the *daughter* who dismissed the servants?' with dawning incredulity.

'Aye, yes, well, she's been more or less running the estate this past year. Sir Hugh had a set to with his agent, over the state of the tenantry and the debts piling up, I fear. Sent him packing and set Juliet to take his place, so I heard. Always liked her better than Neville. Often heard him say he wished she'd been the heir! Did everything better than the boy. Parson even taught her Latin and Greek! Sir Hugh insisted on trying to give her another Season last year, but she refused point blank. Knew what the situation was by then, naturally. Pity, a sound marriage would've saved the estate.'

The two riders remained in silent thought as their horses trotted along the lane towards some rather dilapidated wooden gates standing open, which heralded their destination. The duke was considering everything he had learned. It seemed he now knew the identity of the chance met lady. What he was failing to decide was if this had indeed been the case.

THREE

Of lawyers and hounds.

A sombre clothed, rotund lawyer sat regarding the two ladies who were the only other occupants of the dark, extremely cold stone room. His late client had deemed this to be fit enough to serve as the agent's office. The frail lady, wreathed in black shawls, lifted a mittened hand to dab at her eyes with a black edged wisp of a handkerchief. She emitted a weak moan. His expression softened as he looked at Lady Hugh - the Dowager Lady Cecily Dempster, rather, his legal mind chided him. Such a gentle, delicate lady, not a bit like the slim figure facing him across the oak desk. She appeared to have finished reading the rows of figures he had set before her and sat drumming her fingers in a most unladylike manner. He had been shocked on his arrival at seeing the sprigged muslin dress, over which she had draped a dove grey shawl. She had noticed his look and said, curtly,

'I doubt the estate could run to two sets of mourning finery!' Casting a disapproving glance at her mother's widow's weeds. 'My father would not have wanted me to add to the mire we find ourselves in!' she had added as justification.

Privately, Mr Peal thought that Sir Hugh would not have considered the estate at all, if he had desired anything for himself. But that indeed, was the difference between father and daughter. And between daughter and son - yes indeed. He sighed more loudly than he had intended, causing Miss Dempster to give him one of her direct looks.

'Is this everything now, Mr Peal? There are no other debts of any description?' She fixed him with her bright gaze as he coughed delicately, shooting a glance at the now steadily weeping widow.

'Mamma, I feel sure that you should find Nanny and lie down in your room.'

She shepherded her mother towards the door, as this lady muttered disjointedly, 'alone! - a man - unseemly!' into her lace.

'I can manage perfectly well, mamma.' Firmly closing the thick, aged door.

Mr Peal visibly relaxed. It really was quite disconcerting, but Miss Dempster seemed to be able to handle this sad state of affairs almost better than he could himself.

'Well now,' he began, 'as you may have gathered, it is a little delicate.' Pausing, he cleared his throat. 'It is a matter of a house...or rooms rather, added to which ...er - hem - dressmakers' bills, outstanding.'

'Of what are you talking!' The young lady's well-modulated voice seemed to bounce off the bare, cold walls bereft now of the hangings which had once adorned them. 'Mr Peal, whatever my father's faults, I am sure he never kept a mistress, so.........'

'No, no, no, no!' This came out as a series of horrified squeaks as the worthy man reddened, shaking his bewigged head. That a gently reared young lady should mention such things, and in relation to her own father, made him curl up inside, bachelor that he was.

He cleared his throat once more mopping his forehead, now beaded with sweat, despite the chill.

'No, dear lady! Horses, cards, dice, yes but no - I er - it's - er - the new squire. I mean Sir Neville.' He found himself unable to meet that direct amber-eyed gaze.

Quite distinctly he heard the quill she had been holding snap.

'I understand. Do you have more information?'

Really, he wished the will had not named Miss Dempster as executrix! All perfectly legal and binding. Another example of Sir Hugh Dempster's eccentricities but to name a one and twenty year old spinster as guardian to her brother and trustee for her mother!

'I believe the liaison was begun last year, in Oxford. The rooms are there, certainly, but the dressmaker is a London address. I am afraid the bankers wrote to your father when Mr - er - Sir Neville overdrew on his allowance, once again. However, the letter arrived after the accident.'

She tapped the paper she held, 'So, as well as tailors, potmen, ostlers, gaming hells, coachbuilders and bootmakers, my brother has squandered his allowance in other ways?' She smiled tightly at the lawyer.

'A pity Papa was riding Greyfriar, was it not?'

Noting his puzzlement she elaborated, 'He had to be shot, you know. Unfortunate, as he would have fetched enough to cover my brother's more pressing debts.'

He looked so shocked at her callous reference to the hunting accident which had killed her father, that she felt quite sorry for him. Gradually the enormity of the whole situation was being brought home to her, making her more outspoken than ever. She passed a shaking hand over her eyes.

'Forgive me Mr Peal, I meant merely to point out how Fate tricks us. Indeed, it was Papa who made such a remark about Greyfriar just before….'

'There are other horses and hounds still to be sold, are there not?' He ventured to suggest, at a loss as how to deal with tears from this young lady who had been in charge of tenants and the estate for over a year now.

'Oh yes,' she blew her nose - a remarkably forceful sound, 'but that will only serve to cover the more pressing of the debts. I had hoped to keep the Manor itself.' She looked at him directly once more.

'I know my brother is feckless but he does love the place, in his own way. He wishes to keep it too. Of course, he enjoys London too much to give it real care at present. Do you think we might possibly save it, Mr Peal?'

His lawyer's mind overruled the man's: 'Dear lady, we must take one step at a time. We have managed to clear most debts within six months, but I am afraid the gambling ones - debts of honour you realise! - must be settled as soon as they arrive. I would be failing in my duty if I did not point out that your brother's creditors will become more pressing, now that they know how things stand. The publication of the will, you know,' he added as she looked at a loss for the moment. 'If I might suggest,' he paused and pointed to a clause in the will as it rested on the desk between them. '...your mamma's house in Half Moon Street, left by her father for her lifetime. It is let by the season, I believe. If you were to move there, it being available at present, it might serve. Running costs would be considerably lower whilst you might get a tenant for Solworth. Being in deep mourning, no one would expect you to....'

She cut him short, 'Oh, excellent Mr Peal, I fear that I am too caught up in this to think rationally. But could we not sell Half Moon Street,' she began pacing the small room, 'an excellent position for a moderate family wishing to acquire a Town dwelling which would surely…' she stopped, midsentence as she saw him shaking his head.

'I am afraid any monies from a sale would revert to your cousin's family, it is the way of the entail, your mamma has use of it for her lifetime only.'

She inclined her head. 'Of course, foolish of me. Well, we can add the carriage horses to the contents on the bill of sale. One can walk in London much more easily than in the country, do you not suppose? Now, will you partake of some refreshment? Only ale I'm afraid.' Her determined chin came up, defiantly, 'I plan to sell the remains of the cellar too. The Claret and Port should attract some interest.'

Smiling slightly, he asked, 'What does Sir Neville say to that?'

She looked her blandest as she replied, 'He does not know. Nor shall he, until it is done. The Manor means more than crushed grapes!'

The lawyer looked shocked at hearing Sir

Hugh Dempster's famous cellar thus described. Then he began to laugh, a dry unused sound.

'Indeed, Miss Dempster, if anyone can keep the Manor in the family, I feel it will be you.'

'Believe me, sir, I am determined to try my utmost to ensure that is the case' she uttered with a vehemence most unbecoming in an unmarried lady.

Chafing his hands together, Mr Peal took out his pocket watch. He would be pleased to leave the penetrating chill of this room for the spring sunshine outside.

'I fear that I must depart without refreshment, Miss Dempster. There is the final bill of sale to prepare for the auction. If you are sure there is nothing else to note?'

Ruefully she shook her head as she opened the door, 'No, nothing. Mamma refuses to part with anymore furniture. Although the paintings in the hall must go, no matter what. You will add the carriage now, of course. I would also suggest Neville's curricle, however I believe the coach builder may be persuaded to take it back, it's so new.' She noticed the man's horrified face.

'Oh, never fear Mr Peal, I shall inform my brother first! He is due to arrive here soon, now that he has finally been brought to realise that his sojourn at Oxford is at an end.'

She crossed the uneven flagstone floor to the heavily studded oak door which stood open, letting in a shaft of sunlight. Having watched his coach depart down the unweeded drive she turned to contemplate the portraits of which she had spoken. Several generations of Dempsters stared unseeingly back at her. Over the fireplace hung one painted on her parents' marriage.

'Oh, Papa! So many debts! What were you thinking!

Her slim shoulders began to shake under the old grey shawl, as tears coursed unchecked down her cheeks. After a few minutes, she angrily dashed them away with her handkerchief. Shakily she took a deep, steadying breath and retrieved a list she had been making from the Jacobean chest which stood beside the huge stone fireplace. A delicate oval miniature was the only other object on this chest. Picking it up carefully, she angled it towards the sunlight, tracing the long hair, pointed beard and lace collar points.

'Time to part with this!' Resolutely she wrote with her pencil; Van Dyke locket, containing note written to Sir Rupert Dempster from Charles 1st. It pained her to part with this treasure, especially as her father had insisted it was hers to wear and keep for her children. Shaking herself, she thought, 'Neville will only pawn it!' This too, would have to be placed in the auction. Laying it gently on its velvet wrapping, she heard the sound of hooves approaching. Almost imperceptibly she straightened her shoulders, lifting her head and rubbed at her face with her shawl before walking with great purpose to the door.

She was fully expecting to see her brother's canary yellow curricle standing outside. She did not expect to see two gentlemen on horseback. Fleetingly she considered calling to her mamma but in reality, if it were more creditors, she could at least spare her mother that humiliation. With these thoughts, she stepped boldly out into the bright sunshine. The contrast from the interior gloom dazzled her eyes and for an instant she failed to recognise her closest neighbour, Lord Roger Hitchley. Holding her hand to her brow against the glare, she regarded the other gentleman. It seemed to be the same person whom she had met that morning by the ruins. She stepped out onto the gravel and dropped a curtsy to Lord Roger.

'My Lord, what can I do for you?' She caught the quick lift of the other's brows at her want of manners to himself.

'Please to come in.' A slight flush crept up her pale cheeks as she hoped they would not take her at her word. There was little hospitality she could offer, in their present circumstances and with the Manor in such disarray. The riders dismounted but remained standing on the unkempt drive.

'Forgive our unannounced visit, especially during your period of mourning.'

She felt her colour rise again as it seemed to her that the other gentleman was glancing askance at her lack of mourning attire. In fact, she was overly sensitive as his look had been to register recognition of the sprig muslin dress he had noticed earlier that morning.

'Firstly, allow me to present you. Miss Dempster, Charles, Duke of Vénoire. Vénoire, Miss Juliet Dempster.'

No fault could be found in the elegant and precise depth of her curtsy this time! Vénoire bowed over her hand taking it to assist her in rising. He made no reference to their previous meeting, and she felt discomforted by this.

'Your servant, mam'selle.' The froideur in his tone belied the statement. Had this morning's encounter really been by chance? This thought occurred to him once again.

'I am honoured, your grace.'

He could not fail to note her irony. Did he really expect her to find importance in his visit, she could not help thinking.

For a bemused moment Roger looked from one to another, failing to comprehend why there should be such an uneasy atmosphere. Both stood stiffly regarding each other.

'Yes, well...It's about the hounds. Heard the pack was for sale.'

Juliet turned her shoulder to the duke, virtually snubbing him, whilst responding to Roger.

'Why, yes that is certainly the case.' She gathered herself together. 'Are Papa's hounds of interest to you, my lord? I collect you and he were often at outs about their breeding! If you wish to view them, they are in the kennels at the rear of the house. Please to follow me.'

Without waiting for confirmation, she set off around the side of the building.

Once again, Vénoire found himself following her straight, slim figure. Her glossy chestnut hair was caught back from her face with a plain black ribbon, yet there was an innate elegance to the way she carried herself. Certainly, her hair was chestnut he realised, despite the auburn tones he had at first noted. Easy to have mistaken her for an upper servant he again thought, yet she wore a certain air of authority. He was used to most young ladies being flustered or coquettish on first being introduced, not bristling with indignation! It piqued and intrigued him.

They had tied their horses to the rings along the stable wall as Miss Dempster opened the door to the huge kennels. It was patently obvious that the wood here was in much better condition than that at the entrance gates to the estate. All the names on the interior doors were also picked out in gold leaf.

They followed the lady to the far end of the kennels where the whole pack of hounds lay behind a makeshift partition.

'Having them all in one stall makes it easier to care for them.' She stated, defensively.

The obvious leader of the pack was already jumping at her skirts but she seemed oblivious to any harm he might inflict on her dress. Indeed, she even knelt in the straw to fondle the ears of a sleepy young hound.

'They are getting sluggish for want of a run, I'm afraid.'

'Does your kennel man not see to them?' The duke loftily inquired. Even to his own ears, this sounded condescending. He had meant it as an inquiry of concern for her obvious worry.

Hitchley tutted repressively but before he could interject Miss Dempster shot back,

'I am the kennel man!' Covering this impetuous disclosure with an attempt at social conversation, she inquired, 'Do you breed your hounds, your grace?'

'I have no hounds, as yet.'

The young lady looked a little at a loss, glancing at Hitchley who began,

'I thought... that is, Vénoire thought... we'd take a look.'

Abruptly she stood, provoking a low growl from the hound who had had his muzzle in her lap. She brushed straw from her shabby shawl fringe, saying in a tight, low voice,

'I thank you for your concern, Lord Roger, but it is misplaced.'

Roger gave her a blank look. 'I don't quite follow?'

Vénoire filled the ensuing strained silence with his studied drawl, 'I think the young lady is attempting to tell us that she does not wish to accept an offer made out of... ah... neighbourliness.' He managed to prevent himself from using the word compassion.

As understanding dawned, Roger began a flustered explanation which was becoming very tangled. His friend spoke again in order to end it.

'It is indeed I who wish to acquire your hounds. Not for hunting, nor breeding. I have a notion that I will set a fashion: if I have one attend my person no matter where, then I would be amused to find out how long before others follow suit. It will become the talk of this Season. Certainly a way to lift ennui!'

So saying, he turned to look at the pack as if to choose, hence failing to see the indignant glare she threw at him.

'The pack is for sale as a whole, or not at all!' Why did she find this gentleman's attitude humiliating? She knew from her brother and his friends that such starts were only too usual. For some reason, that a man like the duke should want to indulge in such base frivolity raised her indignation. A careless frippery with scant thought for cost. How far apart were their situations!

Detecting the steel in her tone he turned one of his piercing gazes on her face. Under her proud look he caught a glimpse of vulnerability.

'Then I shall take the pack!'

'London would hardly seem the right place!' She could not prevent herself from riposting.

There was an undercurrent to this interchange which Hitchley was still failing to comprehend. Bored civility was usually Vénoire's watchword, there was no sign of boredom nor very much civility that he could detect in his words. He was even more shocked at his next pronouncement.

'Shall we come to the matter of price?' asked with icy hauteur. To Vénoire's own ears this seemed painfully crass. What had become of his well-schooled manners was his thought.

Miss Dempster seemed to hug her shawl more tightly to herself. With none of the warmth nor ease which she had shown by the ruins she rigidly suggested, 'Perhaps you would come inside?'

Such was her tone and demeanour that the duke replied at his most sarcastic,

'Haggle in the drawing room? Oh, surely the stables are more appropriate. You do have a price in mind, I would expect?' Again, he was shocked at the words he was uttering. That a gently reared young woman had been forced to think about debts rather than on what to spend her pin money seemed iniquitous. He could not explain to himself why it had stirred such rancour.

She found herself unable to form a temperate response. What right did this arrogant creature have to judge her? A man of his rank and wealth could have no concept of the straits she found herself in.

Lord Hitchley coughed, appalled at his friend's ill-mannered remark. He could not understand such a lapse. In fact, he disremembered ever seeing the duke thus in public.

Vénoire's next words were even more shocking, 'I will pay any sum you care to name. My grooms will come to collect the pack to take them to Denbrugh as soon as I receive your price.'

He found himself bowing to the rigidly presented back of the young lady as she resolutely took Hitchley's arm before he realised that he had offered it. They walked out towards the waiting horses.

The duke remained rooted to the spot. One of the hounds was snuffling at his boot through the partition. He lifted the dog's head, regarding its intelligent brown eyes. The growl it emitted made him lose his tight grip. He felt in the throes of an inexplicable anger. A choler which he had been trained to suppress behind suave, well-mannered social skills. He knew that he had been intolerably rude to a defenceless female who had done nothing to provoke him. It was her situation which had provoked him! A situation over which he had no control. What had happened to his noted sangfroid? He tried to bring some order to his emotions as he was used to do; to recover his usual well-mannered demeanour, but found he was unable to overrule his seething feelings. This was disquieting. A slip of a girl, very much below him in social standing was affecting his equilibrium.

He strode into the stable yard where he found Roger mounted, waiting for him impatiently. There was no sign of their hostess.

'Demmit it all Charles! What is the matter with you? I told you how it was here before we came. She's mortified at having to do the necessary without you making it seem more sordid!'

The blazing anger he saw in his friend's face at this remark served to silence him. Before Roger had time to ask more, Charles had vaulted into the saddle, gathered his reins and kicked his startled horse into action. Hitchley was left to stare after the bay gelding's heels as it took off in a spurt of gravel.

FOUR

Thoughts of the duke's cousin.

The duke had passed a fitful night, irritating for one who was normally a sound sleeper. He had been uncharacteristically short in his response to Ferris when the latter inquired what attire he wished laid out. In consequence of which, a silent valet had begun brushing his master's coat of French-blue broadcloth. He knelt to help the duke into his low heeled, plain buckled shoes.

'I apologise Tom. I seem to be severely blue-devilled this morning.' He allowed his man to set his pearl pin in his plain cravat before shrugging into the well-tailored coat.

'Perhaps it's the rain, sir. Doesn't seem likely to stop anytime soon.'

Vénoire nodded, absently. Tom Ferris cast him a searching look. He had already surmised that the duke had slept badly. On entering the bedchamber, he had found him already seated by the almost dead fire, with a guttering candle stub for company. The duke was rarely ill and led an active life, therefore insomnia was not something he was generally acquainted with.

'Tell me, my good Thomas, would you recognise thyme?'

This provoked a pause, then, 'Recognise time, your grace? I apologise but I don't follow.'

With a rueful shake of the head, Vénoire repeated his question, in French, adding, 'It is a bush.'

'Oh, your grace means the herb. I'm not sure I would. A kitchen maid or the cook would for certain.' Hoping this was helpful.

'Ah, as always you are invaluable!' He walked thoughtfully towards the door. When Ferris would have opened it, he stayed him briefly, 'Would you ask the cook for…a branch, a sprig….. whatever…to be delivered to the library this afternoon?'

Not by a flicker did Ferris demonstrate he found such a request odd.

'Also, have a message sent to Wilkes. I think it a good idea that the blacks are exercised sometime today.'

After breaking his fast in solitary state, the duke chose to sit beside the library fire. He was pleased to have the solitude in which to try to order his straying thoughts. His behaviour to Miss Dempster had shocked him all the more because of his inability to comprehend his reason for this. Most of his adult life he had acted with due care for his social inferiors, for those weaker than himself and for those dependent upon him, whether family or staff. He had apologised to Roger for causing him embarrassment. What was more important to him now was to offer an apology to Miss Dempster. Somehow it mattered to him that she should not take him for an arrogant boor. Her fine-boned face hovered in his mind, cold and reproving. He singularly failed to conjure it with the smile he was certain had been present by the ruins. The more he tried to reorder his thoughts, the more they behaved like skittish colts. He had tried to turn them to the loss of his emerald ring and the robbery which had caused it. Even this puzzle had proved fruitless. Numerous times he attempted to recall the exact shade of the grey eyes which had confronted him then, instead they were supplanted by angry amber ones.

He was failing to choose a book with which to occupy himself when his cousin entered.

At just above four feet tall, Lady Roger Hitchley, née d'Alvière, was diminutive and delicate. No one considered her height once they were acquainted with her. She had inherited the d'Alvière presence. This morning she was attired in an apple green morning gown, over which she wore a heavy russet cloak. A bonnet which matched the apple green colour covered her black curls which fell in ringlets about her face.

Four years separated Hélène and Charles; initially they had been brought up together at the château de Palombières. This in part explained their closeness. A closeness which had increased and deepened after her marriage to the duke's school friend in 1774. This was the same year in which Charles had inherited his titles, becoming the head of the d'Alvière family. They each valued the other, knowing they could always expect honesty as well as genuine affection. Hélène's mercurial temperament was often tempered by her cousin's comments, whilst Charles cynicism was lightened by her outrageousness.

He stood on her entrance, bowing. In response she sketched a curtsy. He was assailed by the question why did this not offend him when another such had? Was he really so tender about his status?

As always if they were alone together, they conversed in French.

'Roger will be glad the rain has ceased. He and the agent are visiting some of the tenants. I have a sick visit to make. Cook has prepared some beef broth for the Billings. Will you forgive me if I abandon you?'

Vénoire walked to the window, 'You have not ordered your carriage yet? Might I suggest that I escort you? I was wishful to give the blacks an airing so you would be rendering me a service.'

Girlishly she clapped her hands,

'Perfect! If you are sure? Where we need to visit will be a touch muddy, I fear. Your turnout will not be so smart afterwards.' They both laughed. He was perfectly at ease with her teasing. He glanced at her booted feet. A vision of neat, wet stockinged ankles flashed before him. He hoped that his face had not betrayed this.

'Send a message to the stables and I will send to the kitchen. I will not keep you.' She left the room.

Hélène was true to her word. By the time he had on his caped greatcoat and plain tricorne, she had re-joined him. A few minutes after which, Wilkes had driven the carriage round. Her basket was held by one footman, whilst the other opened the door.

Vénoire assisted her into the carriage and the basket was stowed safely below the opposite seat.

'I will attend your mistress on her visit. No need to accompany us.' He stated.

She gave him a questioning look and on seeing the slight shake of his head, she added her own order, 'Have the fire made up in the library and some mulled ale ready for his lordship's return, Robert.'

'Certainly, your ladyship.' Closing the door, he correctly interpreted the duke's nod to instruct Wilkes to drive on.

Hélène settled back against the blue squabs, regarding her cousin curiously. Vénoire was known for his feigned air of ennui. She knew that this was a well-practiced facade, although lately she had begun to fear it was not so much a fashionable trait. Wondering if his suggestion of the carriage drive was a ruse for something other, she smiled and waited.

He continued to stare into the distance for several seconds, then surprised her by asking,

'Am I become insensitively arrogant? Everything in my life is ordered exactly to my requirements. I order my people, they accommodate my smallest need. Tristan and Louise follow my wishes, no matter their own. Society aims to please me and yet here am I kicking against duty and expectations!' This had been uttered in a terse voice, unlike his normal mannered tones.

She sat up, taking his hand, 'My dear Charles, tell me truthfully what besets you? You describe your symptoms not your ills, I think.'

He squeezed her hand, saying abruptly, 'My ills! There's the nub; in reality, what ills do I suffer? None in comparison to you… or…'

He felt her hand tremble within his and he was thankfully certain that she had not picked up on what else he had been about to reveal.

'Oh - ills? - oh - I know not what to call our disappointments! Eight years and still no child in the nursery! Each time I have confided our expectations to my dear Roger, only to see his sorrow when I fail him, again!' Tears glistened now on her lashes.

'You do not fail him! Dearest Hélène, you must never doubt that there will be a child!' He felt keenly this couple's losses, knowing his cousin's yearning to give her husband an heir. They were both healthy and there seemed no reason why her pregnancies failed to come to fruition.

She removed her hand from his, in order to retrieve her handkerchief,

'It has been a year now, without even the hope!' Looking away from him she regarded the distant huddle of cottages which were their destination. Her next utterance seemed forced from her, 'Sometimes, I think that God is punishing us!'

This was too much for Vénoire. 'What utter nonsense! No, what arrant nonsense!'

Like most young French ladies of her status, Hélène had been educated in a convent until her debut. She was goaded into replying with some of her accustomed fire, 'I cannot worship as I would in this God forsaken country!'

'God forsaken? Oh, my dear, King George would disagree with you!'

This slight sally raised a tremulous smile as she straightened her bonnet, sitting back with a sigh. The duke thought seriously about what she had revealed to him. It was another instance of something over which he had no control. And if he were to marry for duty's sake, the Hitchleys proved that an heir was not destined to follow.

Wilkes brought the carriage to a halt as close to the cottage's path as was possible and had the door opened before Vénoire could retrieve the basket. Reaching in, he said,

'If you'll allow me, your ladyship,' and lifted it down and across to the nearby low wall. Then he helped her to descend the carriage step, deftly swinging her over the mud where hens pecked. He then doffed his tricorne to his master and the lady, returning to the horses' heads.

'I will not keep your horses standing long, Charles.'

He watched her respectful welcome by a woman with several small children clinging to her skirts. He was now even more at liberty to think. However, on Hélène's return with an empty basket, he seemed to have made no progress in sifting his thoughts. Once they were on the move again, she repeated her previous question,

'Charles, what besets you?' adding, 'Both Roger and I know you are not yourself.'

Linking his elegant fingers and resting his chin, he offered, 'Of that I am aware, yet I hardly know why.'

He decided it was more than time to confide in someone and Hélène was his perfect confidant. 'I have been ill at ease for several months past. The thought of another Season, another social round has filled me with repugnance. I know that I must marry soon, for duty's sake, for the family, yet…'

She interrupted, 'You hoped to find someone who would become your bride for love rather than titles and wealth.'

He nodded, smiling wryly, 'Foolish, I know!'

She shook her head, 'Not foolish, never that. Unlikely, perhaps. I was lucky that Uncle Louis supported Roger's suit.'

'Oh, I would give myself permission, if the thing came about!' He was attempting to bring some humour to his deepest feelings.

Abruptly he demanded, 'Did the Dempsters know of my visit to Stanford?' The gleam of humour had been extinguished.

'No. They are in deep mourning, as I'm sure Roger explained. Lady Cecily and I do not favour each other's company. Roger and Sir Hugh were wont to hunt together. I have extended invitations to include Miss Dempster in the past, but we have never been in each other's pockets. What makes you ask?'

'I have not told Roger about this.' He twisted his bare ring finger whilst thinking about what he wished to reveal. 'I met Miss Dempster on my morning ride, before we went to inspect the hounds.'

'Oh, yes?' She realised this statement was reluctantly made. 'I believe you have purchased the pack?' Her comment was laden with irony. 'For some foolish fashion start? Really, Charles, you are better than that. What were you thinking?'

He remained tautly silent beside her, then blurted out, much against his will, 'My wish was to help! How could her father have laid such a burden on her slight shoulders!'

She regarded him carefully. A slow enlightenment was emerging from what she was hearing. In truth he did not realise the import of his words, she surmised.

'I was abominably rude to her but that was not my intention.' Suddenly his smile lit his face, 'At one point, she snubbed me expertly! She has spirit!'

'Indeed. If you were ill mannered I am shocked. You owe an apology, surely?' Hélène was determined not to mention her true thoughts forming about his behaviour. He was behaving irrationally due to never having encountered such a young lady as Miss Dempster. She must favour Roger with her ideas.

'Of a certainty I owe the lady an abject apology.'

The carriage was slowing as they reached the house. The duke's habitual demeanour had returned. His discussion with his cousin had seemed to be of benefit. For his cousin some things were becoming clear.

On hearing the return of the carriage, Ferris had emerged from the servants' domain. Ostensibly, he was ready to receive his master's driving coat and hat. Vénoire was surprised at this until he caught a distinctive aroma.

'The desk in the library, if you please, Tom. I sincerely thank you.' This was spoken in a lowered tone as his coat was removed. Hélène was busy ascertaining if Lord Roger had returned.

The duke soon found himself once more seated in the welcoming library of Stanford Park. Here, he began composing a heartfelt apology. This consumed a fair amount of time and several crumpled sheets of paper. Eventually satisfied, he folded his missive, enclosing a generous sprig of thyme leaves, under his seal. The heat and the pressure caused by its sealing produced the pungent aroma which he now recognised. It also evoked the delightful picture of a slim figure in a faded muslin dress, her amber eyes seemed to be mocking him!

FIVE

The duke's brother brings tidings.

A rather lathered looking horse was approaching the front of the house. On it sat a young gentleman with the unmistakable d'Alvière features but without an air of boredom about them. Instead, he wore a certain look of fatigued preoccupation as he tied his purebred bay to the ring in the post by the shallow steps. Mounting these slowly, the oaken door opened to reveal the stately figure of Westock. The butler cast a pained glance towards the horse; in his opinion the stable yard was the only suitable place for horses. The face he presented to the visitor was bland as he greeted him politely,

'Lord Tristan.' He bowed. 'I had not been informed that we were expecting you.' Taking his slightly damp cloak from his lordship's shoulders before passing it, with his tricorne, to the footman, he continued,

'I shall endeavour to find Lord Roger.' His tone carried a slight reproof. No matter that the estates of Stanford Park and Denbrugh Place were separated only by a dozen miles, casual visits were not something the old retainer condoned. 'Perhaps you would care to wait in the library.'

Tristan followed his measured tread across the checkered hall, to be ushered through the door with it then being firmly closed. The fire burning brightly in the fireplace was most welcome. His riding clothes showed evidence that he had endured the rain showers which had persisted. It was a comfort to warm his hands at the hearth. He desperately hoped that his brother had not cut short his visit here, yet he would have avoided the coming interview, if he could. Chafing his hands again, he helped himself to a glass of brandy. He had just tossed this off when the door clicked open softly.

An even softer voice asked, 'To what do I owe this singularly unexpected honour?'

The duke leant against the now closed door, arms crossed. He regarded his brother as he was pouring his second glass of brandy.

The younger d'Alvière ran a hand through his already dishevelled locks, pulling more strands from the confining ribbon of his queue. Squaring his shoulders he stated, 'I thought I should inform you that Louise and I are now at Denbrugh. We arrived yesterday.' His blue eyes seemed to be fixed on the wooden panels of the door behind his brother's head. Louise, their seventeen-year-old sister, had been living in France in the care of this brother, at their elder's decree.

Not by the flicker of an eyelid did the duke betray any emotion. In the same neutral tone he had been using, he asked, 'Indeed, forgive me. It seems my memory is not what it was. I had thought to find you both at Grosvenor Square, one week from now. Was that not what we had arranged? I must assume that you have good reason for changing my plans.'

He removed the decanter from Tristan's

reach, as his brother swallowed a third glass.

'I was caught in some rain you know! I don't want to risk a chill!' Even to his own ears, this sounded petulant. On receiving no other response than a raised eyebrow, he reluctantly continued, 'I did not know what else to do. I tried my best in Paris, Charles, I really did but short of cutting the man dead and causing a scandal...I could think of nothing else! He is after all, an acquaintance but being aware of his reputation... I really had no idea that.... Oh, it's all such tangle!' He stopped short, suddenly seating himself in the chair facing the window.

Vénoire moved to join him, 'My dearest brother, I fail to comprehend what it is that you are attempting to explain. Except that none of it is your fault. Which one knows it never is!' He raised a hand to still the reply, ' Acknowledging the fact that you cannot help your own incompetence, do try to give a more lucid explanation.'

Eyeing his brother warily he blurted out, 'Well, its Aldersleigh, of course!'

'Ah, now things are becoming much clearer to me.'

To all who knew the duke well, his deceptively calm tones betokened rising anger. 'Has Louise found ways to continue meeting him?'

Tristan shifted uncomfortably in the chair, 'I had thought, only unavoidably in public, as was agreed. Instead, I discovered that they had been meeting secretly in Notre Dame! I had no suspicions other than she was going to early Mass with her maid. Then last week, at a bal masqué held at Versailles, I discovered them alone together in a private ante-room. I threatened to call him out but Louise began to cause a scene there and then. That gossip the duchess de Lucre heard the fuss and found us. We all passed it off of course. Give Aldersleigh his due, he replaced his mask swiftly enough...... he doesn't want a scandal either.' He paused. 'Not a bit of use taking her to Grosvenor Square, she threatened to run away!' He ventured a look at his brother's set face.

'Yes, my dear, I quite see that you have surpassed yourself! How comes it that you are exemplary at managing Palombières Tristan, yet now you arrive in England bringing chaos in your wake? No, spare me an explanation, I fear I could not stand it!'

There was a lengthy pause, then Charles's sarcastic tone changed to a more interrogative one. 'Who else might have seen them together? How did you discover their meetings in Notre Dame? We must see what is to be done.'

Tristan's high colour receded somewhat, 'It was Jules saw them in church, so I'm sure of his discretion.' Jules was Tristan's valet. 'I saw the duchess de Lucre talking behind her fan to…. de Langon!' He waited for his elder's reaction.

Vénoire looked very grave indeed. 'Then it is worse than I feared. You know how that man hates us. He would delight in damaging our sister's reputation. I don't like it at all! You travelled directly to Denbrugh from Paris?'

Tristan nodded with an expression of distaste, 'Paid a merchant to take the carriage aboard his boat…. thank the Lord for a short crossing and calm seas!' He was not a good sailor.

'I assume Nounou has taken charge of Louise, she will keep her close. You removed her maid, I take it?'

'Certainly I did! Charles, I meant to keep her in check but…' he shrugged apologetically.

'Yes.' Grimacing, Charles added, 'A pity our sister could not have been more like our mother in character as well as looks! I will not have her flout me like this! The answer seems to be that I must bring a match about for her, this Season.' He noted his brother's incredulous look. 'You don't agree?'

'She'll never agree to marrying anyone else whilst she imagines herself in love with Aldersleigh! Charles, please be…' he stuttered at the enormity of contradicting his forceful elder, '…be careful she don't elope with him!'

Charles regarded him fixedly, 'Dear me, does it run so deep? Louise is but a child. I cannot allow her to ruin herself with such a one.'

His frown had grown heavy and menacing. His little sister reminded him forcefully of memories of their mother. He felt most protective of her, desiring a good match. Aldersleigh could not be considered. Despite a large fortune, he was dissolute, residing mainly in Venice where he was rumoured to have several mistresses and numerous offspring. His lineage was ancient, but he held no land in England and retained his fortune by maintaining gaming hells. Not a suitable alliance for Lady Louise d'Alvière! Vénoire was somewhat perturbed to know what game he was playing. The rules were fixed; one did not entrap the fragile heart of an innocent.

'Of a certainty, it seems it is time to bestir myself.'

Tristan had been watching his elder brother's face. At five and twenty he was perfectly at ease in his world, yet he remained in awe of the duke.

Their father had insisted that this son remain in France for his education. A perverse rather than a loving notion. Thus, a succession of tutors had prepared Tristan to be a perfect French aristocrat. He knew exactly where he stood within his rank; he could be enraptured with fabric and wig styles. He had been eight when his mother had died. His father had brought him to Versailles to act as page to his great friend - the duc de Langon. Not well planned. De Langon had been a rejected suitor of she who became Catherine, duchess de Vénoire. He grew embittered after she had made her choice. One night in his cups, he had vilified her in Tristan's hearing. A footman had prevented Tristan from stabbing the duc and the duc from beating his page senseless. Both still bore the scars.

The younger d'Alvière spent the remaining years of his father's lifespan running wild on their Loire estate. He was eighteen when his brother inherited and he himself took possession of the annuity left to him by his mother. All to the good. Vénoire took his brother in hand; he removed him to Oxford, for a belated education befitting his rank in life.

The two were in actuality very close. However, Tristan remained wary of his brother's moods. He was at his happiest living the life of a French country gentleman, running the estate at Palombières, much to the derision of such as de Langon. Ever more spiteful in his old age.

Until this latest start, Louise had happily resided in France, too. Rising and hoping to emulate his brother's tone, he asked, 'Yes but, may one possibly enjoy a change of clothes and some food first?'

Vénoire laughed at this sally, 'You have brought a change? I see no sign of Jules.'

'Oh, I packed a cloak bag. Ferris will despair but my aim was discretion!'

Swept along on a fog of fatigue, Tristan allowed himself to be led upstairs to his prepared bedchamber.

It was in a slightly better frame of mind that Tristan joined his family for dinner. Ferris had been sent to his chamber, in order to help him dress. Tristan's packing had resulted in a sad mixture of styles and fabrics - silk breeches, brocade waistcoat and velvet jacket.

Hélène threw up her hands on his entering the salon.

'Ah, Roger, I fear you are sadly out of style! See, the latest fashion at Versailles!'

Vénoire, elegant as ever in sapphire velvet and lace, regarded his brother over the tips of his joined fingers, 'You must let me have the direction of the tailor from whom you purchased that extraordinary... waistcoat.'

Tristan brightened at this, 'Oh, certainly. I was convinced you wouldn't find it to your taste...' he tailed off as he encountered his brother's eyes.

'Oh, you devil! I might have known!' He laughed, showing no rancour at being baited.
'It looks a deal better with the scarlet jacket and gold breeches it's meant for.'

His elder gave an exaggerated shudder, 'No, spare me!'

And he and Hélène led them into dinner.

The gentlemen did not linger long with their port. Hélène dismissed the servants, once the tea tray had been brought, then the duke explained the circumstances of Tristan's unannounced arrival.

'Roger, would you give your leave for Hélène to act as my hostess, certainly for the ball?'

'Happily, if she wishes it.' He noticed how her face was alight with enthusiasm. 'I can easily return here if it were to be required.'

Vénoire spoke again, 'A Court presentation could be aided by Great Aunt Barbara's influence. She tells me Queen Charlotte remains a regular correspondent. I must pay her a visit at Lessing Dower House.'

The Dowager Countess of Lessing was the youngest sister of old Earl James. She had also been Lady Catherine's Godmother. Vénoire visited her regularly.

Tristan then shot him an assessing look, 'Will you write to Louise with the news?'

His brother smiled, silkily, 'Oh, no. I insist that you are the bearer of such good tidings!' His tone brooked no argument.

Hélène suggested, 'I will travel to Denbrugh with you, Tristan. Louise and I can discuss her new wardrobe. What young lady could rail against such a delightful prospect?'

SIX

Miss Dempster's brother brings concerns.

There was to be seen much bustle of departures and arrivals upon the morrow around the lanes and roads surrounding these estates.

Firstly, his grace the duke of Vénoire set off, in tolerable style, to cover the forty miles into Hampshire to visit his ageing great aunt at Lessing Dower House.

Lord Tristan d'Alvière and Lady Roger Hitchley accompanied by her maid, left in her travelling chaise for Denbrugh Place. No great journey.

Unknown to these travellers, a canary yellow curricle came at a swift pace along the road from the Oxford direction. It turned in at the gates to Solworth Manor, amid a great scrunching of gravel and flashing of high-bred hooves.

Watching this arrival from her gatehouse room above the entrance hall, Miss Dempster stifled a sigh. She replaced the ledger she had been scanning onto her small escritoire. Squaring her shoulders, she descended the spiral stone stairs into the hall below.

Here, flicking through letters left for later attention, stood her brother. She regarded him from the bottom step. Her view was unobscured as the tapestry which usually hung there was awaiting the auction. What she saw, made her brows contract into a frown and her lips change to a grimace of disapproval.

Her seventeen-year-old brother was of medium height with moderately handsome features. These were marred at present by a look of dissipation and also a wary, hunted quality. Her sighing made him start guiltily, turning to see who was there. A smile lightened his face and he looked the boy he was again as he greeted her.

'Why Ju. I was just attending to the post!'

He had swiftly pocketed one of the letters, she observed. Giving him an appraising look she picked up the remainder, folding her arms. 'I'm glad you are come at last, Neville. We need to talk!'

Avoiding her eyes, he crossed towards the agent's room on the other side of the door.

'Yes, well. I have spoken with Peal you know, and I think we shall come through.'

He made a point of sitting behind the desk, smiling serenely at his sister as she stood before him. Keeping her tone even, Juliet sat perforce on the facing chair.

'Mr Peal told you that?'

He was unable to meet her gaze directly, yet continued in the hearty tone he had chosen to adopt. 'Not as such but he explained what you have planned for this week and I think it's the right decision.'

He missed the flash of anger on his sister's face as he continued, loftily, 'I've told him now that I am here, he may refer to me and you will look after mamma. He seemed much happier knowing he will now deal with…The Heir.' He emphasised his last words.

'Impossible! You are an insufferable, conceited boy and have no conception of how wretched it all is!' She had not raised her voice but stood shaking with controlled anger. 'The heir or not, papa nevertheless, named me executrix!'

Jumping up, Neville truculently said,
'I shall be eighteen in a month's time and then…'

'Oh, a month! Do you seriously think our creditors will wait as long as that? These are more final demands, Neville!' She unclenched her fingers on the letters she held. 'I have done what must be done in an attempt to repay all that is owed. Once the auction has taken place, we may just be solvent, but we must get a tenant for the Manor. Mamma's annuity will be enough to keep us, nothing more!'

He shook his head, smiling still, 'I have been planning too. Friends have made a good offer for the pack of hounds and the remaining hunters. I have also paid some of my debts of honour.' He waited for the praise he expected his sister to shower upon him.

Instead, she regarded him in stunned silence before stating, 'The hounds are sold already.'

'But they can't be! I promised… he swore he would wipe…'

She caught his arm as he paced towards the window. 'What are you saying? Neville, the estate can no longer pay for your weaknesses!' So saying, she whisked the letter he had previously abstracted out of his pocket, twitching away from his grasp.

'No! Give that back! You are not the heir, I am!'

A rustle in the doorway made them both turn, as the thready voice of their mother uttered, 'My Darling Boy, of course you are! How good to see you in your rightful place.'

Then she dissolved into tears.

Neville rushed to embrace her before escorting her to the chair. This enabled Juliet to swiftly peruse the disputed letter. The owner of rented rooms in Oxford thanked Sir Neville for belated payment of outstanding rent. Thoughtfully, his sister handed it back to him.

'How?'

'What?' Holding his mother's hand, he looked more boyish than ever, despite his fashionable clothes.

'I enquired, how?'

Glancing at his mother he frowned back, 'I just did it! What have you done with my hounds?'

Their mother decided to calm the atmosphere.

'Juliet, we would all benefit from some refreshment. Nanny can bring it; she must be appraised of our Boy's arrival.'

Needing time to think, Miss Dempster made no demur at being dispatched in search of Nanny. Impossible that the bank had advanced Neville any money. Their financial situation was so well known by now that there could be no credit. How then had he settled any debts?

Nanny was found in the echoing servants' hall, once the abbey cloisters. She produced a bottle of claret and made to open it. She correctly interpreted Juliet's look.

'Never you fear, this is from the case your father gave to me when The Boy was born, not the cellar.' She sniffed, 'Can't abide it, myself!'

Her tone softened as she became aware of the droop to Juliet's shoulders and the dark circles beneath her amber coloured eyes.

'The brandy he gave me when my girl was born, that's to be opened on the day she weds!'

Briefly, Miss Dempster relaxed against the ample bosom from which she had received her only maternal affection. Dryly she laughed, straightening once again. 'Then you should open it, Nanny! You cannot await a miracle, which is what is needed before your dowerless girl can fulfil that dream!'

Her old nurse simply tutted, placing the opened wine and glasses on a tray.

Then she followed Juliet to the agent's room. Here, Neville presented a perfect portrait of filial affection, standing behind the widow's chair. His sister seated herself behind the desk, leaving him no option but to remain standing. She added the newly received demands to the folder from which she withdrew several sheets of paper, covered with Mr Peal's meticulous copperplate. She deliberately remained with head bent until her mother broke the strained silence.

'My dear, do you not think…….' Her voice faded away as she encountered her daughter's gaze.

'Neville, how have you settled some of your debts? Where did you obtain such a large sum from? Until after the auction the bank will honour nothing in our name.'

A slow tide of red crept up her brother's pale face. 'It's really that bad?' For the first time his gaze was candid and a little scared. His sister nodded. 'I swear I have paid them. I offered the pack and hunters only after losing last night.'

'Well, I will cross the hunters off the auction list. You must inform your friends that the hounds have been sold already.'

'Who bought them, perhaps they might reconsider?'

Unconsciously, she was rubbing a few dried leaves which had fallen from the folder. An aroma of thyme filled the room. Shaking her head she said, 'Oh, I doubt the duke of Vénoire ever reconsiders anything he does.'

Juliet looked up at her brother's sharp intake of breath and her mother's reproach as he painfully gripped her shoulder. He then moved to the window saying flatly, 'So… That must wait until after the auction.'

The dowager lady Dempster surveyed both of her children. The whole of her life had been spent in someone else's shadow. Firstly, her domineering father, then her unloving husband. The arrival of her Darling Boy had given her such joy, removing the necessity of sharing a distasteful marriage bed. Lavishing all her emotion on Neville, she and her daughter had grown further apart. Juliet's character was all her father's; riding fearlessly from the time she could walk, devouring books which the Boy struggled with.

The wedge between the parents divided the children too. By the time Sir Hugh realised that his son was a spoiled, petted milksop, it was too late for any closeness between them. He set about 'making a man of him' but succeeded only in introducing him to manly vices. He praised his daughter and damned his son. He judged his heir and found him wanting. In his widow's eyes, her boy remained perfection, whilst her daughter remained a puzzle.

Attempting a stronger voice, the widow pleaded, 'My dears, we only have each other. We must face the future together.' She held her hands to both, tears still hovering on her lashes.

Deciding the moment was right, Juliet stated, bluntly, 'We can only do so if we quit the Manor. If we secure a tenant, we may come about.' For the first time in her mother's presence, she allowed her tears to fall. 'We must move to Half Moon Street.' She told them of the lawyer's suggestion.

'Oh, what a dear kind man! I must write at once to thank him,' was all the dowager said.

Her daughter looked bemused, as their mother drifted out.

Neville was first to recover, 'I think I may know of a tenant. I need to return to Oxford first in order to be certain, then I will join you in Town.'

'You seem to have found an exceedingly large amount of money from somewhere. Can you not explain?'

Suddenly he was all bluster again, 'Why should I explain to a female! It's my business, I will sort it!'

'Very well! Arrange your tenant by all means, but I will require Mr Peal to check his credentials as to solvency.'

Being unable to remain in her brother's presence and hold her temper, she turned on her heel. Part of her desired to hide in her room, yet the part which set herself at the highest fences when on the hunting field made her smooth her hair and skirts. Calmly, she walked into the oak dining room where the remnants of her childhood home were being set out for public view.

SEVEN

Thoughts of the duke's sister.

In a different house, not so very far away, another young lady regarded another gravel drive. There any similarities ceased. Here the gravel drive was pristinely raked to perfection by the several gardeners who could be seen at work. One of whom was Dan Threadgold, raking against the broad outer steps of Denbrugh Place. This was a perfectly proportioned Palladian building, with its front dominated by soaring columns with a suitably frieze decorated portico. Rebuilt on the shell of the original Tudor house by old earl James, it was considered a model of modern convenience and style.

Lady Louise d'Alvière naturally gave little thought to her new surroundings. Things were as they were. Certainly, she was not considering architectural style at present. Turning from the view she picked up her embroidery once more. Sighing, she began resetting the stitches which she had already unpicked several times.

'Oh! I cannot bear the waiting! This is not good!' So saying, she threw the offending work into the corner. 'It is a rag!'

Then she began pacing impetuously in front of the window, knocking the rocking horse into motion as she went.

Mrs Threadgold reached out to still the creature as it tapped against the wooden floor.

'Indeed, and it is not surprising that it should be a rag the number of times you have screwed it up. Please to pick it up, Lady Louise! When I remember the fine work your mamma produced!'

She smoothed the exquisitely embroidered lawn apron she wore. 'Do you but sit and concentrate!'

This statement was greeted with a torrent of rapid French and a toss of abundant copper-coloured curls. Nevertheless, the young lady retrieved her crumpled embroidery.

'Humph! It's no use trying that temper on me. Please to use the King's English.'

A smile played at the corners of Louise's mouth as she sat over her work again. 'Nounou, I know that you understood. You have not lost your French.'

'I understand a deal more than you think. What I will tell you is he will come when he comes and say what he has to say but he will not eat you!'

Louise gave her a quick look from under her lashes, 'Do you think that I worry about that? Oh, no! I am just so very bored!'

'That's as maybe. Lord Tristan bade me keep you to the house until his grace arrives and so I shall do.' Her tone was gentle as she inquired, 'Did they not teach you the virtue of patience, those nuns of yours?'

'Of course! But I am no longer a child and no one realises it! I cannot just sit in the nursery and sew while…' She bit her lip, 'I just cannot!' Her green eyes filled with tears.

Mrs Threadgold picked up her own sewing, 'Ladies must learn to wait.'

Louise recognised the tone from long ago. There would be no more discussion.

As she plied her needle, her thoughts were very far from being governed. Indeed, her head seemed to be filled with resentment. It seemed to her that anything she had loved was always snatched from her. Her mother she had never known, having died so soon after her birth. Nounou, her mother's nurse previously, linked them but when Louise reached seven years, her father had sent Mrs Threadgold back to England. The replacement governess had been frightful. The nuns had swiftly followed. Her father's death when she was nine had seemed the final abandonment. She had sworn she would love no more.

At fifteen she had returned to Palombières where she had grown to love her brothers again. Tristan had despaired of her behaviour with the succession of companions whom Charles had provided. Then last New Year, Charles had escorted her to Paris for her court presentation at Versailles. Tristan had presented her and then... nothing! A taste of court life and something else snatched away. It was little wonder that such a headstrong young girl was ripe for adventure when she first met John, Earl of Aldersleigh. An aristocrat, true but at six and thirty far too old for a girl of seventeen. He himself had told her this the last time they had met in Notre Dame. Yet... yet, she remembered the look on his face as he had said it. It was not her elder brother's wrath she feared as Nounou surmised but the fact that she might really never see 'Beau' Aldersleigh again.

In such a frame of mind she awaited her brother's coming. In the event, she failed to hear the carriage pull up. A housemaid was dispatched to the nursery floor to inform them of the new arrivals. Louise's hands trembled only a little as she put down her work and smoothed her hair. Mrs Threadgold rearranged the muslin fichu round her charge's neck, nodded and ushered her out of the door.

The newcomers were in the salon which was on the second floor, overlooking the open parkland to the rear of the Place. The late afternoon sunshine emphasised the tones of green and gold with which it was decorated. Hélène rose as her youngest cousin entered the room, they exchanged curtsies whilst the older lady began swiftly, in French, 'Oh my dear Louise, you grow more like your mother than ever!'

She inclined her head towards the portrait between the long windows where Catherine, duchess de Vénoire, smiled down at them. 'You failed to mention her beauty, Tristan.'

Louise glanced around and on seeing only Tristan said, warily, 'I do not understand. Where is Charles?'

Casually dropping an arm around her shoulders her younger brother led her to another sofa and sat down next to her. 'He has not come. Oh, he knows all, never fear!'

'All! Fear! What do you mean?' Her eyes held a warning sparkle.

Tristan gave a dismissive shrug. 'I am unsure myself. Dashed calm about it but not best pleased. Seems to think the answer is to present you at St. James's.'

There was an ominous silence, then Louise started to laugh, 'Oh and what if I refuse? He seeks to divert me, does he? I am not a child anymore to be given a new toy!' She stamped her foot.

'You prefer another plaything?' Tristan asked.

At that precise moment Chambers, the butler, brought in a tray. He bowed himself out as Lord Tristan indicated they would avail themselves. Hélène covered the following stormy silence by talking of the dances, parties, routs and other delights to be enjoyed in a London Season. Louise sent her cousin a calculating glance,

'Well it might be enjoyable; when do we go to London? I cannot choose gowns here.'

Tristan had expected this, 'Nothing simpler, dressmakers and all the rest will be sent from Town.'

She glowered at him, 'Where is Charles, why doesn't he come himself to tell me my good fortune?'

'He had business to attend to.' Swiftly he snatched his cuff away from the ratafia which spilled from his sister's glass as she set it down with a snap. 'Careful my dear. It's not what you imagine. He has gone to visit great aunt Barbara, in the hope she will be able to present you at a Drawing Room.'

The stormy look on the young girl's beautiful face abated a little. To be the centre of attention for a while might prove amusing. Also, she knew that the Earl of Aldersleigh planned to remain in England for a few months yet. She listened politely enough to Hélène's chatter as she accompanied her upstairs to her bedchamber.

Tristan sighed with relief at coming out of that skirmish so sanguinely. He sank back on the sofa to enjoy his claret.

INTERLUDE.

Lessing Dower.

The Dower House, situated upon the Lessing estate in Hampshire, was commodious by any standards. Visitors, though few, were received with as much ceremony as at the main house and perhaps with more style. Vénoire's great aunt was from an earlier era and mindful of her status.

Thus it was that the duke found himself following the stately back of a fully liveried footman into the parlour on the rear of the upper floor. He was announced and with a flourish. Having made an elegant leg to the lady seated beside the fire, he stood waiting politely.

She was regarding him through raised lorgnettes, 'Well, come closer boy, so I can see you! Ha! Ever the image of that stiff necked tartar Catherine fell head over heels for! Handsome, mind!'

He lifted her mittened hand to his lips, 'As you say, Milady. I hope I find you well?'

She chuckled, richly. A surprisingly deep and provocative sound whilst tapping his cheek, 'You did not travel here again so soon after your recent visit to ask after my health! Whatever it is, it can wait until you've taken a glass with me.'

She motioned to the decanter on a side table, 'It's port, if your delicate French palate can take it!'

Charles smiled wryly, 'I will attempt to remember grandpapa's teachings, ma'am.'

He bowed slightly as he handed her a glass, tasting his own. 'Alas, it has not the taste of the '45! A good vintage, nevertheless.'

'Humph! Lessing never did keep the sort of cellar m' brother did. I ensure his cousin keeps mine somewhat up to the mark.'

Savouring her drink she contemplated the duke, 'I was wrong! James looked just so when he wanted something from me! I gather you *do* want something?'

He cast a pained expression at his elderly relative, 'Why ma'am, well you know I pay my respects often.'

'Fiddle-de-dee! Not without first sending a message. It's not two months since your last visit, when you presented me with this pest!' A fat pug puppy lay sleeping on her sleeve, snoring gently.

'Indeed. Forgive my want of taste, ma'am. Had I realised its vulgar habits, I would have brought brandy instead.' He smiled wickedly.

'Cease flannelling me boy! Now tell me what it is you want.' She indicated that he should sit.

'Would you care to pass some of the Season at Grosvenor Square?'

She raised her lorgnettes once more, with an interested expression in her still lively eyes. In her youth she had been considered a shocking flirt; she and the Earl of Lessing had been intimates of Prince Frederick and Princess Augusta of Wales.

'Go on.' Lady Barbara listened to all her great nephew had to recount. Punctuating his explanation with interruptions from time to time such as:

'Silly chit!'

'Aldersleigh? Knew his father - there *was* a man!'

'De Langon? Bad blood there.'

Eventually she said, 'I must write to the Queen. No use thinking Lady Roger would be allowed to present her.' This was a simple statement of fact for, as a Roman Catholic and foreigner, Hélène had never had an English presentation.

'I assume you wish to dine and stay the night?'

Her summons on the bell rope brought her footman. She gave orders for her nephew's accommodation and comfort before inviting Vénoire to partake of a game of cards, suggesting the stakes, and to pour out some more of that delicious port!

EIGHT

An auction, a rental, an encounter.

The advertised sale for the partial contents of Solworth Manor in the county of Berkshire was to be well attended.

The Honourable Miss Dempster partook of a light breakfast in the kitchen as she steeled herself for the day ahead. The dowager Lady Cecily Dempster had been persuaded to set forth on her journey to London, assured by her daughter that to remain would be too painful for her nerves. It had been less easy to persuade her that she should be escorted by Sir Neville, travelling in his curricle. Both parties were of the opinion that the carriage would have been more suitable. Somehow Juliet had triumphed and the carriage now stood in the stable yard along with the remaining horses, awaiting new owners. With promises that he would be in Half Moon Street to welcome his sister, the incongruous travellers had departed

'Now then, my girl, you come and settle yourself somewhere.'

Juliet shook her head, 'I must check with Mr Peal's clerk that arrangements are in hand for the collection of the curricle.'

She walked down the rear passage and out into the stable yard. Parting with the horses was especially hard for her. As she forced herself to pass the remaining animals looking over each open half door, she recalled snippets from her childhood and young girlhood; her first pony, the first litter of pups she had seen born, her father waiting to escort her on her first hunt. Her mind also conjured up a more recent encounter here, in the form of a mocking voice and brilliant blue eyes. On rounding the corner to the front of the house she stopped abruptly. Foolishly she had been caught unawares by the number of still arriving horses and carriages there. Feeling unable to face the pity of so many, she made use of a pause in the steady stream of gentlemen and slipped into the agent's room. The closing of the heavy door silenced the anticipatory hum emanating from the oak dining room.

There lay a copy of the bill of sale upon the desk, beside which sat her battered volume of The Odyssey. She opened it and began to read. After a while the challenge of the Greek gave her respite from her worries and time passed.

Nanny entered, bringing a tray with some cold meats and ale.

'Mr Peal asks if you will see a gentleman. I said after you'd eaten.'

Closing her book and pushing the tray away she said, 'What gentleman? I will see him now, if you please. Will you bid him enter?' Her tone provoked a sniff from her old nurse.

Nevertheless, she removed the tray, returning with a soberly yet expensively clad man of middle years. Nanny seated herself on the straight-backed chair near the door, folding her arms. Miss Dempster found her presence reassuring.

'Good afternoon, sir. I understand that you wish to speak with me?'

He bowed over her extended hand, seating himself opposite. 'Miss Dempster, Mr Peal has appraised me of the somewhat unusual situation in which you are placed. As you may appreciate, I am unused to dealing with young ladies in the realms of such affairs.'

She broke in, 'Sir, do I gather that you are somebody's agent? Have no qualms that I am some schoolroom Miss; I was responsible for managing the estate here before my father's death.'

'Quite.' He unrolled a parchment, handing it to her. 'I hope you do not find the enclosed anymore unusual.' He sat back whilst she read its contents. 'The rental offered is more than generous and I have furnished your lawyer with all the facts concerning my master. If you will but agree to the specific terms, we may proceed quite happily.'

She stood causing him to stand also, 'Let us be clear, your master wishes to rent Solworth for such an amount, solely on the assurance that his privacy will be absolute?'

The sum she had seen betokened extreme

wealth. Who would make such an extravagant offer and for what possible reason, she asked herself.

The agent nodded. 'He insists you sign to this effect and that only Mr Peal will have knowledge of his identity. There are to be no visitors unless he expressly issues an invitation.'

'Indeed, you may be assured that my family and I are not in the habit of visiting anywhere, uninvited. Once I leave the Manor, I have no intention of returning whilst it is tenanted. Having said that, I would be very foolish indeed to refuse such a generous offer. Nanny please be so good as to ask Mr Peal to step in and oversee the signing.'

In a daze Juliet saw the document signed, sealed and the agent escorted out.

'Extremely propitious, Miss Dempster. I can vouch that your new tenant's credentials are impeccable. You need have no worries. My men are just clearing the remaining articles sold and I must assure you that the auction was a great success.'

She looked out of the window and asked, 'Did all the paintings go? The locket too, I suppose.'

The lawyer sipped the ale Nanny had

brought in. 'Why yes, the same buyer purchased most of the library I recall.'

'Ah.' Was all she commented. 'The rent will help enormously.'

'I feel these necessary steps you have taken will help with your retrenchment. If it can be impressed on Sir Neville that he must… ah… modify his lifestyle during the coming two years, then I see no reason to prevent the family returning.'

He made it sound very simple, yet she knew that two years of sober living would seem an eternity to her younger brother. Especially as he had expected to be launched into the Town during that time.

'If that is all Miss Dempster, might I suggest that we meet quarterly in Town in order to transfer the rent. Naturally I will inform you of any changes. Do you go up tomorrow?'

She nodded, finding it hard to speak about her last night under this roof. He sensed her mood, continuing in a business-like fashion, 'The new tenant wishes to arrive in two days time. I believe his man was to engage some people from the village to make all ready. His own staff will oversee everything. You leave it in excellent hands.'

Once the lawyer had departed, Juliet walked determinedly into the oak dining room. Her soft shoes sounded loud on the rug-less floor in the surrounding stillness. The linen fold panelling showed bleak patches where tapestries and paintings had hung. The long refectory table looked bare without the pewter candlesticks which had dated from Tudor times. Rather than see it thus, she twitched the covers into place. It was done; there could be no going back, only forward one day at a time.

She found herself in no better frame of mind when later she took a walk to the ruins. Huddled into the folds of her grey woollen shawl, the wind lifted tendrils of her hair. Tears which she had resolutely striven not to shed in the preceding weeks obscured the mass of primroses growing at the water's edge. Half blinded as she was, she found her unerring way to the mossy covered walls where she rested her forehead on the ancient stones. The aroma of bruised thyme wafted up to her, recalling a cool-eyed gaze and words uttered with a faint French accent.

Why in the world should smelling a plant she was so familiar with evoke thoughts of the duke? As she turned to retrace her steps, she was nearly knocked off her feet by a large, panting hound.

'Achilles!' She recognised the lead hound from her father's pack. Grabbing the new collar he wore, she turned to see if he was unaccompanied. Then she heard the sounds of a horse crashing around in the nearby woods and a female voice muttering in French. A rider emerged, reining in at the stream's edge, undecided as to crossing the water. Coming to a decision, the equestrienne urged her mount along the grass, soon drawing level with the ruins.

On seeing Miss Dempster and the hound she said, rather imperiously, 'If you please, my dog.' Holding out a leading rein.

Juliet clipped it onto the collar. 'I believe this dog belongs to the duke of Vénoire?' handing the rein to the rider, who inclined her head.

'He is my brother. The dog runs away!' Lady Louise's expensively styled riding habit had twigs clinging to its skirts as well as mud, which also spattered the coat of her mare. She looked expectantly down at Miss Dempster, obviously awaiting an introduction. Juliet supplied it.

'I am Miss Juliet Dempster.'

Louise nudged her mare towards a mound of fallen stones, swinging herself out of the saddle with accomplished ease.

'Lady Louise d'Alvière.'

They exchanged curtsies. 'Oh, this dog has led me…far!' She was not totally at ease using English.

'I lost my groom and my brother.' She caught the lift of Juliet's chin. 'You know my brother?'

Dryly Miss Dempster stated, 'Indeed, we have met.'

Lady Louise looked puzzled. Just at that moment, another rider emerged from the woods, audibly cursing in French. This ceased abruptly as he caught sight of the ladies amongst the ruins. Rapidly he schooled his features into a polite expression. Lord Tristan d'Alvière dismounted in order to observe the pleasantries, not before throwing an angry glance at his sister. She it was who made the introductions.

Juliet noticed from his reaction that he recognised her name. She was aware of another glance between the siblings and wrongly interpreting it as disapproval of his sister conversing with her, uttered coldly, 'I will not detain you, now that your hound is found.'

He smiled at her. 'My apologies, my sister is at fault for encroaching upon your land.'

The lady in question erupted into a torrent of French, of which Juliet caught but half. Lord Tristan maintained the conversation in English,

'No matter what you swear, Lulu, your behaviour has caused Jim a bad fall and lamed his horse. Got caught out by a rabbit hole when you took off! And he's like to get into trouble with Dickon for accompanying you at all. Charles gave strict orders you were to ride only with me or Dickon!'

Juliet commented, 'The warren lies between here and Denbrugh Place. It can prove extremely treacherous for the unwary.'

She sensed that his lordship was uncomfortable with the trend of the conversation. 'You are familiar with the terrain hereabouts, my lord?'

He was relieved at the turn in the conversation. 'Not on this side of the woods. I hope you will forgive our intrusion.' Bowing again he made to aid his sister to remount, tying the dog's leading rein firmly to his horse's girth.

Then, unexpectedly, Lady Louise asked, 'Do you go to London? Perhaps we may further our acquaintance?'

Lord Tristan cleared his throat, recalling the Dempster's changed circumstances, whilst Juliet blushed. 'That will not be possible. We are in deep mourning for my papa.'

Lady Louise pouted, 'Surely a ride in the park is permissible?'

Miss Dempster shook her head, curtsied and the riders departed. Walking back to the Manor she thought over what she had understood from the young lady's tirade to her brother. Like her Greek and Latin, her French was good. Obviously, the girl was excitable and over dramatic. She had certainly heard the word 'abducted'. Why should anyone think she could be abducted in broad daylight? Another example of this stiff-necked family! Over protective in the extreme. Really the freedoms she had enjoyed under her father's regime were to be valued.

NINE

A missing button, a missing jewel.

Several weeks were to pass before Juliet thought more about the d'Alvière family. The small household in Half Moon Street evolved a creditable routine which suited almost everyone. Nanny ran below stairs with the help of a daily girl for rough work. Miss Dempster saw to the marketing as well as her own and her mother's needs. Filling her days with physical work meant that fatigue prevented her from worrying over much about her brother's activities. These remained unpredictable. He was often absent from the house, not even returning to dine.

The dowager Lady Dempster saw this as normal behaviour for a gentleman, despite their straightened circumstances, refusing to address it. Neville, it seemed was managing to maintain some sort of social life, despite mourning and lack of funds. After a much heated argument, he had relinquished both the curricle and horses back to the carriage maker. He had then stormed out of the house, refusing to contemplate a livery horse, declaring he preferred to walk. Two days later he had ridden up to the door on a showy gelding.

'Bought this from a friend. I've got cheap stabling and it'll save on bootmakers' bills!' Thrusting the receipts into his sister's hand before riding off again. That was a week past.

There were no new creditors dunning them. Mr Peal faithfully reported on their financial situation, more often than Juliet deemed absolutely necessary. Indeed, he had made a point of coming to the house so that there should be no necessity for Miss Dempster to visit his office at Lincoln's Inn, a courtesy she had failed to understand.

Her concern for her brother's absence was increasing.

She sat now at the parlour window, turning the hem of her riding habit, which she wore when buying provisions. Certainly, the light was better here but also she had a clear view to the end of the street, so could observe any arrivals. At present, it was a deserted scene. The neighbouring houses were homes to families who would be taking the air in the park at this hour; the lesser gentry come to a rented house for the Season in order to launch sons and daughters before returning to their rural roles of squire, magistrate or parson.

Shaking out the folds of the heavy navy cloth, she held it at arm's length. What she beheld provoked a sigh: the sunlight emphasised how rubbed the hem was, despite judicious turning. It contrasted with the still smooth broadcloth of her brother's frock coat. The large gilt buttons twinkled provocatively, emphasising how sadly out of place such a garment seemed in their new circumstances. The rent caused by one of these oversized objects having caught on who knew what, must be mended. The offending button appeared to be missing.

More in hope than expectation, she searched the pockets. Her fingers encountered nothing hard; nevertheless, she emptied out the contents. Assorted cards scattered across her skirts. Thinking they were invitations to functions Neville could not now attend, she began to sort them, wondering if any had been answered. The final card was smaller and less embellished than the rest. Her glance caught the word guineas. This caused her to groan aloud. Was this some undeclared creditor demanding his due? Closer scrutiny revealed that it was a receipt, signed by her brother for a very large sum of money indeed! The address was in the City. Bleakly, Juliet realised it must be from a moneylender! She remained stunned into immobility. What had he pawned? She knew of nothing that they had kept which was worth such a sum.

What should she do? She was agitated and distressed by this new development.

Having no idea when, or if, her brother would return, Miss Dempster took the imprudently desperate decision to visit the address herself. She left the house stealthily, managing to remain unobserved by nanny.

Walking at a rapid pace, she reached

Piccadilly where she hailed a hackney carriage. The driver queried the direction but, on hearing the tone in which it was repeated, made no further comment. It would not be the first time he had carried a lady of Quality to such a destination.

It might have appeared that Miss Dempster was confident in her ability to solve this mystery in her usual forthright fashion. The tension in her grip on her reticule told another story. How did one conduct oneself when dealing with a usurer, she found herself mentally asking? Also, was there any connection between her destination and Neville's absence? Aware suddenly of the mustiness of the cushions she sat against she found she had to curb an overwhelming desire to laugh! It proved a great relief when they drew up.

As the sound of the horses' hooves died away, she regarded the building in front of her: plain, similar in style to the offices of Mr Peal. As a man walked past, she became aware that the longer she hesitated the more conspicuous she became. With returning determination she pushed the door open, causing the bell above it to clang. The room in which she found herself was perfectly ordinary. A man resembling a clerk entered through the only other door. His face registered nothing on seeing an unescorted young lady awaiting him.

'How might I be of service?' His manner was less deferential than his words.

'I believe this is your card.' Juliet held it out to him. 'I wish to ascertain what you are holding on my brother's behalf.'

He flipped the card against the chair back on which he had suddenly leant.

'Mmm, well.' He gestured for her to sit down. She remained standing not wanting to feel anymore intimidated.

'Mmm.' He regarded her steadily, a look which she returned. 'Firstly, how am I to be sure that you are this - gentleman's - sister?' He gave her a wolfish smile. 'Would it not be a simple matter to ask him yourself?'

Drawing herself up she responded, 'My brother is out of town at present.' Deciding to try a direct attack she continued, 'I wonder if you realised that he was a minor when you made this transaction? Of course, if you would prefer to deal with our family lawyer?'

A slight flicker crossed his features.

'Well, well.' He removed a key from his

waistcoat pocket, 'No need for lawyers! I don't recollect the gentleman; I see so many. My aim is to be of assistance but not to minors, you should understand! If a gentleman assures me he's entitled to pawn what's his own, who am I to disbelieve him?'

He unlocked a cupboard which ran along one wall to reveal a jumble of tagged objects. Swiftly dismissing these he turned to a drawer being careful to obscure its contents from view. As he pushed it silently to, his whole attitude changed. He turned with an ingratiatingly smug smile, 'Oh, well, yes! A family heirloom I dare say. I do hope your brother is not expecting me to change my special terms? Oh, dear me no, not even for your pretty face!' Smile or no, his voice held a scarcely veiled threat. 'The ring becomes forfeit, mine to dispose of if he don't repay the principle with the agreed interest inside of six months!'

'A ring you say?' She was puzzled, wary and a little frightened, however she would not allow this dreadful man to perceive it. 'What sort of ring? What proof have I that my brother signed what you claim? Our lawyer would be very keen to….'

He propelled her, none too gently, by the elbow towards a large ledger. Opening it forcefully at a page corresponding to the number on the card, he stabbed a rather dirty finger at what was written.

'See for yourself. If that's not your brother's signature, then you tell me!'

Indeed, she had no difficulty in recognising Neville's flourishing style. The description of the ring meant nothing to her: -

'Square cut emerald, surrounded by sixteen diamonds, 24 karat gold mounted, man's ring.'

There followed the details of amount given, rate of interest, redemption time or forfeiture. Keeping her tone even she stated, 'Certainly it is my brother's hand. I assure you there is no question of changing the terms agreed.' Holding out her hand for the card she added, 'Thank you for your time.'

She waited in vain for the door to be opened.

Fighting with her composure, she regained the street and walked rapidly away. Her mind was wrestling with that which she had discovered. One thing remained certain; the family had never possessed such a ring. From where had Neville obtained it? And far more worrying now - where was Neville?

On returning to the sanctuary of the house, she sought the privacy of her room. Her thoughts were in such turmoil that she had failed to notice the discarded tricorne and tan riding gauntlets on the table in the dimly lit hall.

Hastily splashing cold water on her face, she stared grimly into the looking glass. This was much more than devilment. If only Neville would return! She was startled from her brooding by catching sight of her mother reflected in the glass too.

'I knocked my dear,' she drifted, wraithlike towards the bed.

'I have such news! I'm sure you were resting as was I, so you will not have heard the arrivals.'

Juliet never found time to rest in the afternoon but let that pass as her parent continued,

'Both together, so fortuitous.'

'Who, Mamma? Do tell me of whom you are talking!' She snapped more forcefully than intended.

'Oh, how silly of me! Mr Peal and Neville... oh! My dear girl, please!' The dowager yelped as her daughter almost pinned her to the bed post.

'Neville is here?' A most unladylike rage took possession of her. 'He is below?'

'Whatever has put you in such a taking?' Tears choked the fading voice as the widow struggled to stand. 'He is freshening up after his journey...'

Neville's room was situated at the rear of the house. Juliet's knock was perfunctory in the extreme.

'Juliet!' her brother was, with difficulty, shrugging himself into a grey silk coat which she was certain was new.

'Hang it, Ju; no really, you cannot come in on a fellow like that!'

'Where have you been?'

Before answering, he checked his appearance. Satisfied, he smiled brilliantly, 'No need to start hectoring me. I've been in Oxford, at my books; thought you'd be pleased.' He offered in mitigation. 'I also met some fellows who took me to a splendid place. The cards favoured me the past three nights. See, I bought this for you.' He held out a grey gauze scarf.

She snatched it from him, twisting it into

a ball in her distress. 'Oh Neville! Where did you get the money to play?'

His smile turned truculent. 'I told you, friends who don't want repayment.'

'That will not wash, Neville. Even generous friends would not lend you funds to cover the amount you have been spending!'

Petulantly he stalked to his saddle bags, tossing out soiled linen and nightshirts, he grabbed a handful of paper, thrusting it at his sister.

'Look, receipts! Everything paid for… even my new coat!'

Juliet saw that what he said was true. In her turn she gave him the pawnbroker's card. 'Is this not the true source of such bounty?'

His hand holding the card began to tremble as all bluster fell away, 'Oh dear God, Ju! What am I to do?'

Suddenly he was sobbing. Not the demanding tears of childhood but harsh, racking, masculine sounds which chilled her to the marrow.

Then there was a hammering upon the door and Nanny could be heard, 'What's to do, you two? You can be heard from the hall! Your mamma's in a faint all over Mr Peal, poor man.'

Juliet reassured her saying they would be down presently, by which time Neville had composed himself somewhat and at his sister's prompting disclosed the truth.

'I had no intention of pawning it. I did it for a bet but that didn't cover everything, so I put it all on a hand of cards. Carshaw gave me the address of the moneylender. I signed the special clause.'

'But what did you pawn?'

He would not meet her gaze, 'A ring - an emerald ring.'

She remained bewildered, 'A bet? I really do not understand.'

Taking a deep breath, he stood up, 'Will Carshaw's brother made a bet that I could not take the duke of Vénoire's emerald ring.'

The whole room faded briefly as Juliet came near to fainting. Steadying herself she heard him continuing.

'I played the highwayman to steal the Denbrugh emerald. No one else would try for it. I was foxed when I agreed to the bet, thought it would be a great lark.' He was staring out of the window, unseeing. 'Carshaw's brother promised to return it but how can I redeem it?

It's all got out of hand, I'll end up in the Fleet…
or worse.' Absently he fingered his cheek where
it met his wig. A faint red scar was just visible.
'He took a shot at me that night!' Looking
helplessly at his sister, he pleaded, 'What am I to
do?'

Several images flashed across her mind
yet no coherent thoughts. Steely blue eyes
regarded her with contemptuous anger; thyme
mingled with the smell of rain.

'I need time to think. We must join
mamma if Mr Peal is downstairs.' She stated
flatly.

'Swear you will not tell her! It would kill
her!'

They agreed to carry off their argument as
nothing out of the ordinary. Mastering their
emotions, they entered the parlour, now lit by
candles. They lent a luminosity to the dowager
which she normally lacked. She was about to
deliver another shock to her daughter's
overwrought nerves.

'I have hit on a scheme for even greater
economy. I have asked Mr Peal for his aid in
renting this house out.' She shook her head at

their surprised interruptions.

'I received a letter from my cousin Charlotte, who resides at Tunbridge Wells for her health. She suggested that I might benefit from a rest cure. She will happily allow us to reside with her in return for a little attentiveness from Juliet. Neville will of course need to remain at Oxford.'

Mr Peal filled the stunned silence by enumerating the amount of rental which could be gained. He beamed down at the top of the widow's head, where he stood behind her chair, elaborating that he thought the dear lady's health should be of primary importance.

In a low aside in his sister's ear, Neville begged her not to abandon him. Before she felt able to make any comment Nanny entered to announce dinner. Airily, her mother disclosed that the plump, still beaming lawyer was joining them whilst taking his arm and allowing him to escort her the short distance across the hall into the dining room.

Juliet ate without tasting her meal. She felt far from her normal, resilient self. Her relatives were continuing to make demands of her whilst no one thought to ask what she wanted. Perhaps she should simply acquiesce to serving as cousin Charlotte's unpaid companion, leaving her brother to his fate. Looking across the table at him, now deep in conversation with their mother, it would appear he had not a problem in the world!

'That is such a splendid idea, mamma! A sensible marriage would be the perfect answer.' He turned his regard expectantly on his sister.

She remained silent as her mamma repeated that cousin Charlotte was acquainted with several eligible widowers, in need of a chatelaine, whom she would be happy to introduce. Incredulously, she heard Mr Peal point out that such a gentleman would no doubt favour a quiet wedding. Neville concurred that mourning would not then be a disadvantage. He also opined that income from the Half Moon Street rental would cover other disbursements, sending a deliberate look at Juliet. Her astonished bemusement continued, as the lawyer was heard to offer his carriage and escort to Tunbridge Wells in order to defray costs.

'May I at least meet these gentlemen before I am escorted to the altar?' She was unable to prevent herself from asking.

Mr Peal laughed over heartily at her sally, detecting the hurt which lay beneath.

Miss Dempster knew that her brother would once again take the easy option, disappearing to his rooms at The Blue Angel, ignoring the whole sordid affair until it was being cried through the Ton. There would be no recovery for the family name from such a scandal. All her efforts at retrenchment would have been in vain. So, was it truly her duty to make a marriage of convenience? Having been her own mistress for so long would it be possible for her to subjugate her will to another's, especially someone she had no respect for, let alone love?

Suddenly she stood, 'Make your arrangements then, mamma. You must excuse me if you please. I am afraid I have the most fearful headache.' So saying she stumbled from the room.

The headache was no ruse. She swallowed a decoction of herbs and wine brought to her by nanny whom she allowed to undress her before gratefully sinking into her feather mattress and slipping into oblivion.

TEN
May 1782

Revelations at The Ball.

A chance to seek oblivion would have been welcomed by most of the servants, and at least one of the gentlemen, now residing at the Vénoire Town House in Grosvenor Square.

The preparations for the coming out ball of Lady Louise d'Alvière were gathering a momentum not seen in its precincts for several years. From the kitchens where Monsieur Samson was driving his staff hard, to the attic where the lowliest maid sought her rest, the bustle of activity was permanent. Naturally, none of this was allowed to impinge on the family. The gentleman's desire for oblivion stemmed from the topics of conversation in the drawing room: menus, invitations and dressmakers!

The duke was at present seated at his ease in his library. His appearance as was to be expected, was perfection attired still in top boots and plain riding coat. His slender fingers caressed the silky ears of Achilles, his hound. This animal now accompanied him wherever he went; lying beneath the carriage of an evening, awaiting his master's return from his entertainment.

The aroma of coffee filled the room, but a cup stood, untouched, at his grace's elbow. He was thinking on other things. Thrice now, since his arrival in Grosvenor Square with the dowager Lady Lessing, had he presented himself at the earl of Aldersleigh's rooms only to be told on each occasion, that the servants were unaware of their master's whereabouts. That they were expecting him was made clear but seemingly he had vanished in the interim. If one came to London for the Season, one did not forego its pleasures. Gambling came high on Aldersleigh's list of these, yet he had not been seen in any of his usual places of play. More tellingly, Louise did not act as if her heart were broken by the lack of the earl's appearance. Vénoire desired to know what game he was playing.

'I am surrounded by mysteries.' He murmured to the hound, who whined in reply, cocking an ear as the door opened.

It was Tristan who strolled in also wearing riding apparel, 'Ferris said you were in here with the coffee pot. You were out damnably early; I had intended to ride with you.' He yawned hugely.

The previous evening, they had held a family dinner followed by a musical interlude from the ladies before some deep play at cards. This had been preceded by Louise's afternoon presentation at a Drawing Room, under the aegis of Lady Barbara. Vénoire had escorted them, finding himself as bored as he had expected to be.

Tristan informed his elder that he was hoping to make his escape for a few hours. When asked from what, he reminded Charles that the final fitting for Louise's ball gown was due to take place today.

'Also, the gardeners from Denbrugh seem to have taken over the ballroom and I heard Samson screaming even through the backstairs door! I feel it prudent to absent myself from the circus.'

Vénoire made the suggestion that Tristan should join himself and Hitchley on a visit to White's.

'Roger believes the club will refuse entrance to my companion.' His gaze dropped to the dog. 'I have wagered that he maligns them. After all his pedigree is impeccable, unlike some members.' Laughing, the brothers parted.

Later, when the duke was changing, he sensed that all was not well with his valet.

On being asked, Ferris began, 'Your grace, far be it from me…'

'Oh! As bad as that, eh? Come Thomas, I see that something troubles you.'

Ferris bent to pull off his master's top boots before stating, stiffly, 'I am afraid it is Lord Tristan's waistcoat… it clashes, your grace.'

Charles's lips quivered, 'I'm very much afraid most of them do, Tom but you, thankfully, are not responsible for his turnout.'

'For which I am grateful!' He compressed his lips, having said too much.

Finally, unable to stop himself he uttered, 'It's salmon, your grace!!'

Vénoire allowed his new cravat to be put into place, arranging it with care before asking, 'The colour of the fish? Dear me! But what of the coat?'

As Tom deftly pulled his master's hair back, securing it with his preferred black ribbon he went on to explain that his problem was the effect against Vénoire's chosen outfit for the ball. Salmon would not compliment emerald silk. It had taken much planning to ensure the hoped for éclatant display tonight. Agreeing that something must be done to prevent talk for all the wrong reasons, Vénoire promised to speak with his brother. On enquiring, out of interest, what colour the proposed coat was, Ferris answered flatly but with a quiver of his lips, 'Jules assured me it is called 'Cœur de cerises' but I'd call it puce, your grace.'

Giving an exaggerated shudder, Charles concluded, 'Of a certainty, it would not have done!'

Suitable raiment was also the topic of conversation for the ladies of the family as Louise's final fitting was taking place. Not, you will understand, the clashing of colours. The heated debate taking place in Louise's bedchamber concerned the degree of décolleté permissible on a debutante's gown. It was taking place in rapid and heated French between the young girl and Hélène. The dressmakers stood with pins at the ready. From the doorway, the dowager Lady Lessing surveyed the tableau. It was not until the pug added its high-pitched yelping to the cacophony that her presence was noticed. She thumped the floor with her cane.

'What the deuce is all this racket? I did not leave Lessing Dower to take up residence in a bear garden! Well, explain yourselves.'

Colour flooded Hélène's face as she started an explanation. However, Lady Barbara was quick of understanding.

'No sense in becoming the talk of the Season for the wrong reasons.' Carefully she rearranged the fichu of lace over the frill of chemise at the top of the boned bodice.

Looking mulish, Louise was still prepared to argue, 'I wore lower at Versailles! I am not some ingenue!'

'Well you'll do well not to go telling that to any of your partners tonight! Ingenue carries all sorts of overtones to most of the men I've known and all of 'em wanted one for a wife!'

Standing back to critically appraise the gown and its effect, she caught the petulant gaze of her great niece.

'La, child if you can but school your features into one of your smiles, you will look stunning. Remain like that and you will be hard put for even Vénoire to lead you out in the first set!'

Ignoring Louise's gasp of outrage, she dismissed the dressmakers. The pug was incessantly worrying the tissue cascading from the numerous boxes whilst growling menacingly. Mrs Threadgold seized him like a recalcitrant toddler, putting him firmly on the other side of the door where he proceeded to whine. Following a nod from Lady Barbara, the nurse passed a rubbed leather box to her. When she opened this, there lay revealed an antique mounted pearl drop. It was the size of a quail's egg and glowed creamily on its velvet cushion.

'There are always acceptable means to accentuate what Nature has given us.' The dowager murmured with a smile, as she pinned it at the lowest point on Louise's bodice, where the lace crossed over on her bosom.

'This belonged to my mother. I wore it at my come-out, as did your mother and my daughters. I give it to you with my love.' The daughters she spoke of had died early.

Louise was genuinely moved to tears as she kissed the old lady's papery cheeks, 'Oh, you are too good to me and I am such a trouble to you all!'

Hélène laughed, saying she predicted that the d'Alvière ball would be formidable as she quitted the room in order to rest before readying her toilette for the coming festivities. The pug came hurtling back into the room as she left. Nounou again scooped him up before he should resume his battle with the tissue or cause damage to the ball gown. His mistress took possession of him. As Mrs Threadgold helped Louise's recently appointed maid to remove the dress, the dowager thoughtfully predicted that not only would the ball be the greatest of successes but also that her great niece would be seen as the catch of the year due not only to her beauty but also to her wealth.

Pausing she added, 'Vénoire will never force you to marry against your will. Don't even think it.'

Louise dropped her eyes to the pin she now held. 'Marry? I do not think of marriage with any of the young men I met in France. I am certain it will be the same here.' She closed the box with a decided snap.

Lady Barbara continued to regard her for a moment.

'True, young gentlemen can be jackanapes. Bachelors of a certain age, who remain unmarried, may have a certain lifestyle which would preclude them from making an honourable offer. That is my experience.' She neither waited for, nor expected a reply to this pronouncement.

Rising from her chair she recommended that a rest would be in order for them all. On this, she and the snuffling pug swept out.

Louise lay down on her bed, draped in her wrapper as Mary Threadgold drew the curtains not quite closed. The door shut noiselessly as she and the maid left the room. The young lady lay very still for a while, intently listening. Once she was certain not to be interrupted, she retrieved a crumpled piece of parchment from the pocket inside her petticoat. It bore signs of much creasing from being crammed into pockets or pressed against stays, safe from prying eyes. Having received it whilst still at Denbrugh, she was able to recite the contents by heart.

Nevertheless, she re-read the now familiar script for the thousandth time:

'Have no fear. I cannot forget you nor my promise. Do as you are bid. Soon we shall be together.

Trust in me, John.'

Martha, her new maid, had slipped it into her hand one night as she had readied her for bed. How the Earl of Aldersleigh had used Martha as his messenger she could not guess. So it was, with this assurance, meagre as it seemed, that she had removed to Grosvenor Square at her brother's behest.

Over two weeks had passed with nothing more. She felt sure that tonight would alter that.

Charles had never mentioned Aldersleigh's name to her but naturally she was aware that all the recent activity had been spurred on by her elder's wish to prevent any more contact between his sister and a well-known rake. Great Aunt Barbara's allusions to Aldersleigh's intentions had caused her heart to flutter. What she had said earlier about marriage was true. At first with Aldersleigh it had been the frisson of daring she had enjoyed yet now, she really did miss being with him. She was forever seeing his smile with the rueful curl of his lips. She had begun to ask herself, if she were never to see him again would that make any real difference to her life and her answer was decidedly, yes.

Despite these growing feelings, she too was worldly enough to wonder at 'Beau' Aldersleigh's motives. Like her brothers she was aware of what was said of his morals and the gossip which surrounded his life. Replacing her secret correspondence in her pocket, she began to drift off to sleep, determined that whatever happened she would enjoy her ball.

The upper floors remained oblivious to the scurried activity on the lower ones. Extra servants brought up from Denbrugh Place helped to ensure all continued smoothly. The change from an exacting bachelor household to one of a family en fête happened with precision due to the impeccably trained staff. It was a matter of pride that this should be so. All had served the duke for numerous years. As they saw it, his successes were their successes. The privileged upper servants were permitted a glimpse of the newly decorated ballroom before resuming their activities.

Mrs Threadgold and Mr Ferris stood together. She was recalling Lady Catherine's ball when the house had belonged to earl James. That had been silver themed to show off her copper hair. Now they were regarding great swags of green silk along the walls, looped back with fresh lilies and gold thread. The gold brocade curtains shimmered beneath their own green gauze. All an illusion of course, Tom Ferris had helped to choose and display it, under the duke's instructions. All would easily be set to rights afterwards. Having regarded his pocket watch Ferris escorted Mary to the backstairs where they went to play their separate parts in preparation for the evening's festivities.

To Ferris's profound relief Lord Tristan had allowed his elder brother to advise him on the matter of the waistcoat. The one he now wore was cream and gold which admirably complemented the cœur de cerise coat which he would not forgo. Puce it certainly was and Vénoire could not refrain from regarding it through his glass as his brother walked towards him at the head of the stairs that night. Tristan's shoe buckles were dazzling in the extreme, containing as they did rubies as well as the more usual diamonds; the clocks on his stockings were threaded with gold and, unfortunately, the same shade of salmon as the rejected waistcoat. The final touch to this whole ensemble was his hair which was powdered and curled to resemble the fashionable wigs both brothers generally despised. Jules had been allowed free rein on his master's hair in recompense for the loss of the waistcoat.

'Salut, dear brother.' Tristan made to greet his elder but Charles held up his hand to fend off this apparition.

'No, I beg my dear! I do not wish to

appear churlish but I choose not to wear powder and of a certainty, I would never choose...' he sniffed infinitesimally, '...attar of roses!'

Laughing without rancour, Tristan corrected, 'Roses de Chine, my good Jules informs me.'

He was now admiring his brother's raiment which was perfectly understated as usual. An emerald silk jacket with ivory small clothes. The lace which foamed over his wrists was as fine as gossamer and its pattern was repeated in the white embroidery on his emerald waistcoat. His shoe buckles were plain gold with his only jewels being an emerald cravat pin and the large family seal, suspended from his pocket. Smiling, he proffered his Sèvres snuff box with a practiced flick back of his ruffles. As he went to partake, Tristan stayed his own ruby bedecked finger saying, 'I see you are determined to understate, Charles. You are missing the emerald!'

Vénoire regarded his bare finger thoughtfully.

'Ah, yes! I really need to be less forgetful. Safe to say, I have mislaid it for the present.'

No rejoinder was possible for at that moment, Lord Roger and Lady Hitchley appeared, followed in stately fashion by Lady Barbara. Hélène wore apricot silk over ivory with Roger in dove grey satin. The dowager cut a resplendent figure from an earlier era, wearing gold and purple brocade with matching plumed dowager's turban covering her hair. Her cane was amber coloured and beribboned. Acknowledging her great nephews' formal courtesies she asked the whereabouts of Louise, adding that their guests would soon be upon them. In the silence which followed this they heard the rustle of skirts along the corridor, turning to observe Louise progressing towards them.

As she emerged into the full candlelight at the head of the staircase she shimmered with each step. Her overdress was white Tiffany which revealed her underskirt at intervals as she walked. This was all lace, the loops of the over skirt secured with bows of emerald ribbon. The same ribbon was threaded through her powdered hair, holding seed pearls, suspended on gold wire.

Stepping forward, Charles took both her hands in his, 'You look very beautiful, my dear sister. Maman's necklace suits the gown admirably.'

He untwisted the strand of pearls she wore at her throat, then beckoned a footman standing in the shadows. He bore on a salver a nosegay of white rose buds, trimmed with green ribbon. Vénoire finished pinning them at his sister's waist just as the sounding of the knocker heralded the arrival of the first guests.

It seemed an age to Louise before Charles led her out in the first set. Her dance card was filled and already two young gentlemen had striven to take her into supper. Roger had intervened in timely fashion which had pleased her; as a relation by marriage, nothing could be inferred by such an escort.

Guiding his sister effortlessly through the steps of the dance, Vénoire regarded those gathered in his ballroom. As expected there were no absentees from this, the first ball ever to be given by the duke in England. He was already satisfied. The decor was suitably frappant, whilst his sister was a decided success. Yet, his inclination was to escape as the all too familiar boredom began settling over him like a cloak. Some devil had prompted him to speak of bringing Achilles into the ballroom, having gained his admittance into White's that morning.

His great aunt, on hearing this, had rung a peal over his head which his grandfather would have been proud of. He knew he must dance with the more prominent young ladies, once only for politeness' sake. That way no false hopes of matrimony could be aroused where none existed. And thus he began the business of acting the perfect partner for the evening. The supper dance was to be Hélène's, then he could lead her into supper. The family were to sit together for this upon a slightly raised dais at one end of the supper room, under a tented ceiling of white silk and green gauze.

Whilst his mind was so occupied, he made no error as he executed the prescribed steps and made polite conversation. Roger, having completed the minuet with Hélène, observed, 'Vénoire looks as if he is sleep walking. Merridew's eldest was looking more and more frosty faced!'

His wife clicked her tongue as she noted his distant response to Lady Merridew on returning her daughter to her side. She recalled, in contrast, the look she had encountered on his face in the carriage ride to the Billings when he had talked of the snub he had received from Miss Dempster. She wondered how to contrive another meeting between these two. Her thoughts were broken into by another aside from her husband.

'Deuce take it if Tristan ain't behaving too much the other way!' Indeed, the younger d'Alvière brother was drawing glances from some of the chaperones as he showed less inclination to retreat from those he had already favoured as a partner.

There was a gleam in his blue eyes and a glow on his cheeks not brought about by terpsichorean exertions. It was simply that each time he went in search of lemonade for his partner he availed himself of some brandy. He had had the forethought to secrete a bottle and glass in a niche behind a gauze swag. Like his brother he longed for the Supper Dance. After the repast he was looking forward to a few hours play in the card room with the fathers of these debutantes, feeling he would have done his duty amply. Replacing the glass, he returned to the ballroom in search of his next partner.

The Honourable Sophia Carshaw was just seventeen and what her mother fondly called 'a sad rattle'. Her father, Lord George Carshaw was a wealthy baronet who desperately aspired to titled matches for all his numerous children, including four more daughters at home. As Tristan bent to kiss her gloved hand before starting the dance, Sophia began to chatter. She proved very amusing although, truth to tell, the rapidity of what she was saying, which continued even when they parted in the dance, precluded him from totally following her conversation.

Some of her comments on the other young ladies were far from kind, yet witty enough for one so young. At one such remark, he was provoked into a wholehearted laugh. He became certain that most of what she said was not original. Indeed, she attributed several sayings to 'James' and 'William' but when 'Frederick' also entered the conversation Tristan felt compelled to inquire who these gentlemen were. Placing her gloved hand on his arm as they followed the duke and Lady Hélène towards the supper room, she explained,

'Why my brothers, of course! Will is two years older than I am, he's at Oxford; Jamie is a year younger than I am, cramming at home with his tutor but surely you know Freddie? I am certain he told papa he was a friend of yours. He'll be impatient to get to the cards, he likes playing deep. He married last year, they live at the Towers with us. Amelia has remained there.'

Tristan was fairly certain he had met her elder brother, the name was vaguely familiar, but she caught his enquiring glance, continuing,

'Well of course, she's increasing. Papa is delighted but would like to get me established quickly.' She threw him a considering look.

'I don't really want to marry yet. Mamma says I shouldn't talk so but I love riding and dancing and James is teaching me all the card games he has learnt from Will. He often goes to Folly Hill… I don't think I'm supposed to know anything about that…' She lowered her voice, conspiratorially, 'It's a gaming house, run by a lady! They take all sorts of odd wagers. I overheard Will talking to Fred about something involving a highwayman! Only fancy! I think I should much prefer to run such a place than be married and have to give up riding, going out and everything that's fun when I….'

Tristan broke in offering to escort her to her seat beside her mamma. She seemed to realise that she had overstepped the mark, refraining from any more artless chatter.

He bowed an apology to his brother for his tardiness, seating himself between his sister and cousin. Louise turned to him and in French confessed,

'Charles was right, I am enjoying myself greatly. I think my ball a success, do not you?' There was an unusual hesitant tone from one who was normally so confident. Tristan reassured her that not only the ball but she herself would be the talk of the Season. She turned to ask her elder brother the same, when something in his countenance gave her pause. He was seated behind a beautiful floral arrangement filling an extremely ugly epergne. Having signalled the footmen to serve the champagne once Tristan was seated, he was idly crushing a sprig of foliage which released a bittersweet aroma. His whole body had seemed to tense for the fraction of a second, then an enigmatic smile played across his lips. It did not fade as he caught her questioning look, in fact it turned into one of his rare open-faced moments, 'It is thyme, you know.'

'Thyme? The herb? Naturally I know, the sisters taught me all the healing herbs. But you, how did you learn of such a thing?'

He had removed the sprig, running it past

his nostrils, 'Why amongst the ruins, naturally!'

His sister was bemused, 'Ruins, what ruins. I do not understand at all. Did you request thyme be put amongst the flowers? That is most unusual. Was it a wager, like your hound? Do you intend thyme to be de rigueur, too?'

Tristan had caught the reference to a wager and joining in the conversation he recounted a decorous version of the strange wagers Miss Carshaw had indiscreetly divulged. As he did so, all vestiges of a smile disappeared from Vénoire's visage. Louise could almost feel the tension of his body beside her. Still as a cat before a mouse.

'Most intriguing,' he drawled, 'Do engage to play with Frederick Carshaw after supper, won't you, my dear?'

Tristan recognised that this was more than a request. 'Why certainly, that was my intention.'

Vénoire inclined his head, 'You know how much you enjoy high wagers and low company.'

His lordship knew better than to take offence at this pronouncement, as yet being unable to comprehend his elder's sudden change of mood. Vénoire turned to his great aunt, addressing her in English as he asked her for her thoughts on the sorts of invitations Louise could look forward to receiving from tomorrow. This effectively closed the previous conversation.

Later when the duke saw his brother seated at a card table which included the Honourable Frederick Carshaw he experienced a feeling of anticipation. He had escorted Lady Barbara to join some other dowagers at a whist table, catching sight of the gentlemen at dice as he returned to the ballroom. He requested a nearby footman to ensure that Carshaw's glass was replenished often enough for him to pass a pleasant evening, adding that there was no need to do the same for Lord Tristan's brandy. His brother detested port, which Carshaw was drinking. He required Tristan to be alert to the conversation he hoped would evolve. He himself continued to play the attentive host, eschewing the gaming room and closing the ball with his sister as his partner once more.

Guests went to their carriages, already calling it the most extravagant event of the Season.

'So, little sister, was it not enjoyable?' He bent to kiss her as she passed him at the library door.

'Oh, yes! Formidable but some of the mamans do not like me, I think. It seems to me they are the ones with not very pretty daughters.'

Her brother laughingly pointed out that it was more how the mamans of the young gentlemen beheld her that mattered. Her own smile faded a little and she gave a shrug as she pointed out their youth. Charles replied that she too was young, recommending she should take herself off to bed.

He thoughtfully watched her retreating back, as he did so he saw his brother emerge from the refreshment room bearing a glass and a half empty bottle of brandy. He smoothly asked Tristan to join him in the library which he obediently, yet unsteadily, did. Downes had brought in a tray with a decanter of claret and glasses; the duke told him to retire as they wanted nothing more. Savouring his glass, Vénoire asked, 'My dear, was your evening with Carshaw fruitful?'

Tristan drained his glass then yawned prodigiously before explaining that he had begun by winning every throw of the dice but then the luck had changed.

He found himself interrupted, 'Dear me! Do not be so obtuse! I wish to know what, if anything, you learned of Folly Hill?'

His brother blinked, 'Is that why you wanted me to play with him? I would have thought that you only needed to ask him. No great secret, that is where he's to be found most nights. Told me if I wanted to get anything back I should join him there. Not your kind of place though, Charles. Carshaw and his set, not your sort at all. In fact, don't think he's my sort. Don't mix my pleasures. Like to gamble but like to choose my own petites-amies. Don't want to find both under the same roof.'

Charles enquired of him if he had ascertained the types of wagers and the stakes. At which, Tristan had become quite heated in voicing his disgust. Limitless amounts could be wagered for a variety of bets, some of them sounding like schoolboy pranks. Carshaw had disclosed that he had gained admittance for his brother William who was still at Oxford and the two of them had got another fellow to play the highwayman. When Tristan had called that bad form, Carshaw had suddenly clammed up.

The now empty brandy bottle slipped from his grasp as he leant his head against the chair back sending a spurt of rose scented powder into the air. His eyes closed before he had time to view his brother's face.

All trace of fatigue had been dispersed as Vénoire glowered into the flames. He wore an alert expression, his narrowed eyes bestowing the look of a hunting panther on him. It was a look with which Tristan would have been familiar, owing as it did a little to their father at his most arrogant and angry.

So, now he knew the loss of his emerald was the result of the bet of a gaming hell. Who, he wondered, could be foolhardy enough to take it? He was pacing the width of the room, as he formulated various ideas. Pausing by the wall where the family collection of miniatures was displayed, he lifted the nearby candelabrum high enough to cast light on them. The candlelight flickered on the faces of numerous maternal ancestors and also several past monarchs. These included a small locket miniature of King Charles the First. He was remembering the situation which existed at Solworth Manor and that the heir was absent due to his studies at Oxford.

Suddenly the candlelight danced macabrely up to the cornice as his hand clenched on the silver stem. He banged it down causing hot wax to fall on his hand. Muttering an impolite French oath, he hesitated momentarily in order to regain his composure then crossed to shake his sleeping brother by the shoulder. Calmly he suggested they should seek their rest, especially if Tristan was to take Sophia Carshaw riding on the morrow. Tristan froze in the action of smothering a yawn.

'Take Sophia Carshaw riding...? no, don't think I promised that.....worst rattle of a female I know'

Vénoire sadly shook his head as he reminded his sibling of the fact that he had told him how much he had enjoyed her conversation, before he had dozed off.

'No that's not the way of it! Awful young lady, wants to run a gaming.......no, no Charles, foxed I maybe but .... you were asking about Folly Hill!'

The duke put a hand firmly beneath Tristan's elbow, helping him to his feet. He retained a firm grip as he reiterated the fact of his brother's interest in both the young lady and the gaming club. In truth, he thought it an excellent idea for Tristan to invite the Honourable Miss Sophia Carshaw to be his partner for the masquerade at Vauxhall Gardens next week. Something of his vehemence penetrated the brandy fumes fogging the younger d'Alvière's brain. He smiled beatifically as he said, 'I dare say. Can't think straight now, p'rhaps you'll remind me what I told you in the morning….and also why I said it?'

'Oh, of a certainty I will! As to why….one of your whims, my dear!'

'One of my whims? Dieu m'en sauve!'

Arms linked, the two brothers mounted the stairs with their unsteady shadows spilling around them.

ELEVEN

A confidence. An invitation.

The Dowager Countess of Lessing sat, straight backed, swathed in a voluminous cloak with her high powdered wig covered by a hat which her companion privately thought hideously old fashioned. Also seated in the dowager's landau was Lady Roger Hitchley as they drove around the park at a sedate pace. The dowager took the air at the same hour each day, thereby meeting the same acquaintances. She stopped only to converse with her intimates, as these were small in number her coachman never feared for the horses' well-being. Since the d'Alvière ball several mammas of hopeful young gentlemen had bowed ingratiatingly at her passing. She was as adept at freezing them out as her great nephew. She had been surprised the previous day when Hélène had requested to join her. Normally she knew that this lady rode in dashing style on a spirited mare with a coat the colour of her owner's hair. As they threaded their way through other carriages, riders and strollers she decided to wait no longer.

'You may as well tell me what is behind this. I am very pleased to have you with me, naturally, but I think there's more to it than conversation!' The older lady thought Hélène looked rather pale.

Her younger companion made an attempt at a smile, 'Oh, I am so afraid that I must let everyone down! More than that, I am just so afraid!' Then she burst into tears, trying desperately to stifle her sobs so that the coachman would not hear.

Lady Barbara poked him in the back with her cane abjuring him to be deaf to all that followed. He bowed stiffly, having been in her service since her marriage. Taking the younger woman's gloved hand she patted it, waiting until she was able to speak calmly. In a tremulous voice her companion explained that all the plans for her chaperonage of Louise as well as undertaking the more arduous activities for the dowager, must cease. She apologised, knowing that Lady Barbara had not been expecting to undertake these either. It could not be helped. Lowering her voice, she confided that she was increasing again at last!

The dowager smiled, 'Breeding, eh? Well, that's right and proper. It goes without saying that you will need to take extra care. No sense at all in you gadding about all over, not with your history. Have you told Lord Roger?'

Hélène shook her head saying she feared he would send her back to Stanford at once. At this point their conversation was interrupted by the approach of three riders: Louise, Tristan and Sophia Carshaw. The latter was chattering animatedly to Tristan, who looked like a fox hemmed in by a hound. Louise simply looked petulant. Her groom, ordered by the duke not to let her ride out of his sight, followed her closely as she approached the landau. She greeted both her relatives enthusiastically, inquiring if her great aunt would have the kindness to spare her cousin to ride with herself tomorrow. The dowager made a noncommittal response, bowing slightly to Sophia and wishing them an enjoyable ride.

Higgs, the coachman drove on at the same sedate pace. The dowager resumed what she had been saying. She gave it as her opinion that the most care was needed in the first few months, that to travel to Stanford Park would be foolish in the extreme when she had all the comfort available at Grosvenor Square, including the skilled attention of Mrs Threadgold. Lord Roger could continue dividing his time between Town and his estate as was necessary and would worry less in such a situation. Also, London had the best accoucheurs should problems arise. As to the matter of late hours, chaperoning Louise, fetching and carrying for herself, it seemed they were in need of finding another companion, but she could not call to mind any suitable relative as yet. Give her time! Someone with a bit of spirit would be the answer.

At that, Hélène looked up, beginning to smile thoughtfully, disclosing an idea which was forming in her mind. She described the situation in which the neighbouring estate to Stanford found themselves.

'Louise has seen her walking in the park early. Greetings have been exchanged. It seems they are to leave Town for Kent soon. They go to a relative in need of a companion. Their lack of funds is woeful, I am thinking that the role of paid companion might be of more benefit.'

'I can see that might be. Do I know of the family?'

On hearing the name, she expostulated, 'What? Hugh Dempster's relicts? Oh, he and I more or less grew up together. He was a devil on horseback! Took me to my first Hunt Ball. I lost all one month's allowance to him once upon a time when I wagered I could ride my hunter to the top of the ruins in his grounds. Dammed animal strained its fetlock on the second brick and threw me! I was married to Lessing the following spring. Dempster's wife was a whey-faced miss when I knew her, most ill matched pair. So, it's Dempster's daughter you're talking of? Like her mamma is she?'

Hélène refuted this, describing Miss Juliet Dempster as rather formidable and a bruising rider like her father. The dowager, liking the sound of this, ordered the carriage to return to Grosvenor Square at once advising Hélène to speak with her husband as soon as possible, whilst she would write to Miss Dempster.

Sublimely unaware of the changes about to take place in his household, Vénoire was trotting across Piccadilly with the ever faithful Achilles loping beside him. He had been for a much needed gallop on the far side of Hyde Park, well away from the sedate fashionable ride. He was to meet Hitchley in Green Park, thence to Tattersalls to view some bloodstock. Also, he wished to talk with him about the planned evening at Vauxhall Pleasure Gardens.

Tristan had inevitably, albeit reluctantly, invited Sophia Carshaw to the gardens and Charles, having imprudently encouraged this friendship for his own ends, was suffering a qualm of conscience.

Both brothers had chosen plain black velvet domino cloaks in the hope that thus covered and masked they might absent themselves from the party, each for their own reasons. If Hitchley would assume the role of host in his absence, then the duke intended to slip away to the house he rented in Soho Square.

Célestine still resided there, yet he had not visited her since that time in early spring when he had felt so despondent. Her tirade at him about the paltriness of the rooms, the unfashionable area and how tired of her wardrobe she was had not encouraged his return. She had resumed her woes even before he had quit her bed. He had left sovereigns rather than the diamond hair clips he had intended her to have. Whilst remaining in Town he had felt no pull to visit her and so had decided the time was right to sever the connection His sense of how one should comport oneself in these situations would not allow him to do so by letter. In the early days of their arrangement, he had passed some pleasant hours.

Becoming aware that he was on the park side of Piccadilly now, he began to scan the horizon for Hitchley. However, all he saw were nursemaids with their charges. Slowing his horse he waited, allowing it to crop the grass for a while. Of an instant, he had to gather his reins swiftly as Achilles rushed under the gelding's belly, narrowly missing a lashing hoof. The hound took off around the bend in the path, baying as if on the scent of a fox. It took the duke a minute to calm his mount, wondering what could have provoked the dog to behave thus. He trotted smartly after it. As he rounded the corner, he saw the wretched animal with both muddy paws planted firmly on the knees of a lady over whom he was attempting to slaver. She wore a plain straw hat on her averted head and much to Vénoire's relief, far from falling into hysterics, seemed to be laughing heartily whilst gripping the beast's collar with gloveless hands.

'Achilles, heel!' The voice in which the command was issued usually brooked no disobedience. Now the hound merely looked at him before returning to his quarry.

The duke dismounted, flicking his crop against his highly polished boot. 'I said, heel!'

The lady spoke and her voice stopped him in his tracks more surely than his commands had stopped the hound.

'Down, Achilles sit! Allow me to apologise, your grace. I fear Achilles must have picked up my scent.'

There, making her curtsy before him, wearing the same sprig muslin dress as on the day he had first seen her, was Miss Juliet Dempster. Her amber eyed gaze seemed a little less direct than when they had last met and he sensed a loss of confidence. Something which he had felt to be an intrinsic part of her. All this crossed his mind as he bowed in response. The hound now lay at her feet, tail thumping the grass.

'I see.' Was all that Vénoire could muster.

Juliet bristled at his cold tone. 'Naturally, he belongs to you, yet a change of ownership cannot blot out everything.'

'I try to ensure that I lose none of my property… in the normal run of things.'

He watched her colour mount as she dropped her eyes. Then he found himself say, less harshly, 'I believe you have made the acquaintance of my sister? My family seem to make a habit of encountering you by the ruins.'

Hearing the smile in his voice she met his gaze once more. 'How does your sister go on?'

Vénoire followed her lead and talked about the pleasures of the Season which Louise was enjoying. He was somewhat surprised when she responded by saying she had found her season a horrid bore, leaving little time to read nor to indulge in a long, satisfying ride.

'Perhaps I could prevail upon you to join Louise and myself one morning? It is our custom to ride to Richmond sometimes.'

'That will not be possible, thank you.'

Suddenly the air seemed charged with an indefinable tension. Achilles sensed this and whined, whilst the horse whickered as another rider approached.

Thinking it would be Hitchley, Vénoire was ready to hail him; instead it was his lordship's Stanford groom. He touched his hat to the lady before doffing it to the duke, proffering him a note which he read at once.

'There is no reply.'

When the man hesitated, Vénoire raised his brows, questioningly, and he explained he had also been asked to deliver a note to Miss Dempster.

By this time, the duke had remounted,

'Then fulfil your duty.'

He clicked his fingers to the hound. 'Come!' This time the dog knew better than to disobey such a tone. 'Your servant, Mademoiselle.'

The French inflection on the last word sent shivers down Juliet's spine, something which she did not care to consider. Inclining her head, she broke the wafer on the parchment she held, as he rode off. The groom had obviously been told to await a reply, so she perused it quickly.

To her bewilderment Lady Roger Hitchley requested that she visit her in Grosvenor Square, at her convenience but also as soon as maybe. The now dismounted groom, it seemed, had been told to accompany her if she agreed.

This afternoon, Mr Peal was due to escort herself and her mamma to Tunbridge Wells and so the visit must be now or never. It was an unusual request; she had had no contact with the Hitchleys since before leaving Solworth.

She pondered what it meant as the groom, leading his horse, fell into step behind her. The idea of visiting the Vénoire town house was made less difficult by knowing that his grace would not be present.

Her thoughts were still in utter confusion as she lifted the knocker. The butler appeared to expect her, bowing her in before requesting that she follow the footman. She had gathered her composure by the time she was announced, finding herself in Lady Hitchley's bedchamber.

Her ladyship did not rise from the chaise longue on which she lay, supported by cushions and covered by a cashmere wrap. Having ordered some refreshment, Hélène set about explaining the situation as well as an idea which might prove of mutual benefit.

Her disclosure of her pregnancy touched Juliet, as their close neighbourhood was well aware of the Hitchleys' losses. She bridled slightly at the mention of a paid post; yet in reality it would be much more practical to accept this offer rather than perform the same tasks merely for her food and board! It might also mean that there was a chance to redeem Neville's pledge in time to save the emerald. However, this would mean living under the same roof as the duke, having to face him daily, knowing what she knew. Enduring those arrogant eyes probing her whenever they met. For probing they were, despite their studied sleepiness. The thought also occurred to her that if they did manage to redeem the emerald, she would be well placed to return it secretly.

There was another consideration, one which helped to tip the balance; if she did not go to Tunbridge Wells no one could engineer a marriage to an elderly widower! It was her claim that she valued her independence, would do anything to regain the Manor; well then, what better way than her own income?

'I would be happy to assist you, Lady Hitchley,' she heard herself saying.

'Hélène, please you must call me Hélène.'

It was suggested that perhaps she should seek her mamma's permission for such an undertaking, which Juliet refuted in her old determined manner, adding dryly that her parent's concern would be alleviated by the fact that her new occupation need not become common knowledge in cousin Charlotte's circles. Despite which, she did need to inform her of the morning's happenings.

Hélène said she would send for a chair and when Juliet tried to decline, she was pleasantly overruled. Arrangements were also set in train for her to return as soon as possible.

Nanny opened the door on Juliet's arrival in Half Moon Street. She stepped into the hallway which seemed full of portmanteaux and coach bags. Her mother had indeed become distressed by the delay, causing her to lie down. This did not surprise her daughter, although the news that Mr Peal was sitting with her did. The lawyer's man was hovering at the back of the hall, so received instructions to start the process of loading the carriage, but that her bags should be left in the house. Nanny looked askance at this, but Juliet continued on her way to her mother's room.

Mr Peal sprang up from his seat at Lady Cecily's bedside. He began remonstrating, alluding to her mother's distress and worry about her absence. Miss Dempster gave him a long look and he subsided in a great deal of confusion. Having drawn the curtains back to allow in some light, she regarded her recumbent parent who had pressed the handkerchief she was clutching to her closed eyes.

'Another headache, mamma? Perhaps you should delay the journey.'

She half smiled at the rapid exchange of glances.

Then the solicitous lawyer helped the dowager to sit up, murmuring soothing words about the benefit of country air, hastily including Juliet in what he was saying.

'Ah, but I am not accompanying you.'

Lady Cecily then fell back with a moan of anguish, unfortunately trapping Mr Peal's supporting arm, causing him to lean very close indeed, in order to extricate himself.

He turned a very pink, puzzled and disapproving countenance on Miss Dempster.

Taking pity on him, she began her explanation, by the end of which even the dowager's moans had died away, leaving a silence.

Mr Peal broke it first by wondering what Sir Hugh would have thought of such a thing. The young lady stared at him; he had the grace to look chastened, then shocked as her stern look broke on a gurgle of laughter. She pointed out that all their problems stemmed from the fact that he was not alive. Her mamma sought refuge in her handkerchief once more, issuing broken sentences all focused on what affects her actions would have on Neville Dearest's social standing.

Gathering all her force - which, truth to tell was rather vapid - she sat up, looking her daughter full in the face, 'You were ever a wilful child, your father spoilt you! Charlotte has written she has not one but two wealthy widowers in mind. Yet you refuse to settle Neville Dearest's problems!'

Holding up her hands in despair she tersely requested Mr Peal to explain matrimonial law to her deluded parent and without waiting to hear if he tried, she stalked out.

In her room, she methodically rechecked that she had all that was needful for her new situation. Reviewing the scene which had just taken place, a thoughtful, dawning smile crept over her face. Was it possible that one of her responsibilities would be shouldered by another person in the near future?

At that moment there was a tentative tap on her door. There stood the lawyer, his wig slightly askew and his cherubic countenance pink once again as he rushed to assure her that he would take great care of her mamma on the coming journey. Indeed, he added that he wished she would rely on himself for everything she might require, now and at some future time.

On this unlooked for utterance, he offered Miss Dempster his hand. She in turn gave him the direction of where she could be found if the occasion arose.

'I will notify my brother. Nanny knows exactly how to handle mamma! Have no fears.'

She turned, descending the stairs before anymore should be said.

Lord Hitchley's groom was waiting on the step by the now open door and she indicated he should load her meagre baggage into the second of the two carriages now waiting in front of the house. She was holding herself in check as she explained why Lady Hélène had sent her carriage.

It would never do to allow Nanny to see that she was not as stoical as she pretended.

Things had happened so suddenly. Only last week she had known nothing of the emerald affair and now she would have to face the duke daily, knowing the great wrong which had been done to him by her brother!

As the carriage set off, her heart seemed

to flutter in her throat, again she thought: I will see him everyday!

Vénoire himself was seated in glacial silence opposite his great aunt in her bedchamber. This had been her room prior to her marriage, altered very little since the duke had inherited the house from his grandfather. The half tester bed and fire screen were still of linen embroidered by her mother.

She moved this screen now in order to have a clearer view of Charles' face.

'Well boy? What's to do? Don't think to freeze me out with one of your looks, anymore than to fool me that there's not something amiss! So?'

He met her astute eyes, unbending slightly but only to state that he misliked the fact that Miss Dempster was coming to act as her companion.

She would not let it rest at that, repeating her searching question. He regarded the finger on which he normally wore the family emerald, then withdrew his snuff box from his pocket.

This he offered to his great aunt and they both partook.

Shaking his head he said, quietly, 'Would that I could explain it.'

'D' ye dislike the girl?'

This brought a smile which lit his eyes, as he dusted the tobacco from the skirts of his velvet coat.

'Of a certainty, no!'

Lady Barbara was determined to probe deeper, asking if it was the family whom he disliked. She pointed out that it was an old name.

Dempsters had been squires of Solworth for longer than they had had ownership of Denbrugh Place.

When he had agreed with her she continued, 'Then it's the present situation they find themselves in?'

She was quick to notice a slight look of pain cross his almost impassive face.

'So. Is it that you do not like to see the lady in such a situation?'

She sat back, placing her mittened hands on the arms of her chair.

Abruptly, he rose, 'Madame ma tante, it is a fait accompli! Press me no further. I cannot like it!'

Bowing swiftly, he quitted the room, almost treading on the pug asleep on a cushion by the foot of the bed. The dog burrowed under his mistress's skirts, emerging closer to the fire which was maintained constantly in the dowager countess's room.

'Heigh-ho! Does the wind sit in that quarter, Perkin? I wonder. Things must be carefully observed if we are to steer them aright. Of a certainty!' She repeated the duke's phrase.

On a throaty chuckle, she closed her eyes for a brief nap before preparing for the evening's masquerade at Vauxhall Pleasure Gardens.

TWELVE

A proposal. A Parting.

The 'feuille morte' domino cloak which had been lengthened as much as was possible, proved a flattering shade for Juliet. By choice she would have worn a plainer colour; also by choice she would have gone unpowered.

Lady Barbara's dresser sent to supervise her dressing had passed the powder box to the young maid attending her with an insistent look. So here she presented the perfect picture of a society lady ready for the masquerade, as she fixed her mask, adjusting her hood over her piled hair. The dresser had returned with a message for Miss Dempster; Lady Barbara asked for her to step into her chamber.

She was acutely aware of being scrutinised by this room's occupant who was wearing an immense purple turban with ostrich plumes and a somewhat old-fashioned gown of similar hue over a heavily embroidered silver petticoat. As Juliet rose from her curtsy the dowager countess let her lorgnettes fall.

'So, Miss Dempster. Well, you look just as you should for tonight's junketing. Pretty too, under that mask if I'm not mistaken.'

Saying that she had no intention of disguising herself at her age she went on to explain that her need was for young eyes and legs in order to keep her great niece in view at all times.

The number of gentlemen dancing attendance on her was immaterial, as long as she did not wander along the dark walks with any of them. Catching a fleeting expression around Juliet's mouth she asked, 'You think Vénoire's over protective?'

Miss Dempster assured her that it was not her place to think any such thing, although her tone said otherwise.

Lady Barbara pursed her lips before reaching a decision.

'You cannot be responsible unless you are in possession of the facts.'

She went on to inform Juliet of 'Beau' Aldersleigh's interest, which seemingly Louise reciprocated having no thought for her reputation. It was possible that all the intrigue had ceased in France, but Louise was a volatile chit who, if handled in the wrong manner, became stubborn and headstrong. She thought that Vénoire had distracted her by giving her this Season but it was imperative that she should be watched closely.

'You've met m' great nephew I think?'

Shocked by this abrupt change of tack, Juliet was glad of the concealing mask as she replied, 'Yes, at Solworth,' refusing to be led.

'I knew y' r father.' Lady Barbara was not prepared to pursue the subject of the duke at present.

Instead she allowed herself to reminisce about her youth, ending by saying enigmatically,

'I'm sure things will come about. Trouble was he needed a stronger hand than Cecily's to bridle him! There was a time…'

She shook her head causing the plumes on her turban to sway perilously close to the candles nearby.

At that moment there was a knock on the door; a figure stood in a silver coloured domino with a black mask. It was Lady Louise asking if they were ready as Charles did not wish to keep his horses standing. Tristan, she said, had gone to escort Sophia Carshaw and was to meet them at the river steps. Remembering her manners, Louise curtsied to Juliet, who responded with the due deference of the daughter of a squire to the daughter of a duke. It was not easy to remain stiff when Louise was in an engaging mood as she now was. She linked her arm through Juliet's, chattering as they made their way down to the hall.

Vénoire stood observing the two young ladies as they descended the staircase.

The candlelight drew gleams from the silver domino, whilst reflecting on the feuille morte. It was the latter which held his gaze, despite its more sombre hue. The manner in which the lady carried her head and the steadiness of her amber eyes behind the mask caused him to catch his breath. Those eyes did not release him as she sank into a full curtsy and he found himself raising her gloved hands to his lips as he assisted her to rise.

'Welcome to Grosvenor Square,' he murmured to her alone.

Whatever may have followed was stilled on his lips as his great aunt addressed him.

'I hope ye've a rug in the carriage, Vénoire. I don't intend to die of a chill caught on the river tonight! If we are to go, let's get on! Those blacks of yours are too fidgety to stand much longer. I expect you ride, Miss Dempster? Your father will have taught you well.'

So it was that the awkward moment of meeting once more, dreaded by both parties, was lost in the settling of an elderly lady into the carriage. The dowager countess sat beside the duke, sustaining a flow of anecdotal conversation until the river was reached. Juliet remained aware that Vénoire's veiled eyes were often cast in her direction.

He did not affix his mask until they

neared the water departure point, where their reserved boat awaited.

Here too was Lord Tristan, in black like his elder, with The Honourable Sophia Carshaw resplendent in the palest of pinks. With pleasantries exchanged, they took to the water.

It was a mild night. The two gentlemen seated either side of Lady Barbara protected her as well as her ample cloak. It did not take Juliet long to deduce that Lady Louise viewed Sophia Carshaw with boredom and disdain. At first fascinated by the unceasing chatter of this young girl, she soon realised that it held nothing of substance; yet it flowed, much like the river itself, until they had reached their destination. She was delighted to be required to sit with the dowager countess at the rear of their supper box. Louise too, dutifully, sat near her great aunt, leaving the gentlemen and Sophia at the front where they could see and be seen.

As expected, several sprigs of the nobility were soon presenting themselves, requesting to escort Louise to the ruins or the cascade, or to have the honour of sitting with her at the concert which was to form part of their entertainment.

Vénoire gave or withheld permission as he saw fit. Louise seemed neither flattered nor displeased by any of them. Juliet had risen to accompany Louise but the duke had shaken his head, sending his sister's maid instead.

Sophia, who had been attempting to identify any gentlemen who strolled past, gushingly asked Miss Dempster if she had seen the cascade which she thought was prodigiously impressive, a thing she had viewed numerous times yet still had no idea as to how it could work. She then suggested that they should all go, but looked appealingly at Tristan. Lady Barbara encouraged the plan, adding that she was happy to remain in the box, listening to the musicians.

Vénoire surprised himself by organising his party to do this, once his sister was returned. Somehow, despite waiting until last, Juliet found herself taking his arm as they stepped out of the box. The walkways were full of chattering couples using the shadows cast by the lanterns to flirt more than was proper, safe behind their masks.

They soon stood with a mass of others before the cunningly lit cascade of water as it gushed over mossy rocks. Juliet wondered aloud at the attraction of it and the ruins to so many people.

'Ah, but real ruins hold no novelty for you. Are you as well informed on cascades?'

In the semidarkness, Juliet was able to detect a smile in the duke's voice. Before she had time to respond, Sophia's uninformed suppositions were being addressed to the group.

This seemed too much for Vénoire and muttering 'Parbleu!' he led Miss Dempster slightly to one side as she murmured about the need to watch his sister.

He dismissed this worry, saying she was safe with Tristan. He turned to face Juliet beneath the light shed by an overhead lantern.

'Let us discuss your ruins. They mean so much to you, you would do anything to recover them, would you not?'

All trace of the earlier laughter in his voice had disappeared, his eyes looked almost black behind his mask.

Juliet was nonplussed by his vehemence, unsure of his full meaning. Nevertheless, she held his gaze with her own, whilst replying, 'Anything? Why, I suppose, yes, anything within my power. My father left me to manage the estate until my brother reaches his majority.'

She paused, continuing more quietly, 'More than that, I feel it is a duty I owe to all who have held Solworth in the past. Dempsters have always been there, no matter what battles have come and gone. Often the women of the family have made great sacrifices. The Manor was held.'

She stopped abruptly wondering again where this conversation was leading.

Still regarding her intently, he inquired, 'Sacrifices? Of what sort?'

Surprised at his interest in her family's history she elaborated,

'Advantageous marriages in the main, or going dowerless to enable the heir to marry well. Why the abbey became the Manor through a marriage.'

She was aware of Vénoire's stillness in front of her and of a change in his breathing.

'And so, you would marry to change your brother's fortunes?'

'I marry? Your grace, I rather doubt that any gentlemen would wish to spend a part of his inheritance to restore mine!'

Her voice had dropped, as had her eyes.

She felt the warmth of his fingers as with gentleness he lifted her chin, pushing back her hood a little. 'If such an offer were to be made?'

He felt her pulse beating in her throat as she murmured, 'A marriage of convenience?' She made no attempt to draw away.

'It would appear so.'

'I...'

Their tableau fractured as Tristan and Sophia rushed up to them saying that Louise and her escort were missing. Whatever response Miss Dempster would have made remained unspoken as Vénoire began a search. He castigated his brother for carelessness but seemed certain of her escort's identity. The brothers set about finding the errant lady having left Sophia and Juliet close to the supper boxes.

Feeling shaken and disturbed by the recent conversation, Juliet was paying scant attention to her companion's inane chatter when she heard her ask, 'Is that not Lady Louise over there,' as she pointed to a silver coloured domino leaning into a darkened box at the edge of the supper area.

Catching up her skirts, Miss Dempster swiftly covered the ground to reach the silver lady. Her low-voiced calling of Lady Louise's name produced a guilty start, proving that it was indeed the duke's sister. She turned from the box, effectively blocking the occupant from view. There was a glimpse of a grey silk domino and a powdered head but that was all. Deciding it would be circumspect to steer her charge back to their box before Vénoire arrived on the scene, she merely opined that her escort had shown a sad want of manners in not returning her to her brothers.

Louise had the grace to blush beneath her mask.

In fact, they all arrived at the same moment and as the servants were laying the supper table, the duke kept his counsel until this was done. Louise's excuse that the gentleman had mistook the box was received with a glacial look.

'Of a certainty, such confusion must be avoided. Miss Dempster will accompany you and your ensuing escorts.'

Both young ladies were relieved by Vénoire's solution: Juliet that she should have no need to remain in proximity with the duke for now and Louise that she could pretend nothing unusual had occurred.

This was far from true.

The man in the grey silk domino was a stranger to her but he had been the bearer of a message from the Earl of Aldersleigh. The parchment he had given her had been hastily thrust down the bodice of her dress, beneath the all-concealing domino. There had been no time to read it, but she felt its crackle with every movement. She hoped it would remain hidden when they unmasked at midnight. With these thoughts, she began her supper of thinly sliced ham, cheesecake and syllabub.

Vénoire toyed with some slices of meat. He was not overly concerned that tonight's escapade was anything to do with Aldersleigh. His reliable information was that the Beau remained out of town. Tristan, he knew, had arranged to meet Sophia Carshaw's brothers to plan a foray to Folly Hill. His plans were evolving exactly as he had hoped, yet he felt thoroughly dissatisfied. Try as he might he had failed to attract Miss Dempster's attention as she busied herself serving Lady Barbara. The sight of her fussing around his great aunt made him angry for some inexplicable reason. Without causing attention, he slipped out of the front door of the box, pulling his domino hood well over his hair as he strode down one of the alleys leading to the water steps.

It had always been his plan to slip away before the unmasking, in order to visit his mistress. He had sent Célestine a courteous message to this effect. The impulse to end their connection had never felt stronger.

He had no desire to be recognised, so remained hooded and masked until Soho Square was reached.

Célestine had not known how to interpret the few words delivered to her by a groom. In the normal run of things, the duke's messages arrived via a footman at the very least; it was not unknown, if gifts were involved, for his valet to be the bearer.

Her maid had readied the room as normal for these assignations but Célestine herself remained fully clothed. She sat by the candelabrum thoughtfully sipping a glass of wine, fingering from time to time the diamond choker she habitually wore. A gift from the duke in their early days. Looking up as her maid showed him in, she laughed.

'Ma foi! The devil himself!'

He did indeed look devilish in unrelieved black. Throwing off his domino and mask he smiled at her joke. He stood regarding her in silence. She was not bothered by this, being long used to his eclectic moods; at times he hardly uttered a word, at others he spent as much time talking with her as making love. He had never beaten her, was always over generous and treated her as a lady. Despite which, she cherished no illusions: she fulfilled a need as did his servants and his horses. Neither had ever thought nor talked of love. She had husbanded many of his gifts against such a day as she sensed this was.

Pouring him a glass of wine she said, without the rancour of their previous meeting, 'So, Monsieur le Duc, are we to part?'

He did not answer at once, seeing before him only a clear amber gaze framed by a black mask. Shaking his head to clear this troubling vision, he swallowed his wine.

His attention was caught by the glitter of the diamonds at his mistress's throat. A valuable gift, given in exchange for the use of her body. Would a marriage of convenience be so very different? He had always known that he must marry.

'Yes, but you need have no worries. All is arranged. Whenever you wish to return to France the yacht is at your disposal, your rooms still await.'

She approached in order to kiss him, but he moved away. She sensed suddenly that he did not want to be touched. His face lit with one of his smiles.

'I hope soon to be married.' He said this as if he was as surprised as she.

Célestine poured more wine, proposing a toast, 'To the lady who has accepted to become your future duchess! Do you love her, then?'

He looked up from his wine glass with a sense of surprise, 'Love her? Why, yes, yes of a certainty!'

She registered his shocked expression.

'Then she is very lucky. For how long has she loved you?'

His face became set again as he uttered in a clipped voice, 'As to that, it is not something we have discussed.'

Masked once again, his face was unfathomable. He bowed and was gone.

Vénoire found himself wandering in the general direction of the river. He wished to walk and most importantly to think. When Célestine had mentioned love, it was as if everything fell into place. All the confused feelings he had been subject to since first meeting the self-assured Miss Dempster by the abbey ruins crystallised. How was it possible that he who had proved impervious to so many lures cast in his direction should fall under the spell of a strong-minded lady from the lesser nobility? Someone, it must be added, who seemed to hold him in disdain; whose avowed goal was to restore her family's fortunes; whose brother, unless he was very much mistaken, had robbed him of his emerald ring; who perhaps knew more of this than she should. No, he no longer had any doubt as to the identity of the highwayman of Stanford woods.

His most pressing problem was what his next action should be. Never, since his schooldays, had he felt so out of control of his own destiny, a feeling which he disliked intensely. It was not his style to confide in anyone. Of a certainty he could not rejoin the masquerade party. A message must be sent for Tristan to escort them home. A night's solitary reflection might aid him to decide what course of action to take.

The look on his masked face was hardly that of a gentleman newly discovering love!

THIRTEEN

An elopement.

The day following the masquerade started ordinarily enough for the household in Grosvenor Square.

It was not the place of the servants to be surprised when Lady Louise breakfasted in her riding habit. Certainly, she often rode early in the park with her groom and approved escorts. Had the hall boy sweeping the front steps been at all knowledgeable concerning horseflesh, he may have noticed that the horse her ladyship rode was a chestnut, not her normal bay mare. Her escort favoured a grey gelding, the colour of his domino of the previous evening and the accompanying groom had never broken bread with any of the d'Alvière servants in his life. When they departed, at a sedate pace, their direction was certainly towards the park but their ultimate destination was to be that of the Oxford Road.

The parchment received last night had outlined this projected journey. It had also contained reassurance that the thing which was planned would not touch her honour, nor that of her family. Its outcome would in fact solve the dilemma they faced, for ever.

Like her elder brother, Louise had been dwelling on her emotional state of late. However, she knew her mind more surely than her brother did. Her taste of society's whirl had served only to strengthen her feelings.

She loved John, Earl of Aldersleigh. He was older than the duke at six and thirty, a rake and gambler, who could ruin her without effort.

Yet she felt safe and at ease with him. So, she felt no qualms setting forth to meet him at his chosen rendezvous. Had she known her destination and what was to follow she would have been less sanguine.

At a much later hour, Lord Tristan d'Alvière set out on his planned journey with The Honourable Frederick Carshaw. They were travelling together to visit Folly Hill. Here, Tristan hoped to further his recent run of formidable luck; dice, cards, wagers - it mattered not of late, he seemed able to do no wrong.

As the day was pleasant the two gentlemen departed in Frederick's curricle with his valet up behind. Frederick, while less verbose than his sister, was not a very deep thinker. He offered to take Tristan across to the Towers for the night if he did not wish to rack up at Folly Hill. His lordship replied that he hoped to sleep in his own bed. His companion returned to the topic of the Towers, asking if Sophia had mentioned it at all.

'Why yes, several times.'

Her brother laughed at that, pointing out that as well as being such a rattle, she had not a brain in her head and had never mastered

French, despite the governess's efforts. He paused expectantly.

Tristan already knew which way the conversation was tending, silently cursing his elder's insistence on the cultivation of the Carshaw's.

On receiving no reply, Frederick made another attempt by saying his mamma was worried that Tristan would not like it but thought that as they had been seeing something of each other it might not matter.

Time to put an end, thought Tristan, 'I realise Sophia is very young. I shall soon return to France.'

Any awkwardness there might have been was avoided by Carshaw sighing audibly before revealing that his father was of the opinion that she could do better. Far from being insulted, his lordship burst out laughing with Frederick joining in.

Amiability was restored.

Unknown to the pair in the curricle, Lady Louise's party was but a few miles ahead of them on the same road. This unbroken ride was starting to pall and she was suffering shoots of doubt as to the wisdom of accompanying The

Honourable William Carshaw, for he it was whose favoured colour was grey. She inquired if they needed to travel much further and the young gentleman assured her that their destination was near.

'Oh, this is famous of you! I will win if we reach Folly Hill before the sunset!'

She reined in her horse.

'Of what are you speaking?' She too could be as haughty as her brother. 'I am the object of a wager!?'

This was not part of Aldersleigh's plan, she felt certain.

William Carshaw was at pains to explain that it was a private wager just between himself and a friend, not entered in an open book. It could have been any lady, as long as they were not properly acquainted. When the Beau had needed a messenger, he had been happy to oblige.

He continued that he was sure the Beau knew nothing of the wager; he might even be vexed if he found out. Beseechingly, he asked her not to reveal his motives. She looked at him scathingly, favoured him with a not very ladylike description of his character in French before appealing to the silent groom, 'May we get on?'

She urged her horse into a canter.

Ere long they turned into an ordinary looking driveway. This led them to an astonishing castellated building situated on a small rise and aptly named 'Folly Hill' by its builder, who had lost it within a week of its completion on the throw of a dice.

The middle-aged groom assisted Lady Louise in dismounting, and when he spoke it was to request that she allow him to lead her to his master, the earl. It was clear that he had been in charge of their little entourage all along and not the callow youth who remained impervious to Louise's disdain. Her supposed escort ran up the steps with scant courtesy for his companion, hammering on the door.

Pushing past the servant who opened it he called in exuberant tones, 'Neville! Nev, I did it! That's ten guineas you owe me!'

The groom steered his charge away from the noisy group of young gentlemen who had surged from one of the rooms on hearing

William's raised voice.

At the rear of the hall, he opened a door marked 'Private', bowing the lady in. The room faced parkland and was lit by late afternoon light. Curiously, Louise looked around. It bore a strong resemblance to numerous small reception rooms she had known and was not at all what she had expected. Here there was brocade and satin as well as - blessed sight - a sofa table laid with lemonade and biscuits. She was totally alone. Thirst and hunger forced her start to serve herself when a concealed door next to the chimney piece opened without noise.

'Louise! My dear love, you are come!'

John Aldersleigh held out his arms to her and it seemed the most natural thing to walk into them. He held her close, then guided her to the sofa, pouring out lemonade. 'I trust the journey went well? You must be fatigued?'

'A little.' She nibbled on a biscuit, 'William Carshaw is so stupid!'

He regarded her with a questing look before asking how Carshaw had annoyed her.

She dismissed this youth with a disparaging remark about his foolishness.

Aldersleigh smiled at his lady, assuring her that she had been safe in Braxton's care as he valued her honour as much as her family did.

Taking hold of her hands he seated himself beside her.

'I realise that bringing you here clandestinely might disprove that, but I could think of no other way. I have tried so hard to avoid your company. I understand precisely why your brother has kept us apart. I have managed to avoid meeting him, too.'

He touched her cheek. 'He would have demanded my oath that it was finished between us. How could I in all honour swear that, when my sole desire is to make you my wife?'

Louise gave a quick in draw of breath and would have spoken but he placed a finger on her lips, going onto one knee beside her.

'Listen, my dear. I am almost twenty years older than you; I have known numerous women, not all reputable. I have several natural children whom I acknowledge and no doubt others I know not of. I own no lands in England; I live by my title and my ability to gamble. The only acceptable facet of my life is my fortune. I am asking you to share this life with me. If you accept then there will be no other women, I give you my oath. If you cannot contemplate the life that I offer I shall understand, yet I could not contemplate that life unless I offered for you.'

He found he could not look at her as he awaited her answer, continuing to kneel with bowed head.

Louise placed a kiss on his hair so swiftly that he thought he had imagined it.

'Me, I am certain of the one thing which matters to me; I love you. I shall only be happy with you! You have told me truths and I must do the same. I am spoilt, headstrong, quick tempered as well as wilful. I am certain we are meant to be together; I would rather be your maitresse than the wife of another!'

At this he did look her full in the face, 'My dear girl, that would never happen! Ideally, I would seek your brother's blessing and wed you in your family chapel at Palombières, but I fear that will not be possible.'

She interrupted rather doubtfully saying that perhaps Charles might withdraw his objections once he became accustomed to the idea. In a firmer tone she suggested that if they were married there would be little he could do. Rather alarmingly at that point, she remembered that her brother was an excellent swordsman! She refrained from mentioning this thought.

The earl continued to kneel, 'Will you give me your answer?'

She fell to her knees beside him and murmured simply, 'Oh, yes,' lifting her face to receive his kisses.

Aldersleigh helped her to rise and explained that he had procured a special license in the hope that she would accept his offer. His confessor, who was always with him, would perform the marriage - no marriage in English law but perfectly valid in France and more important still, in Venice where they would make their home. They embraced with fervour, until John drew back, explaining that they must travel a little more until the wedding could take place.

He had no intention of spending the night under the same roof unless they were married. To this end, he planned to take her to the Manor he had been renting, not far from Denbrugh Place. There was a chapel, a housekeeper and a maid to attend Louise. Becoming serious again he continued that Braxton had brought her to this place in order that she could see for herself this club which was one of his sources of income. He owned others, in Paris and Venice.

At that moment, the secret door clicked open once more, this time revealing a fashionably dressed, middle aged woman. She asked leave to interrupt in a low husky voice. Louise cast her a searching glance then the earl introduced her as Miss Charlotte Fenner, who managed Folly Hill in his absence.

'Lottie, I wish to present Lady Louise d'Alvière, soon to become my countess.'

'Ah, so she has consented, felicitations. I hope you are at peace with yourself at last!'

Correctly interpreting the fire in Louise's green eyes, she elaborated, 'Our relationship is one purely of business, my lady. My brother and I have known the Beau since our teens.'

She beckoned him to one side before she whispered, 'Lord Tristan d'Alvière has just arrived with Freddie Carshaw. They are ready for play in the card room. I thought you should know.'

The earl drew a quick breath, requesting that Braxton should bring the carriage to the rear door and suggesting that Lottie should oversee these gentleman's entertainment herself.

Louise was stroking the plume of her mannish tricorne, reflectivity. She understood that the emotion she was experiencing was jealousy. A jealousy of the women in John's past, determining that she would be the only one in his future. These thoughts showed in her face as she waited.

Aldersleigh registered the look and assured her once again that she was the only woman in his life now and so it would always be. He was at pains to point out that he could not prevent them from encountering his indiscretions from time to time as they travelled.

She in turn offered that she could not guarantee that she would hold her temper in check. There would be times when she did not behave in the proper manner for a lady.

He laughed, helping her to replace her hat before offering his arm to lead her into the secret passage which gave access to the servants' quarters and the rear of the house.

There, Braxton sat on the box of a closed carriage. The earl aided his lady in, safe from prying eyes. He gave the office to his groom and their bridal journey began at a sedate pace.

As his sister was departing, Lord Tristan was settling in for an enjoyable time in the card room.

Miss Fenner acting as banker, seated herself between the Honourable Frederick Carshaw and his guest. She had already issued instructions that the younger, more boisterous gentlemen were to be kept occupied in the larger rooms. It was imperative that Frederick should not encounter his brother William, who was bursting to tell any who would listen of his winning the wager of 'the lady'.

FOURTEEN

To prevent a scandal.

At eleven o'clock on the morning of the same day, Miss Dempster decided to visit Lady Louise in her bedchamber. They were due to ride out to Richmond Park with some other young people, where one of their number was to host a 'déjeuner sur l'herbe'.

The evening at Vauxhall had ended late, so Juliet was not unduly surprised when Louise was not yet abroad. The dowager countess had also kept to her room.

Hoping to organise the arrangements for the rest of the day Miss Dempster tapped on Louise's door. It was opened a crack by her maid. This struck Juliet as odd, so she asked if the lady was awake, adding that the maid should go to the kitchens for a pot of hot chocolate and some bread and butter. Instead of doing so, the maid attempted to close the door. In most unladylike fashion, Juliet thrust her foot in the door, pushing it open at the same time.

The curtains were still drawn close across the windows, enabling very little to be seen of the room. She drew them back and noticed that the bed hangings, which Louise rarely used, were pulled tight. Wondering if she might be ill, she addressed the hangings to enquire.

Obtaining no response, she lifted a corner. The bed was empty. As she turned to the maid, she noted the disorder of the dressing table, Louise's discarded night attire and the cold, congealed cup of chocolate.

The maid looked pale, speaking with a tremor in her voice as she explained she thought her mistress had gone riding early, as her riding habit was missing. When asked if that was all which was missing, she nodded, being quick to add that no band boxes had gone. Sensing that discretion was to be of paramount importance, Juliet concurred, sending the maid to fetch fresh chocolate. It seemed that the present situation required the utmost discretion.

Once alone, she began automatically to tidy the room. She retrieved several articles strewn across the floor, pulled back the bed hangings, tying them in their place and then plumped the pillows. As she did so, her hand encountered the texture of parchment. Withdrawing it, she proceeded to read the few lines inscribed thereupon.

'Ohhhhh!' It was a sigh of resignation.

The message she had read merely confirmed the feeling of misgiving which had commenced upon her entry into the room.

With great calm she awaited the maid's return. It was now her duty to inform and consult with the dowager countess.

The maid, appointed by Vénoire to watch his sister, as well as attend her, was only too thankful to be given strict instructions to remain in the bedchamber.

Lady Barbara had not yet left her bed. She

received Juliet, her explanation of what had occurred and the parchment, still wearing her nightcap. On reading the few lines, signed with a flourish - 'Beau'- she remarked that no pointers were offered as to where the rendezvous was to be. She praised Miss Dempster for her discretion. It was of vital importance now to keep it from coming out. She added, in quite colourful language, that her great niece should have been sent to a convent, not given a Presentation Season!

'I fear that I have failed in what was expected of me!'

'Stuff! You were engaged as my companion, not the silly chit's gaoler. None of this fix is your fault.'

The elderly lady toyed with the ribbons on her nightcap, explaining that it would be best if the household were not questioned as the fewer who knew of Louise's folly, the better the outcome might prove. She regarded Juliet with a piercing look.

'I really feel that it is imperative Vénoire should be informed.'

So saying, she rang the small bell on her nightstand and her dresser entered almost at once. Having sent her to find the duke, she observed the paleness of her companion's face. 'There's naught else we could do. You are not to blame.'

Juliet brushed such thoughts aside with a flutter of her hand, 'It goes without saying that his grace should be informed. I feel there must be a way in which I can repair my negligence. I do not think I can bear the thought of his contempt!'

Despite this being a half aside, Lady Lessing had heard and smiled to herself, thinking that if she knew anything it was not contempt Vénoire felt for this young woman.

Her dresser returned with a rather flustered look on her normally rigid features. She informed the ladies that the duke was not at home. Mr Ferris had told her this and was without, wondering if he may be of service. The dowager demanded her wrapper, commanding her woman to stop pokering up as he was not the first man to be admitted to her bedchamber.

'Well, bid him enter!'

Despite the circumstances, Juliet found a smile playing on her lips as the duke's valet trod silently into the room. He bowed to the dowager countess, inclined his head to Miss Dempster and sidestepped the pug's attempt to bite his ankles. In his normal composed manner, he asked pardon for the intrusion but had supposed there was some matter of urgency.

Glaring at her dresser, Lady Barbara gestured for her to hand the pug onto the bed, where she settled him with the remains of her bread and butter. Then, she dismissed her woman, much to this personage's chagrin.

Without preamble she asked if Ferris knew of the duke's whereabouts. He was unable to enlighten her explaining that his master had changed after his morning ride but had left no other details concerning his day.

Juliet burst out, 'Oh but it is most important!'

Ferris merely shook his head adding that his grace had left the house just after Lord Tristan had departed with Frederick Carshaw for Folly Hill.

Juliet had paled at the mention of Folly Hill.

Lady Barbara decided that Ferris should be told of what lay behind her questions.

Knowing his total discretion and loyalty, she related what they knew: on receipt of a letter from the Earl of Aldersleigh, Lady Louise had gone to an unknown assignation place. It was to be kept from everyone else.

She lay back on her pillows with the rider that she was becoming too old for such intrigue.

Ferris's face brightened, 'Excuse me your ladyship, I believe that I may be of help after all. It recently came to his grace's knowledge that Folly Hill is owned by the earl of Aldersleigh.'

'Humph! Seems a reasonable thing that he should plan to meet her there, then. Vénoire might be at his club, or… well you know his habits better than anyone. Go and find him, no fuss mind! You and I, Miss Dempster are bound for Folly Hill. Oh, this is quite like old times!'

There was a glint in her eyes as she made to get out of bed. Ferris beat a hasty retreat. The dowager countess's dresser was called, and Juliet hurried to her own room at the other end of the house.

The mention of the gaming establishment had revived all Juliet's worries concerning the affair of the emerald. She could not recover his grace's ring but it was just possible she might recover his sister and prevent a scandal. A journey in the dowager countess's carriage would be slower than the same journey on horseback. She never doubted that she could reach Oxfordshire rapidly. She would then be present as a chaperone to prevent tongues wagging if the escapade became common knowledge. The dowager and her carriage could then convey them all home.

Even as these thoughts were occurring to her, she was pulling out her old, worn habit and hat. The dowager had insisted she was to have a new one made but it was still with the dressmaker. Her lack of style would serve well in this. She piled her hair unceremoniously into the crown of her hat, after securing it with hairpins. Drawing on her tan gauntlets - discarded by her brother due to stains upon the leather - she reflected that if she too disappeared without anyone knowing it would cause unneeded worry. Mrs Threadgold's rooms were on the floor above and thence she went to admit the old nurse into her confidence, knowing she would keep silence.

'If you will be so obliging as to accompany her ladyship, Mrs Threadgold, if you please? I fear Lady Louise will be in need of a comforting presence.'

Mary Threadgold shook her head. 'It will

be too late for comforting if his grace finds her first. Foolish, foolish girl. Headstrong like them all.'

She had begun readying her outdoor clothes but paused to add, 'If you go off alone, his grace will have more to worry him. I do hope as you'll take Dickon along as groom.'

Juliet turned in the doorway, 'Why in the world should the duke worry about me? I am quite used to going about by myself, have been doing so for many months. I am not some green girl but I do thank you for your concern. If you will but inform the countess of my intentions?'

She was gone swiftly down the corridor.

Mrs Threadgold listened to her hasty tread on the stairs and shook her head.

'Another headstrong one! Just what this family needs!' She reached resignedly for her cloak and bonnet.

FIFTEEN

Folly Hill.

His grace the duke of Vénoire wiped the handle of his épée with a cloth before freeing his lace from his sleeves. Placing the slim blade in its case, he sat at his ease in a chair near to the table.

His fencing partner poured wine for each of them.

'Faith, Vénoire. I had forgot what an excellent swordsman you are. I'm relieved I had no money on the outcome!'

The duke yawned behind his hand, holding out his glass for more wine. 'And I, Saxby, had forgot what a fatiguing pastime it is!'

The younger man laughed as he began retying his cravat before the mirrored wall. When this was done to his satisfaction he declared his partner should stop trying to bubble him, as Vénoire had hardly broken sweat despite coming close to pinking him twice.

'Oh no, had I come near to pinking you, you would have felt it,' the duke stated in a matter of fact manner as he laced his shirt at the neck then retied his hair. 'I learned young the difference between a good feint and an intended thrust.'

'Lessons from an expert, I assume.'

As he pulled on his top boots, Vénoire recalled the numerous hours spent in the gallery at Palombières, each time his father was at home. There had been unremitting practice and scant praise until the day he had turned thirteen.

He was newly returned from visiting his grandfather at Denbrugh and his father goaded him about his English phlegm and loss of polish as they practiced. Instead of losing the parry to his father's thrust he had feinted under his guard, nicking his sire's forearm. He had felt no fear, nor anger even, just an icy calm. The sixth duke had saluted him before stalking from the room.

Later that day his father had sent him the case of Toledo duelling swords which rested now at his elbow. The accompanying note negligently scrawled had read: 'Touché, mon fils!'

It too lay in the case beneath the velvet covering the blades. Praise indeed from this volatile man who had revealed his softer emotions only to his wife.

Less than a year later Vénoire's mother was dead, and his father fled permanently to Versailles.

Saxby was regarding the closed, inward-looking expression on the duke's face, knowing better than to pursue the conversation. He had started to shrug himself into his coat when a servant appeared in the doorway. Bowing to both gentlemen he announced that the duke's valet was wishful to speak with him.

Leaning back even further in the chair the duke spoke languidly, 'Ah, yes to help me into my coat. You will excuse me, Saxby, until our next bout.'

His veiled lids covered an alertness in his eyes. It was irregular for a gentleman's gentleman to come in search of him in person. Vénoire wished for no speculation as to why Ferris should have done so.

Saxby knew that their friendship rested on his powers of discretion. In tones matching the duke's he commented that no doubt it was another of Vénoire's whims, like his hound.

He gestured to Achilles lying in a lengthening patch of sunlight.

'As you say.' Vénoire raised his glass to Saxby as he quitted the room.

Ferris, on being greeted with the same languid tones recognised the hint of displeasure beneath.

'I must be fading in my memory, Ferris. Do have the goodness to remind me of when I requested your presence and what my reason might have been?' The use of his surname convinced the valet of his master's displeasure.

Stiffly, he apologised saying that he was come on the orders of the dowager countess as she was concerned about Lady Louise.

Vénoire straightened in the chair. 'Indeed.'

Ferris approached the table, having ensured that the door was firmly shut. He helped the duke into his coat as the latter inquired what his sister's latest folly might be. Somewhat obliquely the valet reported that her ladyship had left Grosvenor Square.

His employer straightened his cuffs saying he thought his great aunt had known about the projected ride to Richmond. With a shake of his head, his man opined that he rather feared she had left for good, to keep an assignation with the earl. There was no need for him to give the earl's title. Vénoire seized his arm in a vicelike grip and ground out, 'Aldersleigh!'

'Quite so, your grace. If I may, your grace?' He gestured to his pinioned arm.

The smile Vénoire bestowed on him as he released his arm was glacial, 'My apologies Thomas. Do you have more tidings for me?'

'I fear that I do, your grace…'

Vénoire's smile this time showed traces of humour, 'Be at ease Tom I beg, unlike the Ancients, I do not execute the bearer of ill tidings and please - no more "your grace" - you overwhelm me.'

Ferris permitted himself to return the smile, as with a smart inclination of his head he reported the circumstances of Miss Dempster finding the note concerning the unknown clandestine meeting place. Once he had suggested that Folly Hill might be the destination, Lady Lessing was determined to travel there with Miss Dempster. As he was leaving she had been ordering her coach.

Vénoire was quick to understand that his great aunt wished to lend her countenance, thus foiling any suggestion of scandal. He reached for his sword case, clicking his fingers to the dog.

'A ride in the country is just the thing for such a delightful afternoon, do you not agree, Tom?' The smile he gave this time did not reach his eyes.

'It pains me, but I must send you to the mews, forgive my want of manners. Have them bring round Tenace. I trust the carriage will be ready to depart!'

His trust was misplaced. On arriving at Grosvenor Square, he saw his own landau standing before the entrance with Wilkes waiting at the horses' heads.

He ran lightly up the steps where the door was being held open by a footman. The hall seemed full of ill-assorted people; his old nurse, his old great aunt, her equally aged dresser and a very concerned looking Downes.

The butler's look changed to one of great relief when he caught sight of his master, framed in the doorway.

'Dear me, am I strayed into Bedlam?' His grace's tone belied the jesting phrase.

'At last, Vénoire you are come!' Turning to the butler, 'That will be all Downes. Remember!'

This worthy bowed, looking affronted at the dowager Lady Lessing's injunction to silence. He waited for his master's nod before leaving the hall.

Vénoire wondered aloud why the party was not yet en route. The countess told him in round terms about Miss Dempster's departure, alone. His frown deepened as he queried if she had taken a groom.

'That she has not, sir!' Mrs Threadgold said, heavily. 'I tried to get her to take Dickon but she'd got it into her head she would be quicker alone.'

His already grim face darkened again, 'Then I must set about overtaking her to lend my escort. Must all of my household be put into jeopardy on my sister's account!!'

There being no appropriate response to this, the other participants in the conversation were pleased to see Ferris's arrival. He stated that Dickon was holding Tenace, who was very fresh; that Miss Dempster was riding Tonnerre, at which the duke so far forgot himself as to emit a French oath; and that he would obtain his master's cloak and hat before hurrying up the main staircase.

Meanwhile the duke urged his elderly relative into the closed carriage. She received the rug offered by her dresser, telling her in no uncertain terms that she was to take care of the pug and some mending. Mrs Threadgold would be of more use with Lady Louise. She placed the rug across her knees as Vénoire helped the old nurse in, enabling his great aunt to see his expression. 'I ask myself of the two, whose well-being concerns you more?'

The duke stiffened in the act of closing the door. 'I fail to understand your meaning.'

He turned to mount his restive horse, signalling to Wilkes to depart and so did not hear Mrs Threadgold murmur that she thought he had met his match.

Lady Barbara smiled and nodded, 'I still wonder if he knows it.'

The carriage was setting a smart pace, but it was not long before its occupants saw Vénoire overtake them, urging his horse along the cobbles at a reckless pace.

Miss Dempster, had she been a man, would have been described as a neck or nothing rider. She had learnt to ride as soon as she could walk, at first in front of her papa, thence to ponies and on to spirited bloodstock since her first hunt. The past months without a mount, had been one of the worst aspects of their reduced circumstances for her. Now, she had been only too glad to exchange the restrained trot, expected in Town, for a canter on the outskirts and was now delighted to be indulging in a full-blown gallop. When familiar country-side came into view she did not hesitate to leave the turnpike in order to take a more direct route across the fields.

It served two purposes: it would certainly prove more direct but also there were fewer observers of her hectic progress. A lone figure, on a mettlesome bay gelding. No lady's horse this but the duke's second mount, Tonnerre. Ridden by the duke early that morning he had allowed his present rider to mount, hardly feeling the light side saddle she had put on him. He had recognised sure hands on the reins, had not attempted to unseat her and now, well into the journey, they were moving as one.

The exhilaration of soaring over hedges once again briefly distracted Juliet from the purpose of her journey. Having little idea what she could or would say supposing she found Lady Louise, her hope was that her presence would save her reputation. The speed of her ride and the concentration needed to control her mount also prevented her from dwelling on the duke of Vénoire and the tangled emotions he inspired in her.

She reined in as they breasted a rise. The bay stood blowing, glad of a brief halt. Juliet felt the blood pounding through her body as she straightened in the saddle. She knew exact where she was; if she were to turn right here, she would be on Solworth land within a few miles.

Instead, she turned to the left in order to regain the Oxford Road. Her pace had slowed as she was uncertain of the exact location of the house she sought.

Soon her attention was caught by the flash of sunlight upon glass and she saw what seemed to be the outline of a castle in the distance. Breathing a sigh, she turned her mount in this direction.

The approach she had taken brought her to a hedge which seemed to form the boundary at the rear of Folly Hill. She set the horse to jump this obstacle, then rode him up the slope to where some formal gardens began.

Here she paused to consider her next

course of action. To enter by the main door, inquiring for Lady Louise would be far from discrete. Discretion was the reason she was here. An entrance via the servants' door would also provoke comment. The sole option seemed to be to gain access unseen. With this in mind, she tethered the bay to a bush out of sight of the house making a stealthy approach to the rear. Raucous laughter and loud voices gave her pause. Windows at the far end of the building seemed unoccupied and blank whilst the rest of the windows on the lower floor cast a glow of candlelight mingled with the fading sunlight.

As she hesitated, she realised a long window, just behind the lighted ones, was ajar. Having eased herself noiselessly through this, she discovered it gave on to a rear hallway. All remained silent as she tucked her straying hair back under her hat. She felt dusty and dishevelled, her tan riding gauntlets were hot and she put them on the window sill beside her. Leaving her crop hanging from her wrist, she took a deep steadying breath before moving towards the nearer of two doors which were visible.

Hesitating, she saw that the furthest door was inscribed 'Private.' Naturally the earl would have use of a private suite in his own establishment, what better place for a tryst?

She turned the handle with care, pushing the door open. Hearing no sound she entered the room, closing the door without noise behind her.

It was in semi-darkness, as the last of the day's sun sank behind the trees where she had tethered the horse. Advancing with more confidence, she saw that the room was empty. There remained enough daylight to make visible a tray of lemonade and biscuits.

Of more importance there were two glasses, one of which contained some dregs. Lemonade being a lady's drink, led her to conclude that Lady Louise had indeed been present. She could appreciate the need for a quenching drink, having covered the same distance. Need overcoming prudence, she drank from the clean glass. Looking around, she found no other signs of anyone's presence; all was tidy, still and silent.

Replacing the glass, she determined to explore what lay beyond the other door in this room.

It was a bedchamber, surprising her in its femininity, with no sign of recent male occupation.

Juliet stood, disconcerted. It was becoming difficult to see, yet she could hardly ring for candles! She began to wonder if her instinct that Lady Louise was here, had played her false. If the earl's intentions were dishonourable, as the family supposed, it would be necessary for him to prevent her from leaving once she realised the truth. Having learnt how quick tempered the young lady was, Juliet felt certain the Beau would have to keep her apart from the club members. That being so, these rooms were too close to the public ones. Perhaps on another floor?

Exploring the dimmest corner of the bedchamber, Juliet found a door in the panelling leading to a servants' night stair. It was darker still in the passage; nevertheless, light seemed to be shining from above. Gathering her skirts, she mounted the bare wooden stairs as silently as possible.

On reaching the top, she found the source of light to be a branch of candles set on a table near to the stairwell. This opened onto a small corridor, mirroring the one below but with more doors leading off.

Faced with a choice of four rooms Juliet again hesitated.

That which was at the far end she suspected would lead to the rest of the house. The upper floors of a gaming hell would not be a suitable place for any virtuous lady, so she had no urge to open that! Giving herself a mental shake at her indecision, she grasped the candles and opened the nearest door.

This room too was unoccupied but decorated in a masculine style. It reminded her of her papa's book room, save for the presence of a bed as well as a desk. She could make out paper and an inkstand on the desk.

Crossing the room to look more closely, she wondered if it was here that the assignation note had been written. All parchment looks the same, yet she recognised the crest decorating the inkstand and sander as exactly the same as that impressed in the broken seal on the note. It proved that the earl might be here, somewhere.

She withdrew, closing the door with care. At the same moment she heard the sound of voices and approaching footsteps on the other side of the far door. Replacing the candles by the staircase, she slipped into the nearest room.

She peeped through the crack she had left in anticipation of seeing Lady Louise and the Earl. Instead, the corridor was flooded with more candlelight, held by a laughing, middle-aged lady as she escorted an unknown gentleman dressed in gold satin and lace. His face beneath his powdered wig was lined and haughty. Juliet was surprised that their conversation was conducted in French.

The lady held open the door of the room next to Miss Dempster's hiding place. As the gentleman entered, she saw that he used an ebony cane.

Having grown accustomed to the gloom, Juliet deliberated her next course of action. She should make her escape whilst the couple were in the adjoining room, yet that would lead her no nearer to discovering Lady Louise. In order to see, she inched the door wider to allow in some candlelight. The room in which she stood appeared to be a dressing room. The hall candles reflected off a pier-glass and the buckles on a portmanteau set against the wall. As she looked around, she could hear the couple conversing. Closer inspection revealed that the connecting door was not quite shut. Circumspectly, Juliet placed her ear against the gap.

SIXTEEN

The man attired in gold.

Had Miss Dempster been able to see, as
well as to hear, she would have beheld the
autocratic gentleman standing before the
fireplace in a room large enough to accommodate a bed, chairs, a sofa and a table laid for
supper for two. The lady adjusted the glasses set
upon the table, laughing again at something the
older gentleman had said. Juliet heard her
reassure the man that the companion he was

expecting would be all compliance, addressing him as 'duke'. His response affronted Miss Dempster as he requested not too much compliance, something was necessary to stir his jaded palate.

'I have a girl in mind who will be whatever you wish her to be. Have you ever known me to fail you?'

'My dear Mademoiselle Fenner, I do not brook failure wherever I find myself.'

The pitilessness in his voice sent a shiver down Juliet's spine.

'You keep a clean and honest house where I am little known. I am free to indulge my passions, which is all that is required.'

She curtsied saying she would send the girl up at once.

Juliet no longer intended to linger. Turning with too much haste in the darkness, she stumbled against a chest of drawers and sent the wig stand set upon it crashing to the floor. Consternation caused her to freeze before catching up her skirts and making a dash for the door, the time for stealth being at an end!

Imagine her horror on seeing the doorway blocked by a stocky valet bearing a candle in one hand and a jug of hot water in the other. At the same instant the connecting door was opened by the French duke who was apostrophising his valet Luc, as a clumsy ox. He surveyed the frozen scene. The valet shattered the spell by attempting to explain.

The duke raised his bony hand, his eyes fixed on Juliet, and ordered the valet, 'Back whence you came! Lock the door as you leave. Do it now!'

Whilst physically unable to move, Miss Dempster's mind had been frantically active wondering how to resolve the situation she found herself in. Her instinct was to pretend ignorance of the French language, however when the last command was uttered her eyes flew to the duke's implacable face. He bowed with ironic good manners and gestured to the other room.

'Mademoiselle, if you please. Better to talk in the light.'

Having very little choice, she passed through the open door. How long, she thought, would it be before Miss Fenner returned with the duke's promised companion?

Continuing in the same amused manner the aristocrat begged her politely to sit. When she remained standing, ill at ease, by the main door he smiled thinly and locked it. The smile remained on his lips but there was something other behind his eyes.

'I wish you to tell me why you were hiding.'

The silence between them lasted only a few seconds before he added, 'I do assure you, I am not known for my patience. If you will not sit, I will.'

He bowed and sat, resting his chin on the ebony cane. 'Pray forgive the insult.'

Holding her head high, Juliet sat on one of the two chairs by the table.

The duke had seated himself on the sofa. Inclining his head, he began musing aloud that given her riding habit it was most probable that she had arrived on horseback. He seemed to be enjoying her discomfiture as he quizzed her with his glass. This seemed to convince him that she could not be acquainted with Mademoiselle Fenner.

A thought occurred to him which provoked very unpleasant laughter; here she was sent as a delicious, unexpected diversion.

He poured wine, offering a glass to his captive.

She shook her head, 'I fear you are making a very grave mistake, Sir!'

There was a trembling in her voice which she could not suppress.

His laughter, this time, was even more sinister. 'Me? No, I never make mistakes.'

Proffering the wine again, 'Drink!!'

Seeing no advantage in raising his ire further, Juliet took a sip.

The gentleman's hand brushed her cheek in passing, instantly causing her to stand and move away. With dignity she tried once more to reason with him, appealing to him as an obvious gentleman. Stating that she was here in secret in order to protect a reputation. She would be very much obliged if he would unlock the door and she would trouble him no further.

His only response was to tell her, in English, that she intrigued him and that intrigue was his lifeblood.

He stared at her without blinking, causing her to pale. The next words he spoke were in French again, this time with no attempt to disguise the lasciviousness behind them.

'You are a thing of great beauty, ma poule. I can savour your fear. Such a luscious fruit cannot be allowed to slip away, untasted.'

His eyes, hard and grey as flint, registered the colour flooding her skin. 'So, you understand what I am saying! All the better!'

She had edged towards the dressing room door, the full glass of wine untouched in her hand, once more appealing to him to allow her to find the owner of the establishment.

He continued as if she had not spoken. 'Forgive my lack of manners, before we proceed, I should present myself; Henri de Richelles, Duc de Langon. There now, does that put you more at ease, ma poule?'

The panic and shock which Juliet had been experiencing was now replaced with a blinding anger at the arrogance of the man, 'Understand this, duke or not, I am no man's "poule"!'

He was standing close to her once more. 'Since you have chosen not to enlighten me as to your name, what else should I call you?'

He had begun breathing hard, 'God but you are magnificent standing there! Such eyes! You remind me of a startled hind!'

He attempted to caress her face again. She retreated another pace, remarking with contempt that she reserved her name for use by gentlemen and his behaviour did not match that description.

Once more he laughed without true mirth, agreeing he was no gentleman but an aristocrat, as if that explained all. As he had continued speaking, he had matched her movements pace for pace, away from the door back towards the supper table as she had no wish to be edged close to the bed.

Suddenly she was struck by the absurdity of it all; here was a man, old enough to be her father, infirm enough to have held on to his cane throughout. Why should she fear him? It was the implacability, the indomitable will latent in the lean body which caused her to tremble. She clung to the hope that the lady would return soon. Surely, she could look to her for assistance? In command of her voice once more, she resumed her seat facing the duke and reiterating, 'When the lady returns, I will explain all. Please have the kindness to wait.'

His laughter this time held the rustle of dead leaves. 'Oh, priceless! Oh, I see I must share my amusement. Luc will have informed la Fenner that I am well fixed for a fille de joie this night!'

At this all restraint fled; Juliet forcefully

flung the glassful of wine into his leering face.

Everything then followed with alarming rapidity. He knocked the empty glass from her grasp, bringing his hand across her cheek with a stinging blow, dislodging her hat. Her chestnut curls cascaded about her shoulders in disarray, pins flying across the room, such was the blow's force. She staggered backwards, yet remained on her feet with the table between them still.

'I have ever admired spirit but have a care you do not over step my bounds!'

There was a sinister threat in his tone as he mopped his face with a napkin. He renewed his approach as she moved around the table, grey eyes locked on amber ones.

Then he stopped and sighed impatiently, 'Acknowledge I hold you at bay. It will give me great pleasure to administer the coup de grâce.'

At this point he seized her by the shoulders. His unrelenting grip caused her to cry out, as with his free hand - the cane dispensed with now - he lifted her luxuriant ringlets. 'No hind but a vixen, I think.'

Despite all her struggles he succeeded in crushing his thin, bloodless lips against hers. With a supreme effort she raised the hand from which her riding crop hung and brought it down with vicious intent on his neck and shoulder. The speed with which she escaped his relaxed grip caused the worn material of her bodice to tear, revealing her chemise beneath. Tousled and panting she stood before the fireplace.

Real anger now blazed from the duke's face. 'When I have finished with you, you shall be horse whipped for that!!'

He reached for his cane and with a practiced twist of the handle withdrew a sword. 'I'll thank you for the crop.'

She made a dash to put the table between them once more, flimsy protection that it was. He advanced on her, upturning it, smashing crystal and china. She quaked as the fine blade hovered over her breast.

'Give - me - the - crop!'

On each word he slashed off a button on her bodice, tearing the delicate lawn chemise in places yet leaving no scratch beneath.

Defeated, Juliet complied.

He threw the crop into the empty fireplace, tossing his sword onto the nearest chair.

'Now you have fired my blood! I will have you!'

Grabbing her wrist he commenced dragging her towards the bed. She resisted with every ounce of her strength; somewhere in a still calm portion of her mind she was surprised to hear herself screaming. At the same instant a hammering on the door had commenced.

Seizing both of her wrists in an iron grip, the duc forced her towards the door, using the weight of his body to pin her against the doorframe.

With a lascivious wetting of his lips he whispered in her ear, 'If that is Luc, he can hold you down.'

As soon as the key was turned in the lock Juliet heard, as if from a long distance, Miss Fenner's raised voice, 'I do assure your grace that the earl is nowhere in the house. This is a private room!'

'Allow me the evidence of my own eyes, I beg.' The words died in his throat, as his Grace the Duke of Vénoire absorbed the scene before him.

Instantly, Juliet felt the hold on her person slacken and she broke free, too stunned by her experience to do other than sink to the floor against the wall.

'De Langon!'

'Vénoire!'

The venomous tones in which each uttered the other's title spoke not of friendship.

'A most unlooked for interruption. I must have missed you sending up a card.' This was voiced with frigid irony.

Vénoire continued to survey the disorder of the room, his gaze falling at last on the dishevelled other occupant.

'Juliet!' he breathed, 'You cur! What have you done to her?'

No trace of the indolent figure of boredom remained. There now burned a luminescent fire in his blue eyes, one which de Langon assumed he recognised.

He began fulsome, disingenuous apologies for purloining the duke's piece of goods, calling him "mon gars" whilst adding with a smirk that it made it all the sweeter.

The younger man's face flickered once as he drew a slow, sustained breath, rejecting the description of being this man's 'lad', explaining that the lady was under his protection. This produced a snigger, an excusing wave of the hands and a muttered, 'Of course!'

Through gritted teeth Vénoire merely stated, 'I will take her home now.'

This provoked a sneer from the older man, 'Ah, in reality, it should have been obvious that no son of that thief Louis-François could have enough warm blood in his veins to bed such a one!'

Vénoire bowed with rigidity as he pointed out that he had been taught to respect his elders, otherwise he should not have let pass such a slur on his family's honour.

This remark caused de Langon to almost lose his reason. His face a contorted mask of fury, with spittle flying, he poured out his venomous hatred.

'Honour! What does your family know of honour! Your sire, so besotted of a coquette that he married her!'

The time for restraint now passed, Vénoire flung his riding glove at the vindictive duke's feet. In barely restrained tones he demanded that a place and time be named. De Langon reached for his discarded sword saying they would fight here and now.

Juliet, during the altercation, had remained hunched on the floor. She was shivering uncontrollably, with Miss Fenner at her side having wrapped her in the coverlet from the bed and administered a glass of brandy. This last remark brought the chatelaine to her feet to remonstrate, 'Gentlemen, please! You cannot mean to fight without seconds and in such conditions!'

Vénoire had removed his boots without taking his eyes from Juliet. In a completely level voice he said he wished for no witnesses to Miss Dempster's misadventure, adding he would prefer more space, spoken in tones as if requesting the dice box. De Langon was still emanating hate as he growled he had no wish for seconds as it was not his intention to halt at first blood.

'It seems we must make shift here, then.'

Vénoire stood in his stockinged feet, without coat or cravat, having withdrawn his sword from its discarded scabbard: one of the same Toledo swords used that morning, brought on his journey almost as an afterthought.

Miss Fenner's years of running like estab-lishments had taught her that there comes a point when gentlemen cannot be reasoned with. She requested them to follow her.

She led them to the fourth door which she unlocked with keys hanging from her belt. It was used as a storeroom, with trunks and boxes piled at one end. The evening dusk shed a poor light through the half-shuttered windows. Opening these, she placed her branch of candles on the topmost box, fetching more from the stair and the other room.

De Langon, without coat and wig, looked gaunt and threatening in the macabre light. Candles in place, the two men took up their positions. Exchanging no further words, they saluted formally and set to, each with a cold determination.

Miss Fenner had witnessed many duels; some whose participants were too advanced in their cups to cause much harm, others ruled by rigid etiquette. Never had she seen two opponents more intent on a fight to the death.

She was spellbound by the parry and thrust being played out before her. The disparity of age between the swordsmen dropped away as the fight progressed.

De Langon was the more experienced whilst his grace of Vénoire had fought few duels confining his skill to the fencing salon. To ameliorate this, Vénoire was adept at mastering his emotions; the other's rancour, nurtured over so many years threatened to entrap him.

By degrees, the sounds of the clashing blades penetrated Juliet's consciousness where she still sat on the bedroom floor. The remnants of her shock and fear dissipated as she made sense of the sounds. Scrambling to her feet, she knotted the coverlet over her torn bodice. Shakily she forced her legs to carry her to the end room, where she gazed in horror at the lethal contest which was in progress.

Vénoire was fighting with his back to the doorway but in any event both men were too engrossed to note her arrival. Miss Fenner's restraining hand was unnecessary; Juliet knew enough of duelling to avoid breaking their concentration. Each man was pressing the other to drop their guard; as well as the thud of their stockinged feet on the bare boards, their breathing was now audible above the metallic ringing of swords. Both ladies gasped as de Langon overcame a parry and reached the duke's forearm. He disentangled his weapon from the torn shirt sleeve before Vénoire could penetrate his arm pit. His grace sought to follow through but it came to nought, save for a scarlet stain across the older duke's chest. The latter let out a breath of a laugh, managing to goad, 'Too slow!'

Vénoire remained grim faced and silent as he continued the combat. More cuts were given and received; one to de Langon's face and a particularly vicious one to the duke's shoulder.

As their movements advanced them as one towards the door, Miss Fenner pulled Juliet into the hallway.

'Oh! We must stop them! They mean to kill each other!' Pleaded Miss Dempster, with horror in her eyes.

The chatelaine of Folly Hill agreed with a grim relish. She found their bloodlust fascinating, pointing out that if they had refused to listen before starting the fight it was unlikely they would do so now.

'I must try!' Juliet looked with desperation at the sweating, panting figures. Overwhelmed, she could no longer bear to watch the diabolical scenario. The odour of candle wax mingled with sweat and blood, coupled with the lingering taste of brandy, made her feel suddenly nauseous. Without clear thought, she opened the door into the main floor of the house, resting her swimming head against the cool marble of the doorpost. Never had she felt so desolate in her whole life.

Footsteps mounting the nearby staircase failed to move her. A slurred masculine voice was heard to inquire if his companion could think of a better way to round off such a successful day than with a bit of dalliance. A more sober voice replied that such was not his intention.

On hearing this, Juliet had lifted her head. There formed a look of hope on her tear drenched face.

In a penetrating, drunken whisper, the honourable Frederick Carshaw interrupted the speaker begging him to have a look at the vision of delight standing before them. He prodded him forward as they reached the head of the stairs.

'Oh, Lord Tristan, thank God it is you!' All thoughts of circumspection were forgotten at suddenly finding the younger d'Alvière present.

Tristan released himself from Carshaw's drunken grasp, propelling this gentleman down the opposite corridor where a dim figure waited in deshabillé. With swift strides the duke's brother returned to Miss Dempster, becoming aware of her tumbled hair, strange attire but most worrying, her blanched, agonised face. Without preamble he asked what was amiss

She swayed a little as she uttered, 'It is your brother. I fear for his life!'

He steadied her by the elbow, following her through the private door. As she passed along the landing her heart lurched with a sickening thump, hearing only silence. Terrified at what she might find, she led the tense young man into the storeroom.

Recumbent in Miss Fenner's lap lay the duc de Langon. His chest was covered with blood, more was visible on the tablecloth which the châtelaine pressed to his neck. Vénoire leant against the mantlepiece, his sword hanging inert from his blood stained hand. He evinced no surprise, no reaction whatsoever in finding his brother's concerned eyes upon him. 'He ran upon my sword. I was ready to call a halt. He ran upon my sword.'

Unexpectedly a ghost of a smile played across the blue lips of the dying duc.

All except Vénoire moved closer to hear his words, 'Catherine… she married…life ended… my death… seventeen years… too…. late!'

His words spluttered on laboured, bloodied breath then a final gush of blood soaked Miss Fenner's skirts and his ragged breathing ceased.

Seventeen years earlier Catherine, Duchess de Vénoire had died giving birth to her daughter Louise.

Tristan returned to his brother's side and relieved him of his sword. Wiping it, he murmured that de Langon had meant to die, that his brother must see that. He had wanted Charles to kill him. Vénoire raised his left hand to wipe his brow, wincing. His sword arm still hung nervelessly at his side.

'Ah, no my dear, at first he very much wanted to kill me.'

Miss Dempster had fetched brandy from

the earl's bedroom. Seeing that Vénoire lived had restored some of her composure. She poured a glass for each of them and, as Miss Fenner seemed calm despite being covered in gore, turned to hand the spirit to the duke.

For the first time since the duel had begun he acknowledged her presence.

'Miss Dempster… Juliet… I...' he straightened, lifting his sword arm in order to take the glass.

It was at this moment that pain exploded in his brain, blotting out all other thoughts. He gave a low, animalistic sound in his throat and collapsed at her feet, his head striking the firedogs with a sickening thump as he lost consciousness.

'Oh! My love!' She dropped beside him, searching for a pulse. It was present but beating erratically. Tearing through the bloodied rent in his shirt made by de Langon's first cut, she discovered an encrusted gash from shoulder to elbow. Above it was a deep puncture wound, from which a slow line of blood still trickled. Coupled with his exertions there had been enough blood loss to sap his strength.

With care she gently lifted his head,

withdrawing fingers smeared with fresh blood. She demanded water and cloths with some urgency. Whilst Miss Fenner went in search of these, Tristan lifted his inert sibling with care, following Juliet across the landing to the room which had witnessed her humiliation. A scene of smashed china and overturned furniture met his lordship's gaze as he laid his brother upon the bed.

His look was puzzled as he asked, 'Miss Dempster, what has happened here? I fail to understand why you and Charles should be in such a place as this. As to the duel…'

The lady's voice was low, her face shadowed as she burst out, 'All my fault. His grace issued the challenge, not de Langon.'

A moan issued from the bed and she promised to furnish him an explanation once his brother's wounds were attended to.

She took the basin and cloths from Miss Fenner who begged leave to change. It occurred to Juliet that the dowager countess must arrive soon and so she informed Tristan.

'Mon Dieu! What else?'

Deliberately misinterpreting his question,

she proposed that a hot brick for his brother's feet and a posset of infused wine would be best. As the châtelaine returned she asked if a discrete servant could bring up those things as well as some goose fat if this were available.

Miss Fenner marvelled at the change in the young lady, calm and in control, all trace of shock vanished, it seemed.

Intercepting her look, Juliet gestured at the cut torso of the duke, 'I can do something about this.'

With concern the châtelaine inquired if a surgeon should be sent for. Lord Tristan replied in the affirmative but Miss Dempster interrupted him with a vehement shake of her head whilst adding that his brother would not want that. For his sister's sake they should await Lady Lessing's arrival.

Looking confused he demanded to know what the present situation had to do with their sister. As she tended the duke's wounds, Miss Dempster commenced a lengthy explanation.

SEVENTEEN

To watch and to wait.

The arrival of the Dowager Countess of Lessing via the rear entrance to Folly Hill, occasioned nothing more than speculation amongst the staff who witnessed it. All knew that idle gossip would cost them their place. Miss Charlotte Fenner, having appraised her new, uninvited, guest of the situation in full had resumed her normal routine.

It fell to Lord Tristan to inform de

Langon's man of his master's demise and to set in train the burial. He feared that the duty of informing his sovereign of the manner in which one of his nobles had met his death was also to be his task. At least, he reflected that it was not an Englishman whom Charles had killed. Small comfort this, with his elder still unconscious upstairs.

Mrs Threadgold had seen at once that Miss Dempster was a competent nurse. There being nothing a surgeon could do which had not been done already, it was decided to dispense with this complication. The three women sat now on the righted chairs and cleared sofa, all trace of debris removed from the suite. Juliet's gaze would keep straying to the immobile figure on the bed.

The dowager countess took possession of her hand, gently forcing her to face her, 'My dear, all that can be done has been done. He is resting. We must now endeavour to find Louise. If we fail to do so before this night is past and she is with Aldersleigh, then all this,' her gesture encompassed the day's events, 'will have been for naught.'

Juliet confided that she felt sure Miss Fenner must know the whereabouts of the earl. The events of the last few hours had driven all thought of Lady Louise from her mind. She made to rise but her ladyship still held her hand saying it was no surprise, considering the ordeal she had been subjected to. The young lady shuddered at the memory but insisted that what she had suffered was as nothing compared to... her gaze was again drawn irresistibly to the duke with an anguish which prevented her from continuing.

At a gesture from the Lady Barbara, Mrs Threadgold went to find the servant who now stood guard over the storeroom where the old nurse had laid out de Langon's corpse.

Oblivious to the nurse's departure as well as to the dowager's concern, Miss Dempster tiptoed towards the bed, leaving her plate of cold chicken untouched on the table. The duke's breathing was so shallow as to be almost imperceptible.

She had bandaged his arm as tightly as was possible across his chest to prevent more bleeding should he move; such a precaution seemed to have been unnecessary as he had lain still as stone since before the dowager countess's arrival. The white head bandage stood out in stark contrast to his black hair. His features seemed softer and somehow more vulnerable.

With all her might she was willing him to show some sign of returning to his senses; only then could they know if his head wound had done any lasting damage. Yet! If he were conscious, she would be unable to look at him thus. In her head, she repeatedly heard him use her Christian name as he had done on first recognising her here. She treasured the sound of it. Perhaps, when he had talked of marriage at the masquerade, he had had more in mind than a marriage of convenience? However, her own moral sense would never allow her to wed someone whom her brother had robbed at pistol point, no matter that she loved him!

Tristan's return with Miss Fenner curtailed such thoughts.

Juliet remained seated on the chair next to the bedside, only half attending to the conversation. The physical and emotional exertions of this day were starting to take their toll.

It was through an encroaching mist of fatigue

that she heard the chatelaine say, 'In such circumstances as we are I feel it right to inform you of the earl's whereabouts. He has taken Lady Louise to Solworth Manor, where they planned to marry this evening.'

'Nom d'un nom! Married!' Tristan shouted.

At the same time Juliet had uttered, 'Solworth!' in a bemused tone. 'But of course, Neville's mysterious tenant!' Then she began to laugh in an uncontrolled manner, much to the concern of all present.

'Oh, do you not see? I should have thought! None of this need have happened! My fault, all my fault!' Her laughter was turning to sobs as Mrs Threadgold brought her away from the bed.

Lady Barbara taking her laudanum bottle from her reticule, passed it to Mary saying, 'A few drops in some wine, I think. Come child.'

Putting an arm around Juliet's shaking shoulders she drew her into a comforting embrace. Over the girl's still unpinned hair she addressed Tristan, 'If they are married in truth we are left with no grounds for objection. This family cannot withstand another duel! We need to know all that has occurred, I will accompany you to Solworth Manor, Tristan.'

She handed the prepared wine to a calmer Juliet. 'A circumspect arrival in the carriage will add credence to anything we might want to put about concerning the ceremony.'

Considering, his lordship nodded. If indeed they were properly married, despite his sister being a minor, there was nothing to be done. A scandal was to be avoided at all costs. He still wondered how his elder would react when informed, if indeed he ever could be informed. It suddenly seemed rather unimportant.

Miss Dempster started to say that she would sit with the duke whilst they were gone. She got no further as Mrs Threadgold dismissed the idea in no uncertain terms. She predicted that Juliet would be asleep in next to no time and that she would take care of them both.

As if from a very great distance, Juliet watched as the dowager and Lord Tristan departed. She felt Miss Fenner and Mrs Threadgold help her to rise and slowly, as if walking through mire, she allowed herself to be helped to the earl's bedchamber. Here she dimly remembered being helped out of her torn habit before falling between warmed sheets.

With the aid of the drug and her utter exhaustion Miss Dempster slept until dawn. She awoke to the sounds of birds in the mock battlements above her window, groggily grasping at the trailing wisps of her recollections.

Once fully awake she crossed to the window, drawing back the curtains. Faint pink fringes of the rising sun were breaking the grey night clouds. She shivered, clad as she was only in her torn chemise and petticoats. Spying a wrapper thoughtfully left by Miss Fenner, she put it on. Regardless of her bare feet and tumbled hair, she hurried across the landing, quietly entering the room where the duke lay.

The candles had burnt down in their sconces almost to stubs. The fire, lit on Mary Threadgold's orders, had dwindled to a pile of ashes whilst this lady slumbered in a wing chair placed beside the bed. Juliet drew back the curtains here with care, allowing the rising sun to steal in. Both the occupants of the room slept on. Examining the duke's face in the half light, Juliet was shaken to see it beaded with sweat; as she leant closer, she beheld a new stain on the bandage at his shoulder. Attempting to remain calm, despite her stomach dropping, she dipped a cloth into the basin of cold water on the nightstand. As she bathed his face he moved in an agitated fashion muttering formless words.

As if still tuned to the sound of his voice down the years, his old nurse came awake at once to find Miss Dempster on her knees holding his free hand. She did not question her right to be there, sharing with her the fact that he had become more restless toward the end of the night. The young woman was calm yet anxious and wondered if the bandage should be changed.

Mary Threadgold leaned across the bed sniffing at the bloodstain, 'I think it's clean for the present. We must wait it out. This fever was to be expected; if the wound becomes infected then is the moment to fret.'

Becoming aware that the old nurse was fully dressed, Juliet asked if she had slept at all.

'Oh, I managed. You grow used to going short on sleep in the Nursery.'

Straightening the sheet she looked determined for a moment then smiled, 'I nursed his mamma from two months, brought him into this world, so I've no intention of letting him go from us yet.'

She regarded Juliet with a knowing look, 'And neither do you.'

Without waiting for a response she left the room saying, 'What you need is some hot chocolate!'

Beads of perspiration had appeared once more upon Vénoire's forehead; once again they were wiped away. This time, he made no utterance; his rapid, shallow breathing was the only indication that he was alive, if not sensible to the world around him. Overcome by her true feelings, realising that such a chance might never present itself again Juliet kissed his lips with great tenderness, then brushed the damp strands of his hair from his face. His eyelids flickered for a second but remained closed. She stayed holding his hand until Mrs Threadgold's return.

Mary carried a tray of chocolate and the skirt of Miss Dempster's riding habit over her arm. Explaining that the ill matched bodice she also carried was a loan from Miss Fenner, she held out both raiment. 'Your chocolate will stay hot enough while you dress.'

Juliet made use of the dressing room, it being nearby. If anything, the pale blue gros-grain bodice was a little tight and looked quite incongruous against the serge of her habit skirt.

Being dressed made her feel stronger. She found an assortment of hairpins in a dish by the wig-stand which had proved her undoing yesterday. Painstakingly she managed to secure her ringlets in position on the top of her head. Regarding herself in the pier glass, the effect was to give her courage to face today's problems, despite having no solution to the emerald affair.

On her return she took the cup of chocolate offered to her but refused the accompanying bread and butter. She was chastened into attempting some when Mrs Threadgold pointed out two invalids to care for would be too much even for her undoubted skill, convincing her finally with, 'You can do nothing for him if you are in a state of collapse!'

The old nurse busied herself by folding clean linen and bandages which had been piled on the sofa. Satisfied that the plate and cup were empty, she replaced them on the tray saying that she must suppose the earl kept some clothes here. It was to be hoped that she could find his grace a nightshirt. She removed the duke's own lawn shirt from the pile just folded, declaring it past mending.

'Will you sit with him, if you please Miss, while I take some breakfast and freshen up?'

She left the room, not expecting any reply, carrying the sorted linen with her. The damaged shirt lay where it had been left. Juliet could not resist picking it up, holding it briefly to her cheek.

'Oh, too absurd!' She castigated herself.

Having been washed, it bore no trace of the duke except that the torn fabric mirrored the cuts upon his body. With precision, she began tearing it into strips, rolling them ready for use. Time crawled past, marked by the ticking of the mantle-clock and the duke's breathing.

She had nothing to read and nothing to occupy her hands. After the last weeks of household activities, she found herself glad to have time to order her thoughts once and for all.

If it proved that Lady Louise was really married, then she would have to quit Grosvenor Square. With her source of income gone what possibility was there of retrieving the emerald ring in time? There could be none. This was something which, in her heart she had always known but had great reluctance in acknowledging.

Her way forward was only too clear: she must reveal the truth to the duke, once he was recovered. He would wish to have nothing further to do with such a family, of this she was certain. She must bear the consequences of her brother's actions with fortitude.

Having at last reached some decisions she felt she could endure the coming days.

Then realisation dawned that the rhythm of the duke's breathing had changed. It had increased in rapidity, as if he had ridden hard. His hands which had lain beneath the sheet since Mary Threadgold had left the room were now twitching and plucking. His free hand moved to his bandaged shoulder and a groan issued from his clenched lips.

Juliet moved to cool his brow and his eyes fluttered open. She poured some water from a jug beside the basin and, on turning, found herself fixed by his cloudy, aquamarine gaze.

He allowed her to raise his head and hold

the glass to his lips as she enjoined him to drink.

After a few sips the effort seemed too much and he lay back, eyes closed, face set.

'Can you remember what happened, your grace?'

His eyes flashed open this time, 'Of a certainty I recollect very well, except for the pain in my head.' He spoke in French but with lucidity.

'That occurred when you passed out. Your head struck the fire-dogs.' She had replied in the same language.

As if making a tremendous effort he slowly raised his good arm and gingerly touched the bandage and the swelling beneath.

Grimacing, he relaxed against the pillows, 'How very careless of me.' There was the ghost of his usual ironic tones in his response. 'I wonder; would it be possible to remove the bandage? It may ease the frightful headache.'

Juliet undid the linen with care, easing it away where it adhered to the congealed blood. She insisted that the pad remain in place as it would be unwise to disturb the scabbing.

His face had become ashen against the sable of his hair except for two crimson spots of colour on each cheek. Sweat beaded the whole of his body now as with eyes closed, through gritted teeth he wondered if Aldersleigh kept a good cellar, requesting a glass of brandy.

His pulse proved to be hectic as Juliet emphatically refused him the spirit, suggesting instead a few drops of laudanum being taken in water. She endeavoured to keep her tone light as she apologised for having no cordial to offset the bitter taste.

Still her hand shook as she once more raised his head. His free hand covered hers as he drank and she felt it's heat in her very soul. His eyes remained shut as she lowered him against the pillows.

Replacing the stopper in the bottle, she said matter-of-factly that he would feel more the thing once he had slept again. The dose she had administered was a strong one to alleviate his undoubted pain.

When he made no reply, she thought sleep had already claimed him; as the door opened to admit Mrs Threadgold, she heard him whisper, 'A thousand thanks, my dear Julie.'

His old nurse had heard nothing. Her worry was that he had bled afresh and that he remained unconscious. Miss Dempster led her from the bed to the sofa where they could talk without disturbing the duke.

She explained the reason she had removed the bandage and that he had spoken with lucidity. She desperately wished that she had access to all her herbs. With an attempt at humour, she doubted that Folly Hill had a still-room. Mary Threadgold was in total agreement. A good infusion of the right herbs would help to keep fever at bay, but sleep was as good a medicine as any.

She blessed Miss Dempster for knowing how to act in treating the duke so promptly yesterday.

She had brought in the duke's coat, breeches and top-boots, and placed them in the dressing room. 'I've put a nightshirt on top of the chest. Lord Tristan can help me get him in to it when he returns.'

Juliet inquired if there had been any news. Mary was of the opinion that, rather than trust a servant, his lordship would ride back himself. Until then she suggested that Miss Dempster might join Miss Fenner in her downstairs rooms. When Juliet hesitated, looking doubtfully at the recumbent figure, the old nurse held the door and in tones used in the nursery and rarely disputed said, 'He will sleep now, for a few hours. Miss, do you go down.'

EIGHTEEN

A binding marriage.

Far more than twenty-four hours seemed to have elapsed since Miss Dempster had entered the club's private rooms below.

Charlotte Fenner was seated before a pile of notes and a ledger which she closed on Juliet's entrance.

'First allow me to apologise for my not being present to welcome you on your arrival yesterday. Had you felt able to make yourself known to me, so much that is unfortunate could have been prevented.'

Her enforced guest bridled at the sarcastic undertones. This was no doubt the woman who had recorded the fateful wager which had resulted in such heartache. 'I fear my business was not with yourself.'

Sitting back in her chair, the châtelaine assessed the young lady who was dressed in such an incongruous fashion. She had to admire her fortitude; few gently reared females could have remained so in charge of their emotions after near rape and the sight of a violent death. Yet, here she was, giving her an icy set down.

'Indeed.' A change of subject was called for. 'Perhaps I may reassure you that Lady Louise is safe? I have known Beau Aldersleigh for numerous years and I have never seen him truly in love until I saw him with the duke's sister. She is a fortunate young lady.'

'Fortunate! Her brother brought close to death by her wilfulness!' Juliet could not refrain from expostulating.

The other lady regarded her in silence.

She wondered at her depth of feeling and

guessed that in part, she felt some guilt over the duel. 'You should not blame yourself.'

'How can I not?!'

This burst from her as she turned anguished amber eyes on Charlotte, 'Had I not been so reckless he would not have killed a man, not be lying wounded!'

'Vénoire knew nothing of your presence in de Langon's room. They were known to be antagonists. In the Beau Monde, the long-standing quarrel between their families was well established. You were merely the means which sparked the inevitable.' She stood. 'The Duc de Langon was an evil man, the world is a better place with him gone'

Juliet shook her head, saying that she had no means of being sure. This woman who had long experience of dealing with the less savoury side of gentlemen's lives stated emphatically that she could. Then, handing her a shawl, suggested that a turn in the fresh air was what was required. She added that Miss Dempster's horse had been stabled and fed.

The well-being of her mount was not something which had been uppermost in Juliet's mind. In normal circumstances such would not have been the case, especially after a hard ride on such a valuable animal. She felt an urge to see him for herself.

Miss Fenner directed her to the stables, saying that she need not fear encountering any acquaintance as most gentlemen were still abed, the play having gone on late. Not trusting herself to enter into a conversation concerning the house's raison d'être, Juliet took herself off to the stables.

The sun was warm on her face, acting like a benediction as she crossed the parterre, easing away stresses and strains. From amongst the surrounding hedges came birdsong. These lilting notes full of the promise of life failed to move her.

The surge of certainty which she had felt when evaluating her choices earlier had evaporated. She was left with a dead weight around her heart. The dreadful pounding in her head was only in part due to the laudanum of the previous night. She felt no claim on happiness, now nor in the future. Once the duke's recovery was assured, she would inform him of the whereabouts of the ring and have done. The prospect of joining her mamma at Tunbridge Wells no longer seemed quite so distasteful. She still balked at the idea of marriage to a widower; however, living as her cousin's companion she viewed as a deserved penance. She had endured enough responsibility, longing for a chance to behave in the more usual manner of a female of her age and class.

Assaulted by the familiar odours of the stable; warm animal, leather, soap, hay and dung, her body reacted as if to a tonic. No 'usual female' of her acquaintance was quite so at home with horses as she. It was unthinkable to her that, seeing the bay gelding had not yet been mucked out, she should leave him standing in soiled straw.

Her father had cared more for his horses and hounds than for his wife and family. If his children wanted to ride, then they had to know how to care for their mounts. Neville dully learned, then left such things to the grooms. Juliet on the other hand had scandalised her mamma by seeming to enjoy such menial tasks.

Thus, it was that she was oblivious to the arrival of a rider in the yard outside an hour later. Hearing noises from within, the newcomer poked his head into the loose-box.

'Hey there!' His cry of greeting died on his lips as he saw, not the expected stable lad but Miss Dempster with sleeves rolled up, skirts covered in straw and a piece of sacking fashioned as an apron in front.

Depositing a bucket of fresh water on the now sweet straw she turned on hearing someone hail her to encounter Lord Tristan d'Alvière. A groom appeared from the barn to take charge of his mount.

Drying her hands on the sacking before discarding it, she asked, 'Lord Tristan, what news do you have?'

Offering his arm, he began to lead her through the garden to the house.

'They are married.' He kept his voice low, 'Great Aunt Barbara and I arrived as they were sitting down to dine with Aldersleigh's confessor.'

'They were married by him? Then it will not stand in English law.'

He shrugged pointing out that, as they were Catholic, it was certainly a binding marriage as he had discussed with the dowager countess. In order to deter scandalmongers they had remained overnight, so it could be said that they had witnessed the ceremony. His sister had made her decision and now must live the life she had chosen.

He then became more concerned with his elder's health, changing the focus of the conversation. Juliet was pleased to note that the mention of the duke's name failed to cause her step to falter.

'He has been conscious, but his pain remains.'

Tristan paused at the door of the house to ask if it might be possible to move Vénoire to Denbrugh Place. The fiction that they had witnessed the marriage would not hold water if Vénoire were to be found at Folly Hill. The newlyweds had been persuaded to spend part of their wedding tour at Grosvenor Square.

The earl had been informed of the duel but Louise had not. Tristan thought it time enough to tell her the harm her elopement had caused once Charles was recovered. Juliet coloured at this, averring that the harm which had befallen the duke was due to her actions.

His lordship took both of her hands in his, 'Non, Mademoiselle Dempster. Any man of honour could not allow such that he witnessed to go unpunished! You endured what you did trying to protect our family. It behoves us to protect our own!'

Nodding, Juliet for a fleeting moment wished that it could have been more than honour which had prompted the duke to fight.

On reaching the bedchamber they found Mrs Threadgold in the process of removing the bandage from the duke's shoulder. He remained in a far from peaceful, drugged sleep. His movements had set the wound bleeding once more. Juliet noted that his head had again been bandaged and wondered if this wound too had reopened.

The old nurse greeted his lordship's arrival with relief, asking him to support the duke to enable her to view the wound. Juliet needed no urging to help as much as she was able. It had not taken her long to absorb the meaning of the sweat soaked sheets as well as the colour of the spreading stain revealed as the bandage was removed. This time, it was no pain induced fever. Vénoire moaned heart-wrenchingly as Mrs Threadgold attempted to remove the pad where it clung, with a noisome odour to the wound. Flowing in with the fresh blood were the all too visible signs of infection. A sickly-sweet stench mixed with the ferric smell of bleeding. The clotting had sealed in some infection. Tristan cradled his brother's inert form in his arms.

Mary Threadgold breathed a deep sigh, tears starting in her eyes, 'Oh, if we were at the Place. I have everything there that I need to treat him. There's nothing of use here! I think we must send for the surgeon.'

'But the scandal!' murmured Tristan.

His old nurse so far forgot herself as to snap back, 'Stop a scandal or stop him dying! You must send for the surgeon!'

Vehemently shaking her head, Juliet almost shouted, 'To be bled and leeched? No! He needs no further loss of blood! All the herbs and physic you need are in my still room at Solworth!'

Both women looked to the younger d'Alvière; in the end the decision had to be his. His expression showed he wished this was not the case.

He considered aloud, 'It is but five miles, he has no broken bones. With rugs and pillows around him, it may answer. At least he will have medicine. Miss Dempster will you see if Miss Fenner will provide a carriage for our use?'

Showing some signs of relief, the older lady shooed the younger towards the door, telling Tristan he should help prepare his brother for the journey.

NINETEEN

A bitter-sweet return.

The parlour at Solworth Manor was situated to the rear of the house, issuing off the oak dining room. It was panelled over stone, as were most of the rooms; yet here the perpendicular arched windows - legacy of the abbey chapter house - were abruptly cut off by the Jacobean plaster ceiling. Even so, it was a cosy room, filled as it was by sun for most of the day. The furnishings had been chosen by Lady

Cecily on her marriage; those which remained after the auction were sadly outmoded. It was here that Lady Barbara had chosen to sit on rising and was now passing her time in playing a game of patience.

Into this tranquil setting burst her great niece not yet having the demeanour of a married lady. Her attire was her riding habit of the previous day. She had been vociferous in refusing to wear anything from the new wardrobe, thoughtfully provided by her new husband. His assurance that they had all been made for her was hotly ignored as she prepared to argue her point - an argument which the earl curtailed by the expedient of crushing the torrent of French issuing from her lips with his own, going on to prove to his wife of a few hours that there would never be anyone else.

The riding habit had been donned for speed of dressing once John had told her the news concerning her brother. Hence, she now stood before her great aunt, misbuttoned and without her lace jabot, such had been her haste.

'Good morning, my dear.'

Lady Barbara continued laying the Queen of Spades in her rightful place.

Stamping her foot, Louise demanded to be informed of the duel. Holding the pack of cards, her aunt regarded her whilst saying with calm that she had been wondering when Aldersleigh would decide to tell her, adding that Tristan had returned to Folly Hill and there was nothing to do but await him.

Dropping the pack of cards she raised her lorgnettes, 'Not quite morning wear, my dear. We must get you some bride clothes, all those debutante gowns will serve no purpose now.'

'A l'enfer avec mes robes!!'

Gesturing for her to sit down, the dowager countess continued, 'if you wish me to understand you, you must speak more calmly and preferably in English.'

In a small voice Louise asked, 'Please explain to me again… was it because of me?'

'No cara, I fear the fault was mine.'

Aldersleigh had joined them and spoke heavily, 'I should have had the courage to speak to your brother, then none of this would have happened.'

Stacking the cards, the dowager countess declared that she had found truth always to be the best course. Having said that, she continued, neither should blame themselves entirely. Their actions may have precipitated things but Vénoire's own emotions played their part. Not having been present she could not be certain but in her view, no honourable gentleman could withstand the insults offered to his family nor see such violence perpetrated on the person of his lady.

The preposition, detected by Aldersleigh, was lost on his wife as she allowed herself to be drawn into his arms.

The dowager suggested that she should help Louise to find a gown more suitable for the time of day. At this, the bride was ready to explain but was silenced with her great aunt's adroit comment.

'Do you find your new dresses too mature in style, my dear?'

Taking her arm she led her from the room.

Meanwhile the party from Folly Hill had commenced the relatively short, yet agonising journey, between the two houses. Tristan had decided that Miss Dempster should ride ahead.

His reasoning was twofold; a strong arm would be needed to hold his brother across the carriage seat and Miss Dempster was best placed to prepare all at Solworth Manor. It did concern him that once more she must ride unescorted, but she gave such misgivings short shrift saying she was wont to ride these fields from an early age.

As the carriage lurched over the uneven surface of the road he felt his decision was vindicated. Setting aside the impropriety, his brother's leaden weight was an effort to hold safely, even for his strength.

Mrs Threadgold worried about Vénoire's shoulder wound for the entire uncomfortable journey. She had administered another dose of laudanum which served to keep him unconscious. The coach was the well sprung travelling one used by Miss Fenner for long distance travel and the coachman was following his orders to take the greatest of care.

Miss Dempster had made good time in reaching the Manor. She left the sweating bay to the ministrations of Aldersleigh's surprised stable lad, walking rapidly to the kitchen entrance of the house.

With no thought of announcing herself, she went straight to the still-room and began extracting various jars of herbs and simples. It was not long before the sounds attracted the attention of the earl's housekeeper.

'Is that you Bob Braxton? What do you mean by… and just who are you?!'

Juliet arose from her task, a frown knitting her brows as she calmly directed the dumbfounded woman to have the Stuart bedchamber prepared at once. The housekeeper caught and held Miss Dempster's arm, preventing her from removing another jar from the shelf.

'Just what do you think you are doing!'

Smiling ruefully the lady prized the woman's fingers from her wrist,

'Of course you may not know it by that name. If you will be so good as to show me to the

Earl and Countess? Or failing that, the dowager Lady Lessing? You are quite correct to remind me of my manners!'

The note of authority in the speaker's voice overrode the housekeeper's fears; even so, she showed Miss Dempster into the book room rather than the parlour where the new countess was. She knew that Father Antonio, the earl's priest was inside.

The Father reviewed the newcomer as she entered. He was an Italian who had spent the last several years travelling with the earl. The marriage which he had conducted yesterday seemed the answer to many prayers. The sudden arrival of an unknown lady was an unlooked for complication.

Usually when travelling in England he wore sober yet fashionable clothes. Here, in seclusion with the earl, he had felt at liberty to wear his cassock.

Juliet realised at once who he was, saying, 'Oh you must be the earl's confessor.'

Holding out her hand she continued, 'I am Miss Juliet Dempster.'

On this, the door opened to admit the earl himself and a still perplexed housekeeper.

Having caught her introduction, Aldersleigh turned to his servant, asking that she prepare whichever bedchamber Miss Dempster instructed.

With rapidity Juliet explained which chamber she required, that the sheets must be warmed and a fire laid, adding she would join the woman there soon.

After Mrs Braxton's departure, she sank into her curtsy, begging the earl's pardon for the manner in which she had arrived, but emphasising that all preparations should be speedily done.

The earl indicated that she should take a chair, as the priest resumed his seat and his book of devotions. Aldersleigh asked her pardon for not making an instant recognition of her name. This brought a slight blush to Juliet's cheeks as she felt uncomfortable at this reference to his tenancy. 'I think I now understand why your agent insisted on a clause for solitude!' She was a little brusque.

He smiled at this, pointing out that his need for discretion had vanished since yesterday and any service he might offer was little enough.

Before he could add anything, Lady Barbara and the new countess entered. Louise was now attired in a Polonaise of leaf green lustring with a ridiculous lacy cap on her curls proclaiming her married state. She demanded to be given news of her brother at once. With a curtsy to both ladies, Juliet told them of what had been planned. The dowager wished to know if a surgeon was to be sent for and Juliet found herself explaining once again why this was not expedient. Louise was inclined to dismiss herbal remedies used on the Dempster's tenants, but the dowager interrupted her protestations,

'The old remedies often have great merit. I recommend, Miss Dempster, that you see Mrs Braxton has done all that is required, then you will join us for some refreshment. I think dinner should be put back to four o' the clock, my lord. By then the carriage should have arrived.'

Aldersleigh was only too happy to agree, asking his wife with a smile if she would inform Mrs Braxton. Louise looked shocked and hesitated. Her great aunt told her, in sharp tones, that having chosen to enter into the married estate so precipitously, she now had certain obligations, advising her also to inquire if the meal could be stretched to accommodate the extra guests. Looking contrite, Louise pulled the bell-rope.

Juliet made her way to the Stuart bedchamber. It was indeed the Manor's guest room but her chief reason for choosing it was the size of the adjoining dressing room. It contained a servant's bed and would prove ideal for night nursing. Checking that the warming pan was in place, she cleared the surface of a chest by the window ready to receive her herbs and ointments.

Hearing footsteps in the corridor, she was surprised to see Father Antonio, his cassock looped through his belt to enable him to carry the tray of simples as well as the ewer of water requested by Miss Dempster. Having placed these on the chest he asked in what other way he might be of assistance. Juliet indicated a wing chair which needed to be closer to the bed. He paused in the doorway, 'I have some skill in tending the sick, should you need aid.'

She thanked him, grateful for his look of concern, adding that his prayers might be of help. He replied that they were readily offered.

Both paused in their conversation as the sound of a carriage on gravel reached their ears. Juliet flung wide the casement to lean out, seeing Lord Tristan's head emerging from the window of the closed carriage, she cried, 'He is here!'

It was sometime before she was able to return to the bedchamber.

Much to her vexation, Lady Lessing had insisted that she should remain with herself and Louise whilst the gentlemen and Mrs Threadgold settled the duke as comfortably as was possible. Good manners and good sense kept her below whilst her true feelings urged her to fly to his side, to ensure that he suffered as little as possible. The conversation between the ladies was stilted as they all waited for Lord Tristan and the earl to rejoin them.

Having given an account of the journey to them all, Tristan was attempting to explain the reason for the duel to his sister when Juliet rose as if impelled, 'You must have family... that is... things to... I must see him!'

The door closed on her precipitous exit.

Tristan and Lady Barbara exchanged glances as Louise urged him to continue.

The bedchamber was redolent with the

bloody, putrid odour of fouled bandages. Father Antonio was inspecting the duke's wound with the help of Mrs Threadgold. Without hesitation, Juliet began pounding rosemary leaves in the pestle and mortar on the tray. The noise, coupled with the discomfort he was enduring, broke through his drugged haze and in French, Vénoire demanded to be left in peace. His voice was slurred.

All present looked to the figure on the bed, then Father Antonio began a soothing monologue also in French. Placing the soiled linen into the basin, Mrs Threadgold said she would make a chamomile infusion as she thought he had had sufficient laudanum. She smiled encouragingly at Juliet whose stock of prepared herbs and remedies had met with her stringent requirements, before leaving the room.

Having finished her pounding, Juliet approached the bed for the first time. The duke whilst attending to the priest's soothing voice had fixed his eyes on her. They appeared almost black in his ashen face. Father Antonio held the affected shoulder steady, giving a nod to Miss Dempster who sprinkled powdered rosemary directly into the wound. Vénoire caught his bottom lip between his teeth but otherwise lay still enough. She explained to the priest that she wished to bind comfrey leaves in place with a light bandage. If they could stem the bleeding without sealing the wound then the powder might cure the infection. The priest nodded in agreement whilst sponging the duke's brow.

Suddenly the duke's voice came clear, 'Of a certainty, that devil's sword was as infected as his brain! May he rot in hell!'

His tone was so venomous that Antonio crossed himself. Noticing the action, Vénoire became fully aware of what manner of man had talked him back to consciousness.

'My apologies, Father, but he was past all prayers.'

The slight irony made Juliet's heart to lift despite the harsh intake of breath which he gave as she pressed the herbs into place.

Next, she asked to inspect his head wound and touched his scalp with gentle fingers. She felt him withdraw as she found the scabbed lump. Whether from pain or some other emotion, she could not decide.

'I have a poultice which will aid the swelling to reduce.' She sought what was required on the chest.

Vénoire murmured to the priest that he thought his family would like to hear how he went on. Settling the sheet across his chest, Antonio saw the faintest suggestion of a smile play across his drawn lips as the duke added that the lady was quite safe with him.

With a more serious look he asked, 'And perhaps you would also offer a prayer for my recovery?'

'For your soul also, my son.'

Vénoire grimaced, 'And for my soul, mon père.'

Juliet was somewhat surprised to see the priest leave the room. Being very aware that the duke was the least delirious he had been since receiving his hurt, she was thrown into a confusion.

Her hands began to shake no matter how hard she tried to still them. Only once they were steady did she turn to find him watching her intently. She had no wish to meet that candid gaze, so was glad that in order to bandage the cold poultice he must face away.

The room was filled with a deafening silence. As she tied the knot in place she found her trembling fingers caught by his good hand.

'Miss Dempster, you are all goodness. I have not as yet been able to ask you if…' he broke off and Juliet withdrew her hand as if bitten, as Mary Threadgold returned carrying a steaming bowl.

Unperturbed by what she had witnessed, his old nurse offered him the tisane, saying it would calm him and help him to sleep.

Vénoire's response was glacial, 'Nounou, I am very calm. I do not wish for anymore sleep.'

She dismissed his comments as if he were still a child, pointing out that if he was so calm he should tell her why he was covered in a thin sheen of perspiration.

Addressing Miss Dempster, she informed her that Lord Tristan wished to speak with her and that the family were in the parlour. As she ushered her out, she whispered that she was not to worry, that he wasn't yet himself but that they would mend him between them.

As Juliet left the room she heard Mary saying, 'Now my lordling, you are to drink this and try my patience no more!'

He lay quiescent once again, despite initially trying to dismiss the tisane. His long lashes served to emphasise the dark circles beneath his eyes which began to close of their own volition. He forced them to open as he obediently sipped from the spoon held out to him.

'Do you know Nounou, I believe I am in love with her.' No need to pronounce her name.

'Well of course you are.' She continued to give him the drink, 'No matter until you are mending.'

Wearily, he motioned the bowl away, wishing he could at least talk to Miss Dempster. Mary Threadgold smoothed his pillows as she had done innumerable times down the years, then took out her lacework from her apron pocket.

Sitting in the wing chair she admonished him, 'Take advantage of a lady who is nursing you? You were brought up to be a gentleman your grace! The right time will come, you'll see.'

He lay, thoughts in turmoil, on the edge of sleep. Drugs and pain had not obliterated the intensity of his feelings for this unusual young woman. These had crystallised when he had discovered her perilous situation in de Langon's room.

Of a certainty, she was the lady he wished

to make his wife but their situation had grown even more complicated. Through him, she had been as good as compromised, certainly in the eyes of the Beau Monde.

There also remained the emerald affair. How much did she know of her brother's involvement? Tristan had most of the story from Frederick Carshaw. Where the ring was at present remained a mystery. As he drifted into sleep, a thought occurred to him; he knew nothing of her true feelings for him. The only overt emotions she had shown to him prior to Folly Hill were anger or indifference.

The object of his thoughts had not gone straight to the parlour. Instead, she had crossed the upper hall into her own bedchamber, guessing that because of its situation and awkwardness it would not be in use. She was pleased to find the holland covers were still in place. Uncovering an oak carved cupboard, she soon found what she had gone in search of: a brightly figured Indian chintz gown, not worn since the previous summer. She was glad of it now, thankful also that she had found a change of linen.

Having performed a quick toilette, she

hung her habit in the cupboard with care. Along with a white silk gown worn in her debutante year, these were her only available changes. Feeling less the poor dependent in her own home, she went to join the duke's family with returning poise.

The earl offered her a glass of wine, having escorted her to a seat beside the dowager. Sipping it with composure she listened as Lord Tristan explained the plans which had been made. In order for the whole of the Ton to believe that there had been nothing clandestine about the recent nuptials, they had to convince that the family were au fait. They simply must lie! Lady Barbara added that if the lies were convincing no one would dare to gainsay them. Muttering behind their back could be dealt with. Once Louise and John left the country, as they soon would, any talk would die away. A sojourn in Town as part of their bridal tour should still tongues, especially if it was ensured that the family arrived together.

Laughing, Aldersleigh said, 'If we appraise Carshaw, then the deed is done!'

Tristan agreed, saying that despite having quitted him in somewhat of an abrupt fashion at

Folly Hill, he knew that his plan had been to visit his wife at the Towers. He would ride there to deliver the news. He chose to ignore Miss Dempster's blushes at mention of the gambling club. Their planned ostentatious arrival in Grosvenor Square would be seen and word soon spread.

'But what of the duke's absence?' Miss Dempster ventured to query. 'Will that not lend credence that he opposed the match?'

The dowager gave one of her deep chuckles, explaining that Tristan must give Carshaw another juicy on dit; Vénoire had been thrown from his mount and was abed with a broken collarbone!

This outrageous suggestion was followed by a chorus of protestation. Juliet's voice overrode this by suggesting it would not be believed as the whole of the Ton knew he was an exceptional horseman. The chuckle remained as Lady Barbara admonished them all to have no fear. She would delight in telling all who listened that she was highly amused that such a nonpareil could be caught out by a rabbit hole!

'He may never forgive you,' warned Aldersleigh.

'That I can endure better than he should if news of the duel became known. There is only one flaw in our plans.'

The dowager countess turned to Miss Dempster with even more bluntness than usual. For their ruse to work, everyone would need to return to London. Ferris would join her and Mrs Threadgold as soon as was possible, meantime could she continue helping to nurse the duke, unchaperoned?

There was no hesitation in Juliet's assent. To be alone with him in her old home was an unlooked for joy, a thing to treasure against times to come. The earl's voice broke in on her reverie as he insisted that Mrs Braxton should remain for as long as Miss Dempster deemed necessary, adding in a much lower tone for her eras alone, that the timing of the rental contract would remain unchanged. Giving him her candid gaze, she accepted; the estate still needed the rental income, especially she thought, as her services as chaperone to Lady Louise were no longer required!

She emerged from these thoughts to find the dowager once more disposing of her relatives. Tristan was to ride to the Towers and return in time for dinner. Louise was to take herself off with Aldersleigh as Lady Barbara wished to talk privately with Miss Dempster.

For a while the two ladies sat on in the ensuing quiet. Juliet was straining to hear any sounds from above. Her fine profile was presented to the dowager for her contemplation. She saw a straight, delicate nose above a generous, curved mouth, surmounting a firm chin. Her chestnut ringlets, piled high on her head, revealed small ears and a high brow. There was just a faint suggestion of freckles across her warm skin, evidence of days spent out riding with scant care for a lady's complexion. The dress she wore showed off her trim figure to advantage; firmly rounded breasts perfectly balanced with her hips. She was no more attractive than many of the stunning young ladies paraded for Vénoire's choice, so what was it that had attracted him? For his great aunt like his old nurse had realised, even before he had himself, that this lady was his Nemesis.

Juliet raised her unusual amber eyes to the dowager's face, making her think perhaps that they had played their part.

'My dear Miss Dempster, do not concern

yourself. All will be well.'

'Oh, ma'am, you do not understand!'

Her voice was attractive too, even in distress.

The dowager said, obliquely, that she rather thought she did, continuing that should Miss Dempster's family needs remain as they were, then she would be grateful for her companionship at Grosvenor Square. This suggestion served to agitate the young lady, therefore she did not press her point. Aware that this young person preferred to be occupied, she suggested that she organise a bowl of broth for the duke when he should wake. Juliet followed her suggestion with alacrity, leaving the old lady sipping a glass of Aldersleigh's port.

TWENTY

Misconceptions.

The relationship between Mrs Braxton and Miss Dempster soon developed into an amicable one.

The housekeeper was quite used to being separated from her husband when the Earl of Aldersleigh moved from residence to residence. They had met in his service and the arrangement suited them well enough. So together, she and Miss Dempster had removed the hollands from the lady's bedchamber on the previous evening. It was there that Juliet was roused from a very deep, natural sleep by sounds of departure.

It was a calculated, ostentatious show. The Earl and Countess of Aldersleigh were traveling in a light curricle, with the earl's crest emblazoned on the panel and he held the reins himself. Braxton was driving a traveling berline containing the baggage, the recently engaged lady's maid and the earl's valet. In the duke's landau sat the Dowager Countess of Lessing enveloped in a thick cloak, determined to leave the hood down in order to be seen. She was accompanied by Lord Tristan d'Alvière and Father Antonio, dressed now as any country gentleman. Wilkes sat upon the box resplendent in full livery and caped driving coat; he had ventured to inquire after his grace's health, rumours of the rabbit hole already circulating in the vicinity.

His grace, too, lay listening to the sounds of departure without fully comprehending what he heard. On Tristan's return from Carshaw's house the previous evening he had paid his elder a visit, finding him attempting some of the chicken broth which Miss Dempster had sent up. Mrs Threadgold was also present as Tristan outlined the family's plans. He awaited his brother's reaction with some trepidation, a little concerned, truth be told, when his elder praised what was planned and requested that the Earl and Louise should step up.

This sparked words of protest from Mary.

'Calm yourself, Nounou. I desire solely to offer my felicitations. Who am I to gainsay love?'

Louise was shocked into tears by his pallor.

With truth rather than any affectation, he urged her not to cry as it was too fatiguing. Her sobs induced a feeling of lassitude and Nounou took the new countess outside, leaving the two men to confront each other. Aldersleigh was the first to speak.

'I sincerely wish there had been another way. I regret everything else but believe me when I swear that I will never regret marrying her!'

'How very rash!' murmured Vénoire. 'There will be times, no doubt, when you will! We are not easy to live with, d'Alvières. Ensure that **you** never cause **her** to regret marrying!''

He had leaned forward on these words,

offering his good left hand which Aldersleigh had gripped.

'Put yourselves about as much as possible whilst at Grosvenor Square. I await with pleasure your entering White's with me.'

The Beau laughed suddenly, 'Oh, I am refused admission!'

The duke's smile was little grim as he lay back on his pillows; attempting his normal ironic tone he stated that they had admitted his hound, so why not a wolf? His efforts were proving too much for him as he lapsed into French on a hiss as he moved again. 'Désolé!'

A concerned Aldersleigh had recalled Mrs Threadgold before bearing his wife off to dine. The duke had spent a fairly restful night and his nurse had been quite encouraged. She now brought in a tray of milk, bread and honey as well as more chamomile tisane. He drifted awake to the sounds of coach wheels on gravel and the rattle of curtains being drawn back. The awful ache in his head seemed to have relented for good and he felt stronger; so much so that he made to sit up unaided.

He was shocked into immobility by a pain in his shoulder akin to the initial thrust and

Nounou's shout to lie still. She raised his pillows and settled him with the tray across his lap. He looked at it with disdain demanding to be informed what the bowl contained. She mixed the pap once more before raising the spoon to his mouth as she told him it was good and nourishing. He responded that it looked disgusting and closed his lips firmly. She tried cajoling as they eyed one another and almost thankfully recognised the glint of steel in his eyes. Sighing, Mary offered the tisane instead.

Acknowledging the compromise he swallowed the drink, then offered in a mollifying tone that he should like something else light to eat. She sniffed her disapproval but uncovered some slices of crustless bread and butter, brought for herself. Once he had eaten most of it, she offered to remove the bandaged poultice from his head wound. Its removal brought a sigh of relief as he ran his left hand through his hair, locating the cut.

'Yes.' She confirmed his thoughts, 'You are lucky to still have your right senses. If Miss Dempster had not known just what was called for, or had gone off in a swoon like most, you would be in a far worse case now.'

He smiled, 'She has rare qualities, does she not?'

'I did wonder if you had noticed.'

She began helping him to freshen up when he passed his good hand over the several days of blue-black stubble on his chin and asked if it were possible for him to shave. She picked up the tray telling him that she would have to do it, should anyone have thought to leave him a razor.

Mrs Braxton was a little disconcerted by the request, apologising for not anticipating it. Her chagrin was such that she mentioned it to Miss Dempster when she took that lady's breakfast up.

Juliet recalled that there might be an old, blunt razor in the wig cupboard in the master dressing room. Whilst the housekeeper went to search, Miss Dempster used the time to dress in the same chintz gown from the previous day. She pinned her hair high on her head again. The severe style served to emphasise her slender neck and the sweep of her jaw.

On carrying her own tray down to the kitchen, she found Mrs Threadgold conversing at the back door with a young man of about fourteen who seemed to have brought eggs, milk and butter. On seeing Miss Dempster she offered her a good morning and introduced the lad as her youngest grandson Daniel, an under gardener come from Denbrugh with some produce. He bowed with care in response to her greeting and when asked if he had arrived by cart, he affirmed this adding that his brother, Jim the duke's under groom, had also brought a mare for her use. She suggested that both would probably appreciate a drink of ale when Jim was ready.

Mary began to usher him out when a thought struck Juliet, 'Tell me Daniel, would you know how to strop a razor?'

He affirmed that he did, seeming perplexed by the question.

'Well that is indeed splendid. If you will but wait a moment, I will have one for you to prepare and then you may shave his grace.'

The youth's jaw dropped as he protested that he was just his grace's under gardener. She smiled wryly at him, 'And you do not need to shave?'

His response was to blush and nod, adding that he had only ever bowed to his grace. At this point his grandmother spoke up. She thought it a good idea. Reminding the youngster that he still only needed to bow, that his grace would be thankful to be shaved by a male rather than a female and that as Jim had the hands of a smith except with horses, there was no one else.

The razor having been produced and prepared, Mrs Threadgold preceded Daniel to the duke's bedchamber. His grandmother had given him one of Mrs Braxton's aprons to wear over his buff breeches and leather waistcoat. Dan hesitated in the doorway holding the basin of hot water and towels as Mary explained to the duke and motioned her grandson to place the basin near to the bed, remembering to bow afterwards. He was taken aback to hear himself being addressed by his master.

'Fear not Daniel, one face is much like another's. A steady hand is all that I ask.'

The boy approached the bed with an audible plea to his grandmother not to watch; Vénoire nodded his agreement and she left the room.

Meanwhile Juliet had remained in the kitchen, preparing to make more decoctions. Having readied all that was required, she swung the kettle over the huge fireplace. It had boiled by the time Daniel returned in an attempted stately fashion but with a boyish grin on his face. Mary relieved him of the shaving tackle, handing him the promised tankard of ale. The kitchen was filled with a strong odour of thyme from the herbs that had been set to steep. Dan took up his hat and the empty basket saying, 'Gran, his grace said as how he could fancy a bottle of claret.'

His grandmother snorted but before she could respond Juliet said that chicken broth and thyme tonic would be of more benefit. As she strained the cooling liquid, she was assaulted by memories which caused her to smile at first. The smile soon faded to be replaced by a forlorn expression; a chance encounter, a thyme scented note of contrition - what slender threads to fix one's hopes on!

Pouring the liquid into a glass with care, she straightened from her task, a decisive look on her face. It was time to make a confession to the duke. It seemed he was out of immediate danger if not yet back to his full strength. Already anticipating scathing contempt in his blue eyes, she knocked on the bedchamber door before her courage failed.

His grace of Vénoire sat in the heavily carved bed, propped against lace-edged pillows worked by some long dead Dempster female. His thanks to Daniel had been sincere. Having managed to tie back his grace's hair in a satisfactory manner and used the razor to remove the sleeve of one of Aldersleigh's nightshirts, he had finally helped him in to this.

'Enter! I was becoming bored with my own company!'

He opened his eyes, a brief, indecipherable flicker crossed his face on seeing Miss Dempster. He gave an inclination of his head, 'Forgive me, Miss Dempster for not rising. I would make my bow to you an' I could.'

Setting down the glass she swept a perfect curtsy, 'Your grace. I have brought you some refreshment.'

Taking the glass he held it to the light, observing that the blow to his head must have clouded his vision for, of a certainty, the colour was green. Miss Dempster agreed waiting as he held it warily under his nose.

'It is thyme!' He regarded her across the rim of the glass. The silence seemed to stretch without end before she managed to find her voice.

Clearing her throat she declared that an infusion of thyme was a well-known restorative tonic. Smiling, he asked if the good monks said so? She too smiled explaining that the receipt was an old family one, probably originating with the monks.

Attempting a sip produced a marked grimace.

'Is it too bitter? I can add more honey.'

On reaching for the glass she found her hand captured by his long fingers. Bereft of rings they seemed stronger than before. 'I shall drink it. Will you not sit?'

Knees trembling beneath her skirts, she sank onto the edge of the bed. 'Your grace, I must…'

'Miss Dempster, please…'

Words tumbling from each, but the mutual laughter this provoked was strained.

'Pray continue.'

He released her hand in order to drink.

With both hands now in her lap, Juliet began pleating the chintz of her skirt. Unable to lift her gaze, she became fascinated with the action.

'Your grace, I have a confession to make to you. By rights you should have known it ere now. My shame and the small hope that I might be able to rectify the situation has stilled my tongue.'

Inhaling deeply she failed to take note of his utter stillness.

'My brother stole your emerald ring for a stupid wager!'

'A boy's prank.'

She missed the interpolation as she rushed on whilst still able, 'Not content with that, he tried to raise more money to repay other debts. Your grace, he cannot return it to you - for he has pawned it!'

The pleating action was quite frenetic now, ruining the fabric. Aware of a weight lifted, yet feeling completely wrung out she waited, still with bent head.

His tone was devoid of emotion as he voiced the request, 'Would you look in the pocket of my riding coat?'

She went to the dressing room where the coat had been hung and on searching the pockets her hand closed around leather gauntlets. They were those she had worn on her ride to Folly Hill. Wondering as to their relevance, she proffered them to the duke.

Turning them as they lay under his hand

he said, 'I first saw these three months ago by the light of a coach lamp. They were on the hands of a highwayman who robbed me of one single item.' He traced the rusty stain across the fingers. 'I felt sure that I had winged him.'

Juliet gasped.

'Next, I saw them on a widow-sill at Folly Hill, the very place I expected to encounter the very same highwayman. You see I had guessed his identity, or almost. I did wonder at one time as to his gender...'

'What!'

'...and wondered about the outcome.'

'Now you can be sure.'

'Now I am sure. Your brother is a very foolish young gentleman.'

She was now seated in the wing chair, holding herself very erect. 'Of that I am only too aware.'

Risking a glance at his impassive face, 'I can furnish you with the direction of the moneylender.'

He raised an eyebrow, 'Indeed?'

Nodding she continued, 'Yes. I attempted to retrieve it myself but...'

'You visited such a place?'

Hearing what she took to be contempt she felt her heart shrivel. 'Oh yes, but to no purpose. The family will recompense you, sir, but it will take a certain amount of time. I fear that if the ring is not redeemed soon then the usurer has the intention of selling it. His rates seemed extremely high!' she added with bitterness.

He was filled with such horror at the thought of this lady in such a place that the next remark he uttered sounded brusque and uncaring. 'The debt is of no consequence!'

'To you, your grace, maybe! That is not so to our family!' She became frosty.

Dismissing her hostility, he added 'I was attempting to point out that our family is as much in your debt.'

'I have no conception of how that may be.'

He hesitated long enough to gain some control over the churning emotions he was experiencing: anger, pain, shame, fear.

'By the suffering you endured, having ridden to my errant sister's aid. A fruitless effort as it turned out. Thanks to us, you have been utterly compromised!'

The pounding of his blood had induced pain in his shoulder so violent that he could not continue. He was forced to close his eyes and grit his teeth.

He sensed her rise but did not see all the colour drain from her face. It had never occurred to her that he would think of her as sullied by de Langon's attack. She had not been troubled by thoughts of any repercussions from that evening. She knew nothing untoward had actually happened.

As if to turn the knife, he went on, 'And now, you are nursing me here, alone, save for servants. An unthinkable situation in Society's eyes!'

His voice shook as he finished the sentence. Juliet hardly caught the nuances of what he had said. She stood with her back turned, staring sightlessly through the latticed window. The view of the driveway to the open country beyond blurred dangerously. All she had seized on from his words was that he viewed her as sullied. His underlying emotions of concern failed to reach Juliet. Rigid with tension, having steeled herself to confess, this last fact was the only thing she seemed able to grasp.

Her life seemed to stretch out before her as bleak as winter. She tried frantically to order her thoughts as she heard him addressing her directly.

'Miss Dempster, I wonder: do you recall the conversation between us at Vauxhall Gardens, near to the cascade?'

She had begun tidying the tray of herbs. 'I… I am not certain that I do.'

'We talked of marriage and family.'

The jar of goose grease landed with a crash against the mortar and pestle.

'If you please, it is difficult for me if you will not sit!'

She was unsure if the difficulty lay in expressing what he wished to say or from discomfort from leaning towards her. Unable to refuse without showing a dreadful want of manners she perched on the edge of the wing chair.

'Mademoiselle, I wish… that you will marry me.'

Gone were the few endearments she had heard him use when semiconscious. He did not even use her given name. To hear, in this fashion, that which she longed for seemed a final crushing blow. Everyone knew that he must marry to get an heir but that he should marry her to save her honour was inconceivable.

A marriage of convenience, half measure,

could only mean a lifetime of misery, as she dwelt on what might have been. Also, her family were too much in his debt to contemplate it!

'Oh no! That would be quite impossible!' She voiced her thoughts on this with great vehemence.

His face grew shuttered, his azure eyes like wet slate. 'Impossible. I see.'

To disguise her agitation, she smoothed his pillows and gathered up the half empty glass.

He made no effort to touch her nor to converse more as she left the room in a rush.

The glass fell from her shaking fingers, shattering on the polished wood of the upper hall. Heedless of shards and the spreading stain, she ran pell-mell into her room over the gatehouse, slamming the door. Casting herself upon her bed, she dissolved into wracking sobs.

TWENTY-ONE

Revelations from the sick room.

The duke remained motionless, frozen in time and space. He had thought that she cared for him a little or at least; that he was not repellent to her. It appeared that he had misjudged politeness and a natural, caring nature for something other. The overwhelming relief that she was not complicit with her brother's robbery escapade had caused his spirits to soar. That moment of euphoria had prompted him to make that awkward, impetuous proposal. Fear of receiving just such a rebuff had held him back from an open declaration of love. The emotions he was experiencing were so far removed from anything he had ever felt before. He, whose training had stressed emotional control. The exclamations wrung from him, which had been so wrongly construed by Miss Dempster, sprang from a longing to protect her always from harm. That he had been instrumental in causing her suffering was hard for him to bear. He sighed. Since his come out he had cultivated a persona calculated to be seen as cold in order to ward off female expectations. Wanting to declare his passion, he found he did not have the means. When she had at last confided in him about the ring, he had perceived some right to hope; if she could entrust such a family secret to him then surely she could entrust her person? Even so, she had declared marriage to him 'impossible'! His jaw flexed as he recalled the abhorrent tone as she had uttered the word.

Had Miss Dempster walked into the room at this precise moment then she would have seen the true depths of the duke's feelings for her.

Conversely, the same could be said, had the duke been able to cross the few feet of old oak which separated them. To be sure, he did not sob but raw emotion was writ large across his aquiline features. Lids closed over eyes now coloured like the midnight sky; a trembling hand, held to his pale brow stemmed not from fever but from a visceral sense of loss. His body felt aching, sick and empty. The renewed energy he had experienced on waking had ebbed away, leaving him debilitated and defeated. Even the healing balm of sleep was denied him as he lay restless against the pillows, seeing the memory of her beloved face.

The need to enter into the duke's presence was averted for Juliet by the arrival, late in the afternoon, of Thomas Ferris. He had ridden ahead of his master's baggage which was being conveyed by Dickon, along with Miss Dempster's meagre wardrobe. Ferris had brought all his master's immediate necessities in saddlebags. He was now being appraised by Mrs Threadgold of the duke's progress.

She remarked that he had sent Mrs Braxton's excellent chicken broth back untouched and that Miss Dempster now seemed to be under the weather. Mary had been beating eggs into milk whilst talking.

'This posset will see her right. Not surprising that she's tired after all that young lady has been through. Now you are come Mr Ferris, perhaps she and I can get a proper night's sleep.'

The two d'Alvière servants eyed each other thoughtfully as Mrs Braxton said she had not seen anything of Miss Dempster since she had taken the thyme tonic up for his grace earlier in the day.

The conversation had set Ferris wondering as he went up to his master's bedchamber. Tom was shocked at the change such a few days had wrought in Vénoire. It took him but a few moments to realise that there was more behind the duke's demeanour than an infected sword thrust. Even a dramatic bump on the head could not explain such a lowness of spirits. A detailed recounting of the Earl and Countess of Aldersleigh's arrival in Grosvenor Square elicited no strong reaction.

The only spark of any emotion was generated by an innocuous mug of mulled wine which Mrs Threadgold had sent up. It smelled warmly aromatic as Tom carried it to the bed.

'This should help you feel more the thing, sir. Help with your appetite for dinner.'

Bowing, he offered the tray to the duke but Vénoire knocked it away, spilling most of the contents onto the floor.

'Take it away, Ferris!', he growled in a harsh undertone, 'I want never to smell that again!'

Despite his valet's pained look of consternation, no explanation followed.

'Fetch me a bottle of cognac. A bottle, mind!'

When Ferris hesitated and would have spoken, he ordered, 'Dépêchez-vous!' in a voice which brooked no denial.

As she crossed the hall, Mrs Threadgold observed the tray Ferris carried up the stairs and shook her head. She continued into the book room with her own tray, bearing the egg posset she had made.

Miss Dempster sat pale and straight-backed with an unopened book on her lap. She startled slightly as the latch clicked, shivering suddenly in the cool room. The lengthening shadows had not roused her until Mary began to light the candles from the one she had carried in.

'I thought you might fancy this, Miss, as you did not partake of nuncheon.'

She handed the warm mug to her.

'Mr Ferris has come and is with his grace at present. He brought this letter for you.'

Glad to be able to turn her thoughts away from their inevitable direction, Juliet sipped the comforting brew whilst opening her letter. It was under Lord Roger Hitchley's seal, from Lady Hélène. The kernel of the epistle was that when Juliet was no longer needed to ensure the duke's full recovery, Hélène would be obliged if she would aid in her removal to Stanford Park, remaining until the child arrived. Such an offer! There were debts still to be cleared and the thought of helping in a house which had close d'Alvière connections had a double-edged allure. There could be no doubt that she would see him from time to time yet could she endure all the emotions which went with that?

Mary Threadgold watched in satisfaction as the posset disappeared. She had judged it sensible to add a small amount of sleeping draught. Whatever was troubling the young lady must be cured by a good night's sleep or await the morrow to be sorted. Later she was to wish that she had spiked the brandy bottle in like manner!

Past midnight, she was awoken by a sharp rapping on her door. Mr Ferris on his arrival had taken up the dressing room belonging to the Stuart bedchamber and he it was trying to waken her now. His usual well groomed, calm exterior was somewhat ruffled as he whispered.

'My apologies Mrs Threadgold but would you please to come? I fear his grace is bleeding again and I am unsure what to do for the best.'

Pulling on her wrapper and bundling her plait under her nightcap, Mary followed him across the upper hall.

Inside the bedchamber a scene of havoc met her bemused gaze. The sheets were pulled from the bed whilst the duke sat on the floor, his back against the wing chair with the thick bedcover draped around him. His good arm clasped an empty brandy bottle. The table by the window bore two empty bottles of claret, their dregs spilled amongst uneaten stewed chicken. On the floor beneath the chest holding Miss Dempster's simples were scattered shards of pottery and trampled herbs.

'Mr Ferris! Whatever has been going on here? And you, my lordling! What are you about?'

The duke made no response.

'I have attempted several times to assist his grace into bed.'

He ran his hand over his jaw. 'He attempted to knock me out as I went to lift him bodily. He was on his feet searching through the herbs as if looking for something specific, when I brought up the second claret.'

She glared at him, saying in a repressive manner, 'Claret and brandy in his state! Mr Ferris whatever were you thinking of?'

He gave the old nurse a candid look, 'His mood was such as I have never encountered him in before. I dared not go against his orders. At first, I thought he was fevered by the manner in which he was searching through the herbs. I do not think that is the case.'

Being more concerned with his grace's present condition, Mary paid no heed to the valet's comments. Kneeling next to the now passive figure she was able to see the fresh blood stains on the bandage. With gentleness she pulled it away from the wound to assess the damage. There was still a steady flow of red seeping from the jagged hole in the duke's shoulder. In flinging the herb pots to the floor he had removed his arm from the sling; he had also clung with both arms to the bedpost to keep himself upright in front of Ferris. The healing of recent days had received a setback.

'We can give thanks that he's not fevered at least. I don't know what has provoked this. I do know brandy on an empty stomach always leads to disaster, no matter how hard a head! Do you help me get him up, whilst he's quiet. I can't tend him on the floor. That's if he's left any herbs to use!'

These last words seemed to infiltrate the alcoholic miasma in which the duke felt he was swimming. He gripped Ferris's wrist as his valet went to lift him. 'No, not any herb… le thym sauvage… thyme, wild thyme… can you find it, if you please, Tom?' His look was a rare, pleading one.

Mrs Threadgold stripped the stained nightshirt from him, followed by the soiled bandage, 'Indeed, thyme is the last thing you need. Let's get you settled, and I'll bring you a nice chamomile tisane.'

He lay back. 'Mais non, Nounou!'
His tone was desolate, recalling his childhood with such vividness that Mary held off from her ministrations to look directly at him.

The pain she saw did not equate to the damage he had inflicted on his shoulder.

'She told me it was thyme, wild thyme… now it is gone… lost… I cannot support…'

His chin had sunk to his chest and, thinking he had passed out, Mary began reapplying dressings and bandage. As she tied it into place across his chest, his dark head rested against her bosom as it had done as a babe.

Automatically she patted his back and smoothed the hair from his slick forehead.

'I love her…. ma Julie,' she heard him whisper.

'Well a'course you do, and she loves you!'
She settled him against the pillows which Ferris had restored to their rightful place.

As she stood, he opened his eyes to enunciate with clarity, 'No, no, she will not marry me!'

He turned away from both and his

brandy induced torpor carried him Lethewards.

The two other occupants of the room regarded each other in shocked amazement.

Mary was the first to speak.

'So that's what it's all been about! Eh! What fools young people are! Not a word of what's been said, outside of this room Tom Ferris!' she admonished.

His grace's valet and confident smiled at her instead of taking offence, 'I should think not indeed. It's a pretty coil though, Mrs Threadgold. What can be done to sort it?'

Putting her arm through his and patting it, she suggested that they should both seek what was left of their night's sleep. Easier to sort the room's mess out by daylight. As to how to sort the other tangle out, it needed some thought.

She gave a last fond look at her old charge. 'His grace will sleep late I don't doubt!'

TWENTY-TWO

Sir Neville grasps the nettle.

The Earl and Countess of Aldersleigh had been married for exactly two weeks. Since arriving in Grosvenor Square, they had been seen at as many society events as was possible.

During a brief lull, "Beau" Aldersleigh had visited Folly Hill to order all there with Miss Fenner, prior to departing for the continent. Now that the Ton were convinced that the marriage had the blessing of the bride's family, they were soon to travel to the groom's Venetian palazzo by easy stages.

Finding Sir Neville Dempster in one of the gaming salons, Beau had felt it incumbent upon him to reassure that gentleman concerning his sister's health and reputation. To say that this young man was more shocked than he had ever been in his short life would not be overstating the case. He had known nothing of the preceding events. Miss Fenner had ensured that the requisite secrecy shrouded all. Despite being present he had remained in ignorance of the happenings until now. What he had learned had not only filled him with consternation and chagrin but also with an overwhelming feeling of culpability. This he could only admit to himself; had there been no imperative to retrieve the ring, then Juliet would never have needed to become a companion!

It was natural that Aldersleigh should know nothing of these feelings, envisaging only shocked concern. He continued to confound Neville as he revealed himself to be the mysterious tenant of Solworth Manor. To the young baronet's incredulous relief he went on to explain that despite his imminent departure, he was quite ready to pay in full the remainder of the lease. It was fair recompense for breaking the contract set up between his man of affairs, Mr Peal and Miss Dempster.

Thus, it transpired that Sir Neville was now in possession of the largest sum of money which he had held since his papa's demise. Under more usual circumstances, it would have been paid directly to Mr Peal for the estate. In the gentleman's heightened awareness of the monumental sacrifices which his sister had been making, for far longer than recent months, he knew exactly his course of action. The availability of every game of chance not withstanding, he pocketed the money and rode directly to a certain house in the City.

The following day he was to be found standing before the studded oaken door of his family home. Mrs Braxton admitted him, on reception of his card, saying,
'I am afraid that your sister is out riding, Sir Neville.'
Juliet had taken to visiting their tenants, as of old, as well as ensuring supplies of produce

reached them from Denbrugh Place and the traders in Stanford. She felt herself to be useful but it also precluded her from painful contact with the duke.

'It is his grace of Vénoire whom I wish to see, if he will receive me.'

Vénoire was seated in the wing chair, now placed before the side window of the bedchamber. From here his view was across the herb garden, over the boundary wall and to the ruins beyond. Each morning since deemed fit to leave his bed he had watched Miss Dempster ride off on his mare, his face shuttered and stony.

His attire at present was a blue brocade banyan with his injured arm still held in a sling. The lines of pain around his eyes were slowly disappearing, to be replaced by brooding implacability. He had not repeated the three bottle evening yet his temper was as uncertain as if he had. Even with Ferris there was none of his usual ease nor amiableness.

Now, he grimly regarded the callow youth whom Ferris had ushered into his presence. He beheld fair, unpowered hair dressed in the latest style, grey eyes, a weak mouth and a complexion tinged with red as the gentleman flushed uncomfortably under the harsh appraisal. However, Neville continued to meet that piercing gaze, something which he would have failed to do but a few days ago.

Swallowing, he commenced, 'Your grace. I believe I owe you my sister's honour.'

When the duke evinced no reply, Dempster continued in a fast constricting voice. 'I owe you more than that! I owe you an apology and....' he produced a small leather bag from his pocket, '...this!'

Since the duke made no move to take it, he dropped the bag into his lap.

Still without moving the duke snarled, 'Explain!' He was determined not to make things easy for this puppy.

Dempster fiddled with his neckcloth. 'It is your emerald ring, your grace!'

He went on haltingly to recount his role as highwayman, his reasons for the wager and his subsequent pawning of the jewel. He did not, as Vénoire expected, seek to excuse or justify the act.

'Because of my fecklessness, Juliet was endangered and you killed a man!'

'Yes. Not the behaviour of a gentleman.'

'I see that now, and more besides. I have been selfish and thoughtless. I do not know how to make it up to Ju. She don't know that I am aware of the happenings at Folly Hill.'

'What has become of the rest of the money Aldersleigh gave to you?' The duke's tone remained abrasive.

'I have it here and I fully intend to take it to Mr Peal's office. Perhaps he can help me learn how to be of use to the estate.'

Vénoire gestured to the straight-backed chair set against the wall and at last the young man sat with palpable relief. The duke rang a bell and Ferris was immediately in the room. He was dispatched for refreshment. From the pocket of his banyan Vénoire brought forth the tan gauntlets, last worn by Miss Dempster.

In more conciliatory tones he asked, 'Tell me, was my aim true that night?'

Neville ran his fingers over the scar in his hairline. 'I thank God it was no more true! But… then? … you have known that I was the perpetrator for the whole time?'

'Oh no. Only recently had I started to suspect… but… she told me all.'

Nothing would prompt him to explain

under just what circumstances she had revealed the emerald affair.

'Ju told you! I never thought… she swore that she never could!'

'Your sister has done so much, endured so much for you and your estate, yet you remain ineffectual still!'

Unpardonable words of censure from one who was no relation. Dempster acknowledged their veracity as he expounded on his actions.

'When I found out what had nearly befallen her, I was filled with shame! It was the same when I learned of her visit to the pawnbroker, once she had found his note of hand. So… so I did what I have always done when a thing displeases me: I ran away to hide. That meant more money outlaid as I fooled myself I should regain it tenfold! I didn't know what else to do! Papa never taught me. He always favoured Ju!'

Some of his old petulance had crept back into his account. 'Up until his death I thought I could do whatever I wished and the bills would be paid. Since his death it has all fallen to my sister.'

The duke found he was unable to refrain from declaring, 'It almost cost her honour - and more!' The latter was forced from him.

Dempster gasped.

Vénoire stated that if de Langon had used her on that night she would not have lived. These stark words were uttered with great difficulty.

Capable of innumerable vices the Duc de Langon was rumoured to have gained his pleasure from the pain of others.

Neville stood, distraught, his face bloodless repeating that his sister had suffered because of his behaviour.

'I too must take the blame for allowing her to be exposed to such as he!'

Vénoire stroked the gauntlets. 'And she will allow me to do…nothing.'

Sir Neville started to expostulate that indeed Vénoire had done more than enough, even shedding his blood in order to save her and her honour. In an icy, polite voice the duke assured the youth that the quarrel was the culmination of a feud of long standing.

The look he gave was threatening in the extreme as he enunciated, 'It touches not your sister's honour - **at** - **all**!'

'Oh, be content. No one shall hear to the contrary from me.' He was quick to make that promise to this intimidating nobleman.

The duke inclined his head. There followed a pause whilst Ferris placed a decanter and glasses within reach of the duke's left hand.

In a smooth, less hostile, voice Vénoire lamented the rabbit hole which had resulted in his fractured collarbone. Dempster smiled a little for the first time in his traumatic interview, acknowledging that the earl had told him as much. Passing his guest a glass, Vénoire held his eyes in a haughty stare as he inquired if Dempster's wish to help his estate was a genuine one. In a humble and sincere tone, Neville affirmed that it was.

'You need discipline. You have been allowed to have your head for long enough. Tell me, have you considered the army?'

Indeed, he had. The attraction of a red coat to such as Sir Neville Dempster Baronet, was not to be lightly disregarded! He had bruited the idea several times in his final years with his tutor but to no avail. Lady Cecily had swooned each time he tried to discuss it and Sir Hugh had disparaged the thought of any career for his heir, then dispatched him to Oxford. 'I did once long for a set of colours, your grace.'

'If I were able to purchase such for you, would you swear to allow a managing agent to be appointed for the estate until you reach your majority?'

'Why should you do that for me after all the wrong I have done you?' Dempster looked stunned and puzzled.

Vénoire looked down at the gauntlets he still held on his lap, 'Never for your sake......but for hers.'

A dawning look began to cross Neville's features, followed by a series of inarticulate words which stopped abruptly on seeing the baleful stare on the duke's face.

'Quite so. If you are to flourish as an ensign you must learn discretion.'

He motioned Dempster to pour more wine.

'She is out riding.' He had not once called Juliet by any name.

'You will not wait to see her. I will arrange all with Mr Peal. News of your new occupation shall come from him. She will then be free to rejoin your mamma. Or what she will. Thus, both our obligations are discharged.'

The duke cared nought for this cub, nor for any opinion he might have of himself. What he could never support was the thought of her having to take gainful employment again. She had refused him the right to care for her in an orthodox manner, yet he still sought to do so from a distance.

'I know not how to thank you, your grace. I am forever in your debt.'

His grace held up his finely manicured hand. 'Talk no more of debts! Once I have secured your acceptance into the army you must manage your own pay. If you are indeed grown wiser then you will avoid places like Folly Hill in your leisure time.'

He lay back, suddenly fatigued. 'You might be wise to depart. All will be set entrain, including caretakers for the Manor.'

Closing his eyes firmly he failed to even acknowledge Dempster's bow of departure.

Ferris, having seen his master's guest to his horse, carried up the duke's nuncheon tray on which reposed some trout, fresh caught from Denbrugh's stream.

'Cooked just how you like it, sir.'

Vénoire allowed the tray to be settled across his knees, the gauntlets reposing safe in his pocket once more and the leather pouch on the sofa table beside him.

'Filleted too, Tom! You think of everything.' The tone was light, just what he was wont to use in easy banter with his valet.

Still his eyes remained dull. The grooves around his mouth and between his wing-arched brows were no longer pain etched. Or at least not from a pain which any physik could cure.

TWENTY-THREE

Lady Barbara disposes.

The first intimation which Miss Dempster had of the Dowager Lady Lessing's unlooked for return was the sharp barking of the pug dog as it scratched at the chapel door.

Juliet, as had been her Saturday custom since childhood, was arranging fresh flowers in the altar vases. She had also used the time for contemplation, her most fervent prayer being for the peace of mind which constantly eluded her.

Surprised on hearing a dog, she opened the door just as the older lady entered the chequered hall. Mrs Braxton was emerging from the kitchen passage having also been alerted by the canine voice. The front door stood open to the summer's day, enabling the descent of the dowager's luggage and dresser to be seen.

'Ah, there you are my dear. I've come to see how Vénoire goes on before I return to Lessing. Everything is right as a trivet in Town. Hélène is of course bored and now fretful at the thought of Louise and the earl setting out for Venice. She remains impatient for your arrival.'

Juliet made no comment as she prevented the pug from rushing around the hall by the expedient of lifting it out of harm's way.

'We did not expect your ladyship. You are most welcome. Mrs Braxton will prepare a room.' The role of mistress of the house sat so very easily on her shoulders.

In the last few days it had been a simple matter to allow it to settle there.

'Oh, for a day or two perhaps,' her ladyship pronounced airily. 'I thought I could help with Vénoire's removal to Denbrugh Place as soon as he is sufficiently recovered. Tristan is escorting the Aldersleighs to Dover. I see no point in spoiling all our efforts through lack of any last minute attentiveness!'

Juliet addressed the hovering house-keeper with a request to prepare the pink bedchamber and to show her ladyship's dresser to its dressing room. This had been her mamma's room and so was well suited to the countess's needs. She then ordered some tea to be served in the parlour at which the dowager opined that a glass of canary would set her up much better after her journey.

Still holding the dog, Miss Dempster ushered the new arrival through the oak dining room and into the parlour which was naturally lit as usual.

Lady Barbara settled herself on the sofa, holding out her arms for the pug. As she deposited him on his mistress's lap, the sun shone fully on Miss Dempster's countenance.

'Why, you are looking quite peaked. Not still having to nurse him now Ferris is here are ye?' To the point as ever.

'No, ma'am.'

'Hurumph! So, he is improved then?'

As Juliet replied that he was making progress she sounded unnaturally stiff even to her own ears. She asked the dowager countess to excuse her as there was only Mrs Braxton and Mrs Threadgold to order things in the kitchen. She made her escape, glad to be free from the questing, bright eyes.

The dowager pulled the pug's ears, causing him to growl which she ignored as she was lost in her suppositions. It was Mrs Threadgold who brought in the tray of wine.

Having poured out and given the glass to Lady Barbara her retreat was cut off with the words 'Now then, Mary Threadgold, what is amiss here?'

With reluctance the nurse gave a somewhat less detailed account of events than the dowager expected to hear. Giving her a long look, she commented that it seemed a pretty coil to be sure, that Miss Dempster looked positively hagged and that clearly something must be done.

Mary allowed herself to smile at that and poured another restorative glass of canary wine for her ladyship, offering the accompanying biscuits with the words, 'My own recipe, the one's Lady Catherine loved to eat.'

Despite their differences in station, their exchange of looks might have been described as conspiratorial.

On Miss Dempster's return she found the dowager feeding biscuit crumbs to the pug with a thoughtful look on her face. Immediately her ladyship dismissed any idea that she was in need of entertaining. They had few staff at Solworth as she knew, and so she offered her coachman Higgs to be used as a general factotum. He was often pressed into making himself useful at Lessing Dower.

When she had finished by declaring that she looked forward to a good coze over dinner that evening, Juliet had given her a puzzled look but the dame swept up the pug adding,

'For now, I am going to pay m' great nephew a visit.'

The duke on hearing that his great aunt was come had ordered Ferris to lay out evening clothes. This had brought forth expostulations from his valet; evening clothes had not been sent to Solworth but had gone with the majority of the duke's wardrobe back to Denbrugh Place.

With a calm yet firm intention behind his

smile he repeated his desire, adding that he was determined to dine downstairs that evening. They were seated opposite each other playing chess. He was fully dressed and had been able to move freely, if slowly, about the room today, unaided by Ferris's arm.

When Lady Barbara entered the bedchamber, the valet busied himself in the dressing-room attempting to solve the problem of attire.

'An unlooked-for pleasure, aunt.'

He would have risen to make his bow but she restrained him by placing her hand on his good shoulder and giving him her hand to kiss instead. Having raised this to his lips, he asked her to sit.

She patted his cheek before availing herself of the chair vacated by Ferris.' Still pale, I see. You need to take the air next.'

He acknowledged the truth in this, admitting that he still felt sadly pulled. 'I never thought to be so affected.' He shot her a look from under his brows.

She pursed her lips, then twinkled as she agreed that it had been a great knock.

'We understand each other, aunt. I would not have others read me so well!'

'Oh! Stuff and nonsense!'

She prodded his buckled shoe with her cane. 'You are both looking plucked. Both of you are at sixes and sevens. It's all on account of you not understanding each other!'

His glacial silence was meant as a set down but ignoring that she continued 'I do not know how a man with your address can have made such a mull of it! It seems that you did. I suggest that you try again.'

This time the snub was verbal, 'I thank you for your concern.' His haughty expression spoke volumes.

'Fiddle-de-dee! You most certainly do not...but believe me you will!'

Ferris re-entered carrying a pale blue silk coat and a dove grey waistcoat of a different weave. He spoke in pained tones, 'I ask your pardon your grace, these are all that I am able to suggest.'

It was clear that he thought the combination hardly adequate.

'What's this? Thinking of coming down to dine tonight? An excellent idea, thoughtful of you. I have no intention of dressing and from what I know of Miss Dempster's wardrobe she will not either.'

She did not fail to catch the quick frown which crossed his features. 'Country hours and country manners will do very well, my boy!'

She was determined to have the two of them in the same room. If she could but see them together, she would be certain of their feelings. It would do neither of them harm, either! If things did stand as she thought, then it might be politic for Vénoire to move to Denbrugh as soon as maybe. She voiced this thought.

'I fear I could not endure the journey. Of a certainty, too tiresome for my weakened state!' There was a lift in his voice belying his words which made Ferris glance at him as he was readying his neckcloths; almost the duke's old ironic tones. His great aunt's blunt words had somehow restored his hope.

After an extremely careful toilette he allowed his valet to ease him into his coat. He had insisted that he would use both sleeves, gritting his teeth with determination during the agonising several minutes it had taken to ease the cloth into place. Ferris commented that it was a relief that the chosen coat had been spoiled by the slight miss measurements of his grace's previous tailor. The duke smiled as he remembered Ferris's original castigation of this local tradesman. The arrangement of the duke's neckcloth was next to be subjected to scrutiny. It was his usual practice to tie this himself, though as Tom had taught him the finer points of this art he was satisfied as his valet brought the flow of Mechlin lace to rest just over the top two buttons of his waistcoat. Remembering his aunt's comments, he refused the sapphire pin which Ferris offered, choosing plain gold instead. It remained for the simple tying back of his hair and the duke was satisfied.

He turned from the mirror to see his valet waiting at the door with proffered arm. He raised an eyebrow.

'Tell me Thomas, do you really expect me to take your arm? No, I thank you! I shall manage alone.'

He smiled at the look of vexation on Ferris's face. He refrained from demonstrating any annoyance as he was followed across the upper hall all the way to the foot of the staircase.

Here indeed Vénoire was forced to pause but his man knew better than to offer further assistance. Instead, at a signal from his master,

Ferris crossed the great hall to the dining room door.

Vénoire waited, supporting himself against the carved newel post. The black and white flags of the hall floor seemed to stretch forever in front of him.

Returned, Ferris told him that the ladies were not yet down and suggested that the duke wait in the book room where he would serve him some wine. The chance to cover the distance in two stages was well received. The duke strolled into this nearer room, choosing the first chair he reached then seating himself with care.

It was not long before he was joined by Lady Barbara and her abominable pug. She had decided it would be politic to have the animal present to act as a diversion, should events go drastically awry.

On her slow, reluctant descent of the staircase Juliet saw Mrs Braxton crossing the hall to announce the dinner hour. Seizing on this as a means of avoiding any pre dinner chit-chat, she offered to announce the meal. Despite this, there was no possible way to avoid taking the duke's arm when he proffered it. She attempted to defer to Lady Barbara's rank but this indomitable lady shooed her ahead saying she must take the duke's arm as the pug did not take kindly to men and a bite to add to Vénoire's other injuries was the last thing which was needed.

So it was that Miss Dempster found it unavoidable but to look directly into his clear blue gaze as she laid her fingers on his good left arm. He bestowed upon her one of his rare smiles which animated his taut features and she found it impossible not to respond in like manner. In those few seconds, the awkwardness of the preceding days receded a little. They were able to converse throughout the meal without strain. The dowager countess looked on with satisfaction as they both did justice to the saddle of mutton with peas which was the main dish.

When Ferris brought in the tray of port, both ladies made to rise.

'I wonder, Mademoiselle Dempster, would you remain awhile? Aunt, you will excuse us?'

Juliet looked flustered and sent an appealing glance to the dowager who smiled reassuringly.

She informed them that she would be in the parlour where she would call for the tea-tray in half an hour. This was to assuage Juliet's now obvious agitation.

As Vénoire rose to escort his great aunt to the door, she waved him back to his seat with the somewhat astringent words, 'I remain quite capable of opening a door, boy!'

The slight sound that the door gave on closing seemed to hang in the ensuing silence.

Juliet forced herself to break it, 'There was something you wished to discuss with me, your grace?' She watched him as he poured the port into a glass and lifted it to a candle in order to view the rich colour. His hand was a little unsteady as he carried the glass to his lips.

'Yes. I wished to discuss something.'

The pause was of such a long duration that she forced her eyes to meet his again as she felt them resting on her bent head. This time they were veiled and it was impossible to read what thoughts they hid.

Reaching into his waistcoat pocket he withdrew something which sparkled in the candlelight, placing it before her on the table.

'That, I think, has been between us for far too long.'

She stared at the ring as it glinted, greenly at her. Wondering, she picked it up, turning it over and over in her fingers. 'Is this your emerald ring? But I do not understand! How can it be here when...'

'Please to listen to me and I will endeavour to explain everything.'

Taking her silence for consent, he started with the visit he had received from her brother. Ignoring her shocked gasp, he went on to tell her that the earl of Aldersleigh had informed her brother of their adventures. He stressed this last word with ironic undertones, then said with a certain amount of relish that he did not recall seeing anyone quite so bouleversé nor so contrite as Sir Neville. He then furnished her with the details of his whole interview with her errant brother.

On his recounting of how Sir Neville intended to dispose of the lease money Juliet cried 'Oh capital! I knew that he would grow responsible, eventually.'

'Indeed!' A quirked eyebrow denoted Vénoire's distrust of this statement. 'Your sisterly faith does you credit. However, I prefer to trust that a spell serving in one of His

Majesty's Regiments will instil duty and courage.'

'What can you mean?'

He explained that he had agreed to fulfil Neville's desire to join the army and to find a manager for the estate.

At this she broke in upon his narrative once more. 'How are you able to promise that? I have been left responsible for the estate until Neville reaches his majority and it would be impossible for me to allow you to run to the expense of a set of colours for him. He and it remain under my care.'

Her words were tinged with regret rather than anything more choleric.

The duke had risen at this and found himself standing behind her chair. 'If you could but let me, I would change all that.'

He was struck by the manner in which tendrils of her hair curled in the nape of her neck; unable to prevent it he reached out an elegant finger to touch them.

Miss Dempster jumped as if stung.

Knowing that if she faced him it would be impossible to retain even a modicum of composure, she allowed herself to plead, 'No, please! We have been through this!'

He seemed powerless to stop his good hand from resting on her shoulder, just at the point where the lace on her ridiculously girlish, white silk debutante's gown met her pearly flesh.

This time she did not flinch, instead a tremor ran through her whole being.

'Listen to me, I beg!'

This burst from him in French, then more measured and in English he went on, 'When I asked you if you would marry me you told me it was impossible. Was that because of the wager and the missing emerald? If that is so, they no longer stand between us. Also, if you thought that my offer was made out of obligation for what passed at Folly Hill and your nights spent here, then you could not be more wrong! Of a certainty, I have never met a woman such as you! I make my offer out of love! Think on it, I beg you!'

Bestowing a kiss upon her neck like the visitation of a butterfly, he quitted the room as swiftly as he was able. If she was to refuse him once more, he had not enough strength to hear it for the present.

When neither of them appeared at teatime in the parlour, Lady Barbara came to search them out. She found the dining room empty. In the light of a guttering candelabrum set by the decanter of port she espied the verdant, glittering ring, forgotten in each hasty exit.

Pondering on what it might mean, she picked up the jewel then returned to her solitary cup in the parlour.

TWENTY-FOUR

Truth and promise.

It was a fine summer morning. The shimmering, twinkling stream lay like a ribbon as it twisted its way past the ruins by the Manor of Solworth. Beads of water sprang like diamonds from beneath the delicate hooves of a mare as she splashed along the shallow bed of the stream. The horse whinnied in recognition of a figure who was leaning his back against a fallen pillar, seated with face upturned to the warmth of the sun. He was motionless, discarded beaver hat held against breechen-clad knees by long tapering fingers. The noise of the approaching horse failed to disturb him. It was not until the rider had crossed the expanse of grass separating the water from the ruins that he spoke.

'It is wild thyme.'

A ripple of laughter escaped from the rider who by now had dismounted. She sniffed the air, appreciating the scent which had been cast up by the mare's hooves on the herbs underfoot. 'So it is, I see!'

Vénoire opened his eyes yet refrained from speaking again, afraid to break the spell. Juliet now stood in front of him as he had had a premonition she would, if he waited patiently enough.

'How could you be sure that I would ride this way?'

He shrugged and with a faint smile told her that he had hoped that he would encounter her here, remembering her penchant for the ruins.

'You remembered that as well as the scent of the herb. What a fine memory you have, sir.'

He laughed a little before agreeing, 'Of a

certainty. I would implore you to tell no one else, for the world knows that Vénoire has an execrable memory!'

Sitting on the warm patch of wild thyme near his feet she dropped her crop next to his boot. All that was visible to him as she hugged her knees to her chin was the bedraggled feather upon her hat.

'Last night you requested that I listen to you, now if you please, I would beg the same of you.'

He felt tension coil through him as he waited, suddenly feeling every stone against his back. With slow thoughtfulness, Miss Dempster started to talk.

'You said that nothing lay between us now that you possess the emerald once more. That is not the whole truth. There is our difference in rank. I do not come from your world! I am merely the daughter of a country squire. In the normal commerce of our society, we should never have become acquainted!'

Here he interrupted her, 'Not so! We met last year at a picnic at Stanford Park!'

She looked up, quickly and obliquely, demanding to be told if it was true that he remembered the occasion. This provoked a rueful grimace as he confessed that he had not done so until prompted by his cousin.

'That is exactly my point! Of what use should I be as your wife?'

His hand strayed to her shoulder as it had done on the previous night.

'Had I wished for a "useful" wife I could have married any one from the dozens paraded in front of me down the years! Look at me! Please ma chère Julie, look at me! The reason that I have never married is simple - I was never in love before. You, I do love! You will never bore me! You may never behave exactly comme il faut for a duchess. Of a certainty you will not put up with my devilish temper nor my snubs! En effet, you are precisely who I have been waiting for!'

As he had reeled off this catalogue of nevers, they had both risen to stand within a hair's breadth of touching.

It took no effort at all for the duke to reach out and pull her to him with his uninjured arm, delicately lifting her chin with the other. She felt as if submerged in the depths of his eyes as he kissed her. This was no decorous pre-nuptial kiss, rather that of an ardent and experienced lover. It elicited an equally demanding response from a surprised Juliet. In that embrace everything coalesced with a blinding clarity which rocked them both. Breathless, their lips parted.

'I have not given you my reply yet, your grace!' she whispered with trembling breath.

'Have you not? Is it not this? ...and this?'

He dropped myriads of kisses across her upturned face, which was like a flower seeking the sun.

'Do you still doubt the truth of my love for you?'

She gave her head a slight shake saying that she could not doubt that he loved her but did still wonder if his offer of marriage stemmed from his desire to protect her reputation.

At this he could not refrain from almost shouting, 'Nom d'un Nom! How can you think that! When I saw you at de Langon's mercy, I wanted to throttle him with my bare hands! It was not your reputation that concerned me but you! Until that moment I was in a confusion; I had never loved as I loved - love - you! How was I to recognise this for what it was? What it is! That night opened my eyes and I was horrified that I - who loved you - had brought you to such a pass.'

He traced the repaired buttons on the bodice of her habit, causing her to give an exquisite shudder.

'And I - who loved you - brought you close to death!' With great tenderness she laid her hand on the slight bulge in the shoulder of his immaculate frock-coat. Asking, did not one cancel out the other? She added that she could not help but think that starting out on a marriage where each felt indebted to the other was fraught with danger. As she looked up at him, her heart and soul were reflected in her suddenly serious face.

'So, is that your answer? You do love me?'

'Oh, as to that, sir,' her voice rippled with happiness, 'I fear that I have loved you ever since receiving your written apology, laden with crushed thyme! For it was a very fine apology for your arrogant, high-handed behaviour over the purchase of the hounds!'

He inclined his head thanking her, adding that no one had dared describe him thus to his face before. He was amused as he knew it to be true.

She gave a quick laugh, 'It's all a trick, is it not? Achilles is too wise to follow a fraud!'

He clapped his hand to his brow in mock horror, begging her never to reveal his true character to Society as it was imperative to leave some illusions. Striking an attitude, she requested that he should give her lessons in arrogance if she was to become his duchess.

'Of a certainty, I shall not, for I wish you to remain exactly as you are.'

She gave a demure curtsy, lisping grovelling acquiescence to whatever were his wishes. In laughing reply he wondered if he could believe her when she said that.

'Ah, yes but would that not become exceedingly, tiresomely boring? And is not at least one of your reasons for marrying me a desire to avoid a lifetime of boredom?'

He gave her a mock salute, 'Touché, chérie.'

As he savoured the use of this endearment, he kissed her again. The fierceness with which she returned his kisses brought him to a sense of where this might lead. He drew away saying, in a voice hoarse with emotion that, despite the admiration that they both shared for the ruins, he felt it time to return to the Manor.

Concerned of a sudden, she gestured to his shoulder, censuring her own forgetfulness that it was not yet strong.

Blue eyes locked onto amber ones as he declared that it was not the strength of his shoulder but that of his will which was concerning him at present. Despite the vivid blush crimsoning her cheeks she did not feign ignorance of that to which he referred.

'How long must we wait?' She looped the mare's reins over her arm as they slowly started for the house.

'I will draft an announcement for The Gazette this very day. Then we must inform your mamma.'

'Oh, but she will be delighted to have me off her hands!'

A thought struck her as she inquired if her mother had been told about Neville's plans for the army. The duke gave a disinterested shrug as he said that he would not presume to be the bearer of such tidings. Juliet never for a moment supposed that he should. In fact, the more she considered it, the more she thought that it should be Mr Peal who enlightened her mamma, as then he could be her perfect comforter afterwards. Giving a rueful laugh she finished with a question. 'Have I told you that I am convinced that Mr. Augustus Peal is enamoured of mamma?'

Vénoire dismissed this as of no consequence.

'Oh, but you should rejoice. When mamma is out of half-mourning, there will be no reason for her to live with us!'

He had paused to open the gate into the Manor wall and was at his most disdainful as he stated, 'Such an occasion would never arise. Do not ask me to show anything other than rigid politeness to my future mother-in-law. She has lavished little love on you! Whatever I have done, or will do, in connection with your family stems only from my love for you. Of a certainty, that is their only claim on me.'

Her reply was as fiery as his had been implacable. 'Indeed sir! Have I requested that you should do anything for my family?'

She went to lead the mare to the stables, seething at his high-handed manner. She was halted by the unusual sound of his rich, hearty laughter.

'Mon Dieu! Now *that* is the very tone of a duchess!'

From her seat by the parlour window, Lady Barbara was granted an unimpeded view of the subsequent merriment and exchange of kisses. She let go a deep sigh of relief and pleasure allowing her embroidery frame to fall on to the sleeping dog who whimpered in his dream. 'At last!'

This seeming non sequitur caused Mrs. Threadgold to look up from where she sat sorting her ladyship's skeins of silk.

'Do you have a problem, ma'am? How may I be of assistance?'

The dowager beckoned the old nurse to the window to enable her to share in the scene below. Mary Threadgold so far forgot herself, despite her long years in loyal service, as to give it as her opinion that it was not before time. Unable to school the broad smile from her features she nevertheless gave a very proper curtsy asking leave to tell Mr Ferris to start packing for Denbrugh Place.

'You have the right of it! The sooner we get Charles from under this roof, the less likely they are to produce a seven-month babe!'

The echo of her chuckling followed Mary out to the hall as the duke came in leading Juliet by the hand. He bowed to his old nurse bestowing on her a brilliant smile, 'Nounou, I am the happiest of men!'

Using the privilege of long ago nursery days, she patted his elbow and would have given a curtsy to Juliet but she had covered the old hand with her own, asking that she would wish her happy.

'Oh Miss Dempster, indeed I do.'

She opened the parlour door and, as the couple entered, the dowager began to chuckle again.

'Well my boy, so you got it right at last! You did not really expect me to be surprised did you? I have known that you were right for each other ever since I first saw you together on the night of the masquerade. Now, I had already sent to Denbrugh to expect you tonight. I thought ye'd wish to leave, no matter which way the cards fell. You may count on me remaining here to chaperone Juliet - I may call you so, my dear? You shall call me aunt, I think.'

Vénoire gave a heartfelt sigh. 'I congratulate you, aunt. Your forethought does you credit. Do inform me, am I permitted to visit?'

This was said in his well-recognised ironic tone of voice. All the while he was talking to his aunt, his eyes kept stealing back to Juliet's smiling mouth.

'Well, there is always Lessing's clerk.'

This oblique remark caught both of the other occupants' attention.

'You have the chapel here. I shall find it no great problem to obtain a special license. A private ceremony; no need for Juliet to be fully out of mourning. No matter, you are a Catholic. No need to wait on dressmakers.'

She was fully into her stride now.
'Travel to Palombières for your bridal visit. Fashions are so much more à la mode in Paris; have a new wardrobe made up there. Marriage breakfast at Denbrugh Place, introduce Juliet to all the staff… perfect, don't ye think?'

Without awaiting any response she scooped up the pug, leaving a bemused pair of lovers alone.

Charles led his betrothed to the window seat, enfolding her in his embrace as he asked her if the idea of such a marriage pleased her, or would she prefer to wait for a society wedding when her brother could give her away. At this absurd picture Juliet laughed outright. Her sole desire was to become his wife as soon as was possible, the manner of the wedding mattered little to her, although she added that she had always expected to be married in Solworth chapel.

'Of a certainty, you shall!'

Her lips tasted of summer wine, the duke thought.

She allowed her hands to tangle in his queue where it overhung his collar. They kissed again, Vénoire reluctantly breaking off on a half groan.

The amber eyes which regarded him were brimming with a passion he had never expected to see in one who should be his duchess. Behind the passion was an imp of laughter as she talked of the need to have a care for his shoulder as a relapse would be unwelcome to each. Deciding that it was essential to put some distance between them, Charles poured out two glasses of the nearby Canary wine favoured by the dowager.

Then he went down on one knee beside his love, producing the emerald ring from his pocket, 'Please to wear this until I can have a smaller copy made. Of a certainty, it is too big!'

He reached for a golden skein of silk from the dowager's embroidery bag. Selecting a double strand, he threaded the ring and dropped it over Juliet's head where it rested, glinting against the dark stuff of her riding habit. He reached out a long finger to touch where it lay upon her breast then shakily, he let his hand drop. He rose with care.

'Of a certainty, enough!'

He moved a few paces, turned and made a perfect leg, 'I find I must leave you Julie. It is imperative that I ensure that Ferris has packed my neck-cloths.'

In the same serious tones she agreed that it was naturally an imperative and swept him a perfect and decorous curtsy.

It was a most reluctant couple who later made their goodbyes. The distance between Solworth Manor and Denbrugh Place had never seemed greater. George Wilkes made his first bow to the lady who would soon become his mistress with genuine delight. Juliet marvelled at how news of a private nature spread in such a rapid fashion between servants. That is not to say that his reverence displeased her. Acceptance from Charles's loyal, long standing staff was what she desired. Ferris, who held the carriage door for his master was striving, yet failing, to keep what some might describe as a grin from his features. And so, the only thing which remained was their public farewell; a beautifully measured curtsy, an exquisite bow; however, Vénoire did press a kiss on Miss Dempster's wrist as he took her hand. The description of such a kiss would never be found in any volume concerning etiquette. She felt its heat long after the carriage had departed!

Meanwhile Barbara, the Dowager Countess of Lessing, had dispatched several letters of import, including a request that the Clerk in Holy Orders at Lessing Church should hold himself ready to perform a wedding as soon as he received the special licence.

CODA.
June 1783.

The Duchess of Vénoire's Suite,
Denbrugh Place.

The unmistakable wail of a recently born babe filled the duchess of Vénoire's suite. Bess Threadgold, under close scrutiny from her grandmother-in-law, lifted the swathed bundle from the crib. With care and not a little pride, she surrendered it into the duchess's outstretched arms. Mary Threadgold watched with a shake of her head as this lady stopped the wailing by the simple expedient of offering the baby her breast. Her grace had made it abundantly clear that there was to be no wet-nurse unless her own milk dried up. The child was feeding voraciously and had long fingers entwined in the duchess's hair. Mary could not deny that all seemed well with this new order. A knock on the door sent the nurse to see just who it was who sought admittance.

It was Alice Chambers bearing a pot of hot chocolate and some thinly sliced bread and butter. Alice had been appointed Juliet's maid soon after the latter's marriage. The idea of a dresser in the manner of the Dowager Countess of Lessing's was something Juliet had refused. Much better Alice, the butler and housekeeper's daughter, born and bred at Denbrugh, should grow into the style of lady's maid required by her new grace.

Alice now dropped her curtsy saying, 'If you please ma'am…' over use of her title was frowned upon by Juliet, 'his grace was wishful to visit.'

Juliet looked up from the meaningless dialogue she was engaged in with the baby, her face lit by joy. Mary had known that her assent would be immediate, nevertheless as she quitted the bedchamber, she asked Bess to cover the maternal scene with more shawls.

Descending to the third floor by the backstairs, the nurse was not overly surprised to see the servants' door into the dining room standing open and at the sound of her footsteps the duke himself appeared. She dropped her curtsy and not waiting for him to inquire, informed him that the duchess and their child had passed an excellent night, adding that they would be delighted if he were to step up to pay them a visit. Mary then went to close the door but Vénoire had already passed her and started up the bare wooden back stairs, taking them two at a time.

'Ehh!' Her sigh of disapproval was overlaid with joy for his obvious happiness. The spring of the previous year had seen a great many of the duke's servants and close family despairing over the course which his life was taking. Now all that was changed. Mary was overjoyed for him and delighted for herself; once more, she had charge of Denbrugh Place nursery, a third generation of children in her care. With Bess being appointed nursemaid upon her own marriage earlier in the year to Dickon, the Threadgold connection was set to continue. Being constantly in Bess's company in the last week since the birth, it would not surprise Mary in the least if she herself were to become a great grandmother in a few months' time!

So much new life burgeoning all around. Lord and Lady Hitchley had finally been blessed with an heir upon the birth of the Honourable Frederick, February last. Then in the month of April, news had been received from Venice that the Earl and Countess of Aldersleigh also had a son, naming him Thomas, John. There was a slight regret in her heart that this babe of Lady Louise would never call her "Nounou" but in reality her joy had been unbounded when the duke's child had entered this world. And *so* like him!

The "him" she was thinking of had entered the duchess's suite so hard upon the heels of his knock that only by a dexterous move did Alice avoid showering him and herself with the remains of the duchess's chocolate. She was quick with an apology, but he gracefully accepted that the fault was his, holding the door for her exit. Bess, blessed with tact and a quick understanding, removed herself to the dressing room taking the tiny nightgown she was in the process of sewing with her.

Vénoire edged the chair closer to his wife and child where they lay in the splendour of the embroidered tester bed. The baby was replete, a fine down of black hair contrasting with the white of a lace shawl, familiar long tapering fingers curled through the ribbons of Juliet's nightgown, intense, black lashes fluttering over inky blue eyes.

'Oh, Charles I am so glad you are come.'

Their fingers, each bearing an emerald ring, intertwined as they gazed at the new person in their lives. A shaft of sunlight moved across the bed and as is often the case, provoked a sneeze from the babe.

Both parents laughed, then Vénoire said in a voice brimming with passion and joy,

'Oh, Julie, you have changed my life completely. Until this last year I was a stranger to love and hope. Of a certainty now, all is happiness and contentment.'

'Of a certainty, my lord!' His wife's voice echoed his favourite phrase with loving delight.

Then with gentleness and awe the duke stroked the smooth, warm cheek of his son.

Christophe Charles d'Alvière, Marquis de Palombières born to Charles James, 7th duc de Vénoire, 3rd Earl of Denbrugh by his wife Juliet Sophia, on 18th June, 1783.

- F I N -

Denbrugh Place

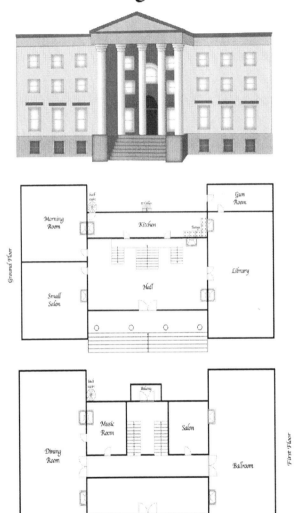

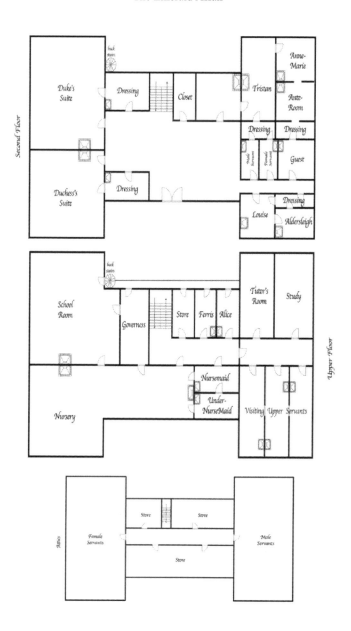

ABOUT THE AUTHOR

Jane Williams was born in Worcestershire. Educated at Stourbridge High School for Girls, Saffron Walden College of Education and The University of Cambridge.

She has always had a passion for Georgian and Regency history, as well as the language and literature of France.

A retired teacher, she lives with her husband, near to their family in the beautiful Chilterns.

Printed in Great Britain
by Amazon